FAST TANGO TO TUNIS

"Everything's been so quick," Tilson said apologetically. "No one's had time to tell *me* anything."

"What contacts in Tunis?"

"None," Tilson replied.

"Rendezvous?"

"Hotel Africa, Les Caravaniers Bar. Code name for the mission is 'Tango.' "

I turned away and an odd thing happened. Tilson got up from his desk. He stood there awkwardly, his plump arms folded as he watched me go.

It told me that however much or little they'd briefed him about this mission, he knew that it could be my last. . . .

"Better than Bond, more interesting, more real." —*Minneapolis Tribune*

"More wildly hazardous than its predecessors!" —*Publishers Weekly*

THE TANGO BRIEFING

Adam Hall

A DELL BOOK

To Jane and Bernard Horsfall

Published by
DELL PUBLISHING CO., INC.
1 Dag Hammarskjold Plaza
New York, New York 10017

Contents

1. Birdseye

I came in over the Pole and we were stacked up for nearly twenty minutes in a holding circuit round London before they could find us a runway and then we had to wait for a bottleneck on the ground to get itself sorted out and all we could do was stare through the windows at the downpour and that didn't help.

Sayōnara, yes, very comfortable thank you.

There was a long queue in No. 3 Passenger Building and I was starting to sweat because the wire had said FULLY URGENT and London never uses that phrase just for a laugh; then a quietly high-powered type in sharp blue civvies came up and asked who I was and I told him and he whipped me straight past Immigration and Customs without touching the sides and told me there was a police car waiting and was it nice weather in Tokyo.

"Better than here."

"Where do we send the baggage?"

"This is all I've got."

He took me through a fire exit and there was the rain slamming down again and the porters were trudging about in oilskins.

The radio operator had the rear door open for me and I ducked in and the driver hooked his head round to see who I was, not that he'd know.

"You want us to go as fast as we can?"

"That's what it's all about."

Sometimes along the open stretches where the deluge was flooding in the hollows we worked up quite a bow wave and I could see the flash of our emergency light reflected on it.

"Bit of a summer storm."

"You can keep it."

They were using their siren before we'd got halfway along Waterloo Road and after that they just kept their thumb on it because the restaurants and cinemas were turning out and every taxi was rolling.

Big Ben was sounding eleven when we did a nicely controlled slide into Whitehall across the front of a bus and he put the two nearside wheels up on the pavement so that I could get out without blocking the traffic.

"Best I could do."

"You did all right."

Most of the lights were on in the building but the place sounded dead as if they'd made up their minds at last that the only thing to do was run. I used the stairs and went straight into Walford's room but he wasn't there and I had to barge into Field Briefing before I could find anyone.

"Where's Walford?"

"Sprained a ball."

"Oh for Christ's sake." I pulled off my trenchcoat and shook the rain off the collar, throwing it on a chair. They've never done anything about the environment at the Bureau: it's a fridge or an oven according to the season and this was August. "Walford told me to get here, fully urgent."

"That's right."

Tilson was always like this: try blasting his eyes and he'll ask if you'd care for some tea.

"You mean he's not in the building?"

"All that matters to me, old horse, is that you are." He picked up a phone, not hurrying. "Quiller's come in. Cancel those last two cables, revamp the board and warn Clearance for tomorrow morning."

He put the thing down and eyed me amiably.

"How were the geishas?"

"Listen, if Walford's not here, who do I see? Who's my director?"

"Director?"

"It *is* a job, isn't it?"

"As far as I know, old horse."

"Then I want some orders."

"What's the rush?"

I turned away so I wouldn't have to look at his pink amiable face. He wasn't doing it deliberately; this was just his character and maybe they'd put him in charge of Field Briefing because that's when your nerves tighten up a whole octave higher, right on the brink of a mission. Maybe they thought his sleepy-eyed approach to the thing would calm us down. It was driving me up the wall.

"Look, they whipped me over the North Pole and spat

me out of the airport and we screamed the place down getting here in a squad car and now you ask me what's the rush, so for God's sake get on the blower and find out."

He rocked gently on his swivel chair.

"Care for a spot of tea?"

"Is Carslake in the building?"

"He's running the Irish thing."

"Well, get me some orders."

It's the routine reaction: most of the shadow executives get it the minute they know there's a mission lined up with their name on it. We call it the shakes, the blues, the doomclangers, but it's the same thing, a kind of sudden love-hate relationship with the job that's been giving you the kicks you asked for all along the line, the same job that's going to kill you off one day when your guard's down or your luck's out or you've finally lost that fine degree of judgement that has so far kept you alive.

So when you know there's a mission you get an urge to run the other way and you can't do that because you're committed, so you run to meet it instead, head down and blood up but with that little cold knot in the stomach.

"The only orders I know, old horse, is that you're to piddle off home."

"What did they get me here for, then, so bloody fast?"

"We just wanted to know you were physically available for this one, and we couldn't be sure of that if you were mooning around Tokyo."

It made sense and the speed went out of me and I crossed to the open window and stood with my back to the rain, watching his face now because I wanted all the info I could get without asking too much.

"What were the cables you just cancelled?"

"We were going to warn Smythe and Bickersteth to stand by. One's in Bucharest and the other's hanging round in reserve on the Pakistan show."

"You were going to pull them out for this job?"

"If you couldn't make it." He flattened his pink hand and tilted it, watching the light flash across his nails. "And now you have. Or have you?"

"What the hell does that mean?"

"Well, you might not like this one." He gave a shy smile.

The knot in my stomach got colder.

"Why? Is it a bastard?"

"Oh, I don't mean that, old horse. Anyway, the thing is you're here physically and all you have to do now is go home and get a good night's zizz." He leaned forward to look at a pad on his desk. "Tomorrow they're running a film show for you at—"

"It would've been quicker to pull out Smythe and Bickersteth, wouldn't it?"

"Oh, yes. Much."

"Someone wants me particularly for this one."

He smiled boyishly.

"That's right."

"Who?"

"Not absolutely sure. Tell you in the morning."

"Is there a director lined up?"

"Sort of."

"Who?"

"They haven't told me. Honestly. Or I'd tell you, wouldn't I?"

"If it suited you."

"That's the way we do things, isn't it? We don't like you people to have too much on your mind. Gives you indigestion. Now why don't you just buzz off and—"

"Where's this film show?"

"Air Ministry. Nine ack-emma mañana—will you be there?"

"All right."

"Room 43, Squadron-Leader Eastlake. Code intro's 'Birdseye,' okay? Then you can tootle back here and I'll give you the rest and you can get cleared."

I stood watching his smooth cherub's face for a bit and thought again about what he'd said—*you might not like this one*—and then got it out of my mind and picked up the trenchcoat and slung it round my shoulders because it was too stinking hot to put it on.

"What's the area?"

"I think you'll need tropical kit."

"Oh, my God."

"It's a shame," he smiled amiably, "in winter they send you to Warsaw, don't they?"

"Why did they want me for this one, specially?"

"It's a solo mission, apart from the director in the field.

You like working alone, don't you? So it ought to suit you down to the ground."

Suddenly it struck me that they'd deliberately got Walford out of the way so that this bland little angel-face could handle me softly, softly, till they'd caught their monkey. This job was a bastard and they'd picked the only one who'd take it on out of sheer bloody-mindedness because he knew that anyone with a bit of sense would refuse. It had happened before and now it looked like happening again. If I let it.

"Get you a taxi?"

"I'll walk."

"In this rain?"

"It'll cool me off."

"We could put it down," he said comfortably, "on the expenses. Let's say the operation's running, as of now."

"From what I can smell about this one you can stuff it, along with the taxi fare."

Her breasts were marbled in the greenish light and her face looked cold and blind. The shadow of the window cut half across her body, leaving her long legs in darkness, silvered with moisture.

The rain had stopped a long time ago but now and then a diamond drop flashed down from the guttering. Taxis were still about, their tyres hissing along the roadway; in here the air was stifling, even with the window open.

She moved and I looked down at her; she'd opened her eyes and they were brilliant in the half dark.

"Okay?" she asked.

"Okay."

She smiled and uncurled herself, getting off the bed and shaking her hair out, moving lazily in the glow from the street lamps, her hands idly smoothing her body as she stretched a little, her eyes closing again as she took pleasure simply in being alive, turning slowly in a kind of dance and forgetting I was here.

I hadn't meant to be.

But Tilson had seemed so certain they'd got me, and he wouldn't be stupid enough to think I'd take on *any* kind of job. He knew enough about the background to know that I'd finally fall for this one after I'd put up a preliminary squeal to show I had a choice.

So I'd gone dripping wet into a phone box and tried four numbers before I could find anyone with enough time on hand to take in a nerve case who wanted a woman and wanted her badly because he knew that once the mission was running he wouldn't get another chance and that if somewhere along the line a wheel came off she'd be the last one he'd ever have.

"You're quiet."

"I was watching you," I said.

She smiled again, just a lazy movement along her mouth.

"You weren't."

Her name was Corinne. I'd only seen her twice before but we liked things the same way, it was a kind of natural.

"There's another job," I said, and found my clothes.

"How long for?"

"You can't ever tell."

She got her cigarettes and held one out and I shook my head and she lit up. "Where is it this time?"

"Italy. Whole coachload, want to see the Tower of Pisa before the bloody thing falls down."

I dropped my keys and she picked them up, stooping naked in the light, giving them to me, smiling with her brilliant eyes: "I just can't see you doing it."

"Why not?"

"I just can't see you standing up with a microphone and saying on the left there's the statue of Marco Polo and on the right there's the Cooperative Spaghetti Works."

"Well, I've got to do something for a living."

The smoke curled across the slanting light, quickening to an air current from the window.

"I wish I was going with you."

"On a coach trip in a heatwave?"

"It'd be a different kind of grind, and there'd be you." She moved around the room, unconsciously making stylised turns on her slim bare feet. "You know something? It isn't the cutthroat bitchiness of the competition that gets us down in the end, it's the strain on the shoulders, lifting our arms to get in and out of the dresses. You're right on the point of throwing it in, then you get a break and see your face on the front of *Go-Girl* so you think you've hit it big, and you're back in the grind again."

I tied the second lace.

"You ought to get married."

"Oh futz, spare me the suds and the sink."

"Someone with a sack of loot."

I got my coat and we kissed and I opened the door and looked back and she was standing perfectly still in the small airless room, the after-rain smell coming in and the light striking obliquely across her, across a thin willowy girl with blue-veined breasts and a slowly dying smile as she watched me go, a girl called Corinne whom I'd met only twice before and wouldn't, maybe, ever see again.

Room 43 was on the fifth floor and I was standing by the window when he came in.

"Sorry I kept you. You're Mr. Gage?"

"Yes."

"I'm Eastlake."

"You've got quite a birdseye view from up here."

"Appropriate word." He was going to add something but the phone buzzed and he picked it up. "Squadron-Leader Eastlake. Yes, I told him to get three while he was at it. Well tell him to pull his finger out, and listen, I'm going along to Projection and I don't want anyone to come barging in, so put someone on the door."

I came away from the window and he gave me a slow probing look, wondering what a nondescript civilian was doing in here with a code introduction. I'd used the name Gage because that had been stuck on for Tokyo and if they'd changed it when they'd arranged this meeting Tilson would have told me.

"Let's go along. Nobody with you?"

"No."

In the small room smelling of acetate and overheated guide mechanism he introduced me to a WAAF operator and three flight lieutenants: "Hinchley was piloting this sortie, Pierce was navigating, and Johnson's the Photographic Interpretation Officer responsible for the analysis of the imagery material. Can we have those curtains drawn, someone?"

There were three or four rows of tip-up seats and we sat down and the WAAF hit the button and threw a desert on the screen and I remembered Tilson saying "I think you'll need tropical kit."

Eastlake said: "Ask what questions you like as we go along, will you? We did this with a cluster of four 35-mm.

Nikons and a restricted field of 25 degrees. Filters were yellow, green and two reds and the film's been cut and joined for continuity, all right?"

"What altitude?"

"Sixty-five thousand feet." He'd hesitated a fraction because it was classified so I thought this must be the Mk II version of the Albatross and started looking for missile installations dolled up as mosques.

But so far there was only desert, a sugar-brown terrain filling the screen and looking like a sheet of corrugated cardboard with a fold here and there.

"What are those rocks?"

"Shale upthrust, nothing very high, perhaps twenty or thirty feet."

The pattern of dunes and rills span slowly as we circled clockwise so I focussed my eyes on the centre but couldn't see anything.

"This isn't a dummy run?"

"No. These are the pix we went for."

I still couldn't see anything interesting on the screen but I was beginning to see a lot more of the job that Tilson and those other bastards were trying to pitch me into: a stinking Robinson Crusoe lark in an area defined on this frame scale as three miles across with nothing in it but a bunch of rocks and something else so small that only people like these could see it.

The ground resolution looked close on ten tenths, with a shade of grain on the light-exposed side of the shale upthrust but the rest very clear, and I began getting frustrated because they'd sat me down to show me something and they knew I couldn't see it and I felt a bit of a lemon.

"Have you got those rocks on a static 3-D viewer?"

"We have, but I wouldn't bother."

Eastlake had obviously been briefed. Last night Tilson had just told me to keep the rendezvous and that was all, so I hadn't reported at the Bureau this morning on my way here; but they'd briefed these chaps to run this film without telling me what I had to look for and there must be a good reason.

The desert span and tilted, the group of rocks changing shape as the angle of view turned through its conic vector, the light-and-shadow corrugations of the dunes shifting definition like water flowing in slow motion. It was all I could see.

"Can we have a few stops?"

The squadron-leader spoke to the girl and she began breaking it up into ten-second runs and I still couldn't get it. The whole scene's slow revolutions were becoming mesmeric and I shut my eyes to prevent strain, viewing for a few seconds and trying to coincide with the rhythm of the stops, resting at intervals and waiting till the afterimage had faded under my closed lids. I knew now why they'd been warned not to tell me what I was expected to look for: the interreactive process of eye and brain can play tricks and sometimes you can see things only because you've been told they're there.

"Would you like some runbacks?"

"We can try."

He told the girl and the scene began swinging anticlockwise at precise intervals with five-second stops. It didn't make any difference: I was looking at the same thing in a mirror. There's no point in runbacks unless you think you've spotted something and want to recap and I hadn't spotted a bloody thing and I was getting fed up. The heat of the projector was adding to the heat of our bodies in here and there was nothing much left to breathe and I thought it'd be nice if a girl came round with a tray of Dairymaid.

The dunes flowed under my eyes.

Swing. Stop. Runback.

The projector droned.

I kept wanting to look at the rocks but Eastlake had said it wasn't worth bothering with. They weren't interested in the rocks. And it was no good asking them for a clue because the object of the exercise was that I should see the target for myself, avoiding the risk of conditioned illusion.

Swing. Stop. Runback.

The dunes were becoming a mirage. The dunes and the rocks and the flow of light and shade across the scene were beginning to swirl in a slow-moving vortex and I was losing track of perspective.

"Would you like us to back-project against a—"

"What? No. Run it back. Run it back, will you?"

The scene swung to a stop.

"Tell me when—"

"Yes."

Anticlockwise. The shadows flowing and the angle—
"Stop."
"This frame?"
"Back another fraction."
The sprockets whirred again and stopped.
"Yes, that's the one. I've got it now."

2. Overflight

"It didn't take you long."
"You're joking."
The WAAF shut down the projector and we all
stretched our legs.
"It took us a bit of time ourselves," said Eastlake,
"even though the navigator had seen it through direct
binocular vision." He showed me a couple of dozen stills
and blowups and filter-screen montages on the static view-
ers but they weren't any clearer, and even the still they'd
taken from the frame of the movie strip didn't have the
same definition. I asked Johnson about that. He was the
Interpretation Officer.
"It doesn't seem possible," he said, "does it? When you
look at the still you're looking at exactly the same picture
as the one on the strip—but there's some data missing, all
the same. The eye hasn't got anything for immediate com-
parison. It's the movement through the projector that
leads the eye over the changing pattern till it suddenly
sees an inconsistency. That's what happened with you."
Eastlake cut the viewer lamp and someone pulled the
curtains and stopped sharp when I said: "What sort of
plane is it?"
Someone gave a nervous cough.
Squadron-Leader Eastlake said: "Don't you know?"
"If I did, I wouldn't ask."
It was perfectly all right if the Bureau had its reasons
for pitching me in here without any briefing but if their
idea was to get me steamed-up about this thing then people would have to answer the questions I wanted to ask
them or it was no go.
"Thank you, Phyllis. That's all we needed to see."
When the WAAF went out and shut the door the pilot
and navigator and photo-interpretation bod stood looking

at their shoes and Eastlake said:

"Mr. Gage has been fully screened."

They relaxed a bit and one of them offered a package of gum round and nobody wanted any and the pilot said:

"We were told to look for a medium freighter."

"You think this is a medium freighter."

We were grouped by the static viewer. On the blown-up still it didn't really look like an aeroplane at all but now that I'd seen it on the movie strip I could accept the smudgy configuration on the sand as an aircraft with one wing dislocated at the root end.

The Interpretation Officer didn't day anything. The navigator shrugged.

"All I'd say from the pix is that it could be. From what I saw through the binocs I'd say it's not military and not very big. If I had to bet on it I'd put it down as a light or medium twin-prop short-haul commercial transport."

"Not just because that's what you were told to look for and expected to see."

He smiled lopsidedly. "What can we ever do about that? Once we're told what kind of target to look for, we're to an extent conditioned."

I was finding it difficult now to look away from the static viewer. In the illuminated central frame the picture wasn't very big: it had been blown up to the point where the grain would start blurring the definition. The ribbed background of dunes was perfectly clear but the grey ashy smudge could be anything—or nothing, just a fault in the processing—but even from sixty-five thousand feet they'd seen it was some kind of aircraft and now that they'd found it the Bureau had cabled Tokyo fully urgent and I was here looking at this vague configuration on the photographic plate that was the focal point of the mission they were trying to sell me.

"Where is it?"

Eastlake spoke before the others could start worrying. The people with No. 2 Fighter-Reconnaissance Squadron R.A.F. spent most of their time taking the sort of pictures that nobody really wanted to reprint as postcards for the tourist trade. This was one of them.

"Longitude 8°3' East by Latitude 30°4' North."

"Tunisia?"

"Algeria."

"When did the plane come down?"

"We weren't informed. Our job was to look for it and take pictures if we found it."

"From sixty-five thousand feet?"

"It's the highest we go."

"You could've gone lower."

Someone coughed again.

I thought I might as well push them right up against the wall so that they'd either have to answer my question or throw me out.

"Did you get official overflying permission?"

I counted up to seven.

"Did we what?"

Very slowly I said: "Did you get official permission from the Algerian government to overfly their territory and take those pictures? Or did you go up to the maximum operational ceiling because the view was better?"

This time I was at nine before the pilot said:

"Actually, neither."

It was just their natural disinclination as secret reconnaissance men to trust an unknown civilian with the whole score. Eastlake had told them I'd been screened and they'd obviously been briefed to give me all the info they could, but they still didn't like it.

I suppose the pilot thought that if things had gone this far it couldn't do any harm to go the whole way and the squadron-leader would slap him down in any case if he made a mistake.

"You see," he said with a perfectly straight face, "we were tooling around in Malta on a friendly visit and then we got these orders from on high. So we planned a suitable exercise and went in at our best altitude so we wouldn't annoy the scheduled airlines. Then we sort of lost our way a bit and after we'd got back on course for home we found Charlie here had made a silly mistake and left all the cameras running. I really don't know what things are coming to, in this mob."

The squadron-leader was looking out of the window. He didn't say anything.

"You must have been tracked by radar."

"Bound to have been."

"How long were you overflying Algerian territory?"

"Not long enough to sort of cause too much comment."

"Did they put up interceptors?"

"Don't actually know. You see, from that height we can

go rather fast in quite a short time, by pointing things downwards."

It was all I wanted to know and I left it at that.

When Eastlake took me down the corridor he said: "Where exactly do you fit in with this little circus?"

"You can't see much from those photographs. I suppose they'll send me in to have a closer look at the bloody thing."

There was nobody around in Field Briefing so Tilson sat me down and folded his chubby hands and said:

"Well, what shall we talk about?"

I said I wanted to know who my director would be if I took the job on.

"It depends who can get there first."

"Where?"

"Tunis."

"Who's been sent for?"

"I'm not really—"

"You're a liar—"

"Now why should I want to—"

"Oh, for Christ's sake stop poncing me about, will you?"

He sighed gently. "They asked for Loman."

"As my director in the field?"

"That's right."

He looked at his pink shiny nails.

I got up and walked about and thought of saying no, I'm not working with that bastard, but he was waiting for me to say that and I didn't want to give him the pleasure of being right.

"What's the mission, Tilson?"

"I'm not sure I—"

"Oh come on, don't waste my time."

He looked up amiably and said: "Are you in a hurry?"

I turned away and did some more walking and thought of saying no, I'm not in a hurry, but he'd got me and we both knew it and I was fed up because they'd hijacked me into a new mission the fastest way possible: by holding back and keeping off and letting me get interested without anyone coming to interfere.

Yes, I was in a hurry.

We can refuse a mission. We can refuse to work at the kind of thing that's not our speciality or the kind of thing that we've proved in the past to be beyond our particular talents. We can say no, this one sounds too political or complex or dull or dirty or dangerous and we can say we don't like the director or we don't like Bangkok or Warsaw or Tunis. We can say we've got a cold or we can just tell them to go and find someone else without even giving a reason. It works all right because if a shadow executive lets himself be forced into an assignment he's a dead duck and they know that and it doesn't suit their book.

But if we refuse a mission it means we have to hang round and wait for another one to come up and it gets on the nerves, the waiting. So in the end we'll take almost anything if it looks as though there's a break-even chance of getting out alive. Today I wasn't interested in that because the chances are always as good as you want to make them. They knew what I was interested in today.

The ash-grey smudge on the photograph.

It was just a medium twin-prop short-haul commercial transport and all it had done was to come down in the desert but the nearest anyone had got to it was sixty-five thousand feet and nobody else had dared to go any closer.

So I wanted to.

And they'd known I would.

"What's the timing on this?"

Tilson raked for a folder.

"Immediate."

"You mean when I'm ready."

"That's right." He was opening the folder. "So long as you're ready immediately."

"Fill me in, will you?"

He looked up patiently. "I'm afraid I can't, old horse. All I know is they want you to go and take a look at that thing you saw at the Air Ministry. Loman will spell it all out for you when you reach Tunis."

"How long have I got for clearance?"

"There's a plane at 1350 so you'll just have to do everything as quick as you can."

On my way through the building to Credentials I passed Napier, one of our Admin. types.

"Hello, Quiller, I thought you were in Tokyo."

"So did I."

"We're leaving your cover name as Charles Warnford

Gage but there's a change in the cover itself. Excuse me."

While she answered the phone I checked the papers.

C. W. Gage, geophysical consultant attached to Société Petrocombine's South 4 drilling-camp in the Tunisian complex. Specific contract, exploration and preliminary assays, until October, optionally renewable, previous contracts with platinum-prospecting consortia, U.K. and Belgium. Returning from one month's routine leave.

When she'd got off the phone I asked who'd designed this one.

"Mr. Egerton."

"When?"

"It came through late last night."

They'd been so bloody sure of me.

"It's a new camp, is it?"

"First assays, yes."

Egerton had his faults but I'd take any cover he worked out for me. This one was very smooth because a geophysical consultant attached to a prospecting company hoping to strike oil was going to keep his mouth shut: it was the perfect excuse not to talk and that was fine because I didn't know anything about survey work.

In Firearms they wanted me to try out a new club-snout rapid loader they'd just had in from Italy and I told them where to put it.

"Take one of these compacts, then. Slung holster."

"How long have you been here?"

"Me? Three weeks."

"Look, there's my signature, so just put *Weapons drawn—none.*"

"Oh you're *that* one."

Codes and Ciphers gave me a third-series seventh-digit duplication setup with normal contractions, transferred numerals, and no blanks. The alert phrase was "wherever possible."

"Christ, don't they know that one by now?"

"It's never been blown."

"There's a first time for everything."

Accounts had passed their stuff on to Travel and I picked up the Caledonian air ticket, two hundred dinars, travellers' cheques, and an American Express card. The existing will and testament to stand as it was, no new codicil.

Then I went back to Field Briefing but Tilson said nothing fresh had come in.

"Has Loman arrived in Tunis yet?"

"There's been no cable."

"Where's he coming from?"

"Nobody said."

Tilson wouldn't necessarily tell me. He'd tell me precisely what Admin. wanted me to know and nothing more. Sometimes we bitch about this but it's based on logic because if an executive goes out on a mission with his head stuffed full of background info that doesn't directly concern him it'll take his mind off the job in hand and that can be dangerous. Last year Webster was found mixed up with the propellers of a Greek coaster in Trieste because he'd got himself involved in the political aspect of a perfectly straightforward penetration job and blew his cover by sending signals when he should have been concentrating on a fast in-and-out documentation snatch.

If you work for the Bureau you've got to work to the rules and they're strict. The Bureau doesn't officially exist. If it existed it couldn't do the things it's been designed to do: things that could never be countenanced even at Cabinet level. So if you get into a jam in the course of a mission you can count on London to help you but only up to a point: the point where they see there's a risk of exposing the Bureau, of letting it be seen to exist. Then they'll cut you off and you'll know it because the set's gone dead or the contact doesn't show up and then God help you because London never will.

Up to that point they'll look after you and one of the ways they do it is by keeping you short of information that you don't really need at the time.

"What made them pick Loman for this one?"

"No idea."

Loman was a bastard but he was third in the ranks of the really high-echelon directors simply because he was brilliant at his job. The ash-grey smudge on that photograph must be hellishly important for them to send a man like Loman in.

"Did he ask for me?"

"Everything's been so quick," Tilson said apologetically. "No one's had time to tell me anything."

So I asked the only kind of questions he'd be able to do anything with.

"What contacts in Tunis?"

"None. There'll be an Avis car waiting for you at the airport, dark blue Chrysler 180."

"Rendezvous?"

"Hotel Africa, Les Caravaniers Bar on the fifth floor, 1800 hours today. No code, just recognition."

"What do I do if he's not there?"

"Rdv at hourly intervals till 2400 and then send us a signal. Code name for the mission is 'Tango.' "

"Noted." I belted my mack. "Got any transport?"

"Car and driver standing by for you below."

I turned away and an odd thing happened.

There is no ceremony at the Bureau. The only human contact in this ancient and featureless building is made when a shadow executive reports for briefing and clearance or when he comes in from a mission. Nobody exists here because the Bureau itself doesn't exist. We call each other by the names we're given: except to the top echelon people our own names have never been known.

Tilson had been here long enough to lose his soul to the sacred bull: the Bureau. He knew what we really were, the shadow executives: we were so many ferrets to be released down a hole and left there to hunt in the dark, to pursue the sinuous ways of the warren and to emerge blinded by the light, bloodied and embattled, triumphant or dismayed, or never, on occasion, to emerge at all.

Object achieved.

Executive withdrawn.

Mission failed.

Executive deceased.

Deceased or replaced or overdue, or home and dry and drunk as a lord because this time we pulled it off and nothing worse to show than a flesh wound from a glancing shot. No one cheers, nobody grieves. Only the results are important.

The J-class sub in the Black Sea has augmented missile potential and rejoins the Med. flotilla tonight on orders from Tikhomirov.

The Cuban national in Room 39 of the hotel opposite the daïs where General Fernandez will speak tomorrow had a Marlin 336T .35 telescopic rifle with 4X scope among his possessions; appropriate action taken; his sister has identified him at the morgue.

The Temple of Heavenly Light near Kuchêng has a

*central minaret comprising concealed guidance ramp with
17-degree inclination towards the Russian border and ac-
commodation for warhead armament in the Z-phase
ICBM category. These are the photostats taken from the
original designs.*

We are nameless and speak in ciphers; we are homeless
and work among strangers; and if we can claim identity
then it lies in the sacrosanct and classified files somewhere
in this building whose doors are as nameless as we.

So it was odd that Tilson should do so human a thing
as to get up from his desk as I turned for the door, and
stand there awkwardly with his plump arms folded and
his round pink head on one side as he watched me go.

It told me that however much or little they'd briefed
him about this mission, he knew that it was deadly.

"Take care," he said, "old horse."

3. Shock

We began sweating as soon as they opened the door and
by the time we'd crossed the tarmac to the Tunis-Carthage
No. 2 Airport Building the soles of our shoes were hot
and I thought, oh you bastards, sending me to Africa in a
heat wave.

Vous n'avez rien à déclarer?

Rien.

A man in a fez waving a chalked board: PETROCOM-
BINE SOUTH 4. Half a dozen drillers were heading
towards him, bearded and sunbaked and one of them
half-seas over. That was meant to be my mob but so far I
didn't sense any kind of surveillance so I didn't join them
just for the look of the thing.

Avis? Par là, m'sieur.

Merci.

Another chalked board: MR. ROBINSON.

If anyone was here to meet Mr. C. W. Gage they
wouldn't chalk it up on a board and I took the long open
passage to the Consigne and back and then double-checked
the main hall before I tapped at the window and noted
that in Tunis they not only try harder but they look pret-
tier while they're doing it.

"Yes, Mr. Gage, we have a Chrysler waiting for you."

"Any messages?"

London would contact me here if there was any change of plan and you never know your luck: Loman might have ricked his kidneys on a camel and I could go home.

"There's no message."

She led me outside with a light jigging high-heeled step and I studied the blue-black hair and the silky eyelashes and the white flashing smile as she showed me how to open the door and where the steering wheel was and everything, then I clipped the belt on and began butting a gangway through the pack of clapped-out Minicabs towards the main gate.

There was a crosswind along the Khaireddine Pacha and the tall feathery eucalyptuses blew restlessly against the sky. I don't like wind: it disturbs me. I began checking the mirror because in this trade you can't always tell when a cipher's been busted somewhere along the line and even in the first few hours of a new mission you can sometimes pick up ticks.

This evening it looked all right and I started wondering where they'd pulled Loman in from: there was obviously a flap on because they'd bounced me Tokyo-London-Tunis with only one night stop and had to leave the final briefing for Local Control. The last I'd heard of Loman he'd been setting up a classified document snatch at one of the ministries in Bonn and he wasn't the kind of director who'd appreciate being turned round in the middle of an operation. Which was another reason I knew this aeroplane thing must be strictly urgent.

I hadn't been briefed yet but there was one obvious aspect to this job: Control in London didn't only want me to go and have a look at that wreck in the desert—they wanted me to go and have a look at it before anyone else could.

So I kept a routine check on the mirror.

If anyone had ricked a kidney it was the poor bloody camel because Loman was there in the Caravaniers Bar at the Hotel Africa at precisely 1800 hours and he got up right away without looking at me and signed his bill and went out. I waited thirty seconds and followed him.

I know people by their walk. The eyes are expressive but if you're good at it they can be used for hiding things. But there's nothing people can do about their walk because locomotion is a lifelong habit and it expresses their attitude towards the environment.

Loman walks like a bird, his hands behind him like neat tucked wings, his head turning frequently from side to side in case there's something to peck at: he never misses anything and if you get in his way he'll peck you to death.

The Arab room was at the end of a tiled passage and he was waiting for me there, his bland face half masked by the shadows of arabesque screens. There were no chairs here, just cushions massed along the stone plinth and on a dais where incense burned in a brass bowl. Light came from lamps high in the atrium outside where tropical plants grew, their leaves like sword blades and their shadows sharp.

"Where were you?"

"Tokyo."

"You're still under flight-disorientation?"

"I'll settle down."

He nodded and got a map out but didn't open it.

There was a flap on all right and it shook me. The pace was too bloody fast. The minute they'd slung this op at Loman to direct he must have said *I want Quiller for it* and he hadn't even asked them where I was, couldn't care less. The pace ought not to be as fast as this right at the outset of a mission: people could make mistakes in the planning stages and that could be dangerous, could be fatal.

Then I knew suddenly how much the flight had upset my personal clock because there was something sticking out a mile and I'd only just seen it. This wasn't a new mission. It had been running for some time and it had seemed to be blowing up and they'd thrown it at Loman like an unexploded bomb because of all the high-echelon directors he was the one who could stay cool enough not to drop it.

I could feel the whole network quivering.

"Someone's mucked it, have they?"

He didn't answer.

It wasn't a good start because he knew I was bloody annoyed. I watched him while he moved round a bit, his small feet nervous, the light glinting on his polished-looking head and the neat polka-dot bow tie and his brightly polished shoes: and I remembered what I thought about Loman the first time we worked together—I could stand his massaged face and manicured hands and immaculate tailoring and his brilliant reputation for efficiency if only he'd have the grace to make a human gesture now and then, leave his fly unzipped or something.

He still wouldn't answer because he hadn't been given enough time to work out the initial phase of the operation but that was his problem and I wanted to know the score so I said:

"How bad is it?"

He turned on me fussily.

"There's no need to panic."

"Just let me in, Loman."

I knew I shouldn't rush the poor little bastard, but it was the hangover from the Tokyo-London bounce and maybe the wind here, disturbing me. That was for Loman too: it's part of a director's job to kick out any kinks in his executive's psyche and set him running straight when the whistle blows.

"You've seen the reconnaissance photographs?"

"Yes."

"We want you to go and inspect that aircraft. You knew that, of course." He began haltingly, but already I could see he'd decided to shoot me the whole thing before he'd got it set up in his own mind, because yes, I was panicking, and he had to do something about it. "It's a medium cargo machine and its call sign in the phonetic alphabet code is Tango Victor. After a routine take-off in the U.K. one of the Customs and Excise officials noticed what appeared to be a false signature on the freight declaration form. An enquiry was made and subsequently the Special Branch was called in. By this time Tango Victor was reported missing."

Wind gusted across the atrium and the green sword blades quivered. I watched Loman thinking. He thought with his feet, placing them neatly together, turning and taking short steps as he square-searched the data and decided how much to tell me, how much to leave out: because the executive in the field has to go in with his nerves tuned like a cat's and his wits light and if he's been overloaded with too much info on the brink of the mission he's going to sprain his brain when he needs it most.

"The findings deriving from the Special Branch enquiry were significant enough to persuade the Minister that the R.A.F. should attempt to locate the aeroplane, put a fix on it and take photographs. This, as you know, was accomplished."

He talked like a bloody schoolmistress.

"How did they know where to look?"

He spread out the map on the dais.

"Its course was known, and it was last heard of in an area where a violent sandstorm had been reported. The R.A.F. made their initial reconnaissance sortie on the assumption that Tango Victor had been forced down by it. This was proved to be correct."

Carte Internationale du Monde Sheet NH-32—Hassi Messaoud Area—Scale 1/1.000.000—Longitude 6-12, Latitude 28-32—Elevations, dunes, rock outcrops, reefs, wells, oases, camel tracks, so forth.

"Is this the sandstorm area?"

"Yes. The cross is the site of the wreck."

South in the Great Eastern Erg. Nearest camel track almost thirty miles away, Tunisian frontier ninety miles, nothing else but sand, not an oasis, not even a well, not even a palm tree.

"The conditions were unpropitious, highly." His manicured finger whispered across the map. "This oasis, Sidi Ben Ali, is the nearest point of habitation in Algeria itself. Control sent O'Brien there to assess the local situation and report. He was briefed to find out whether any other party knew where Tango Victor had come down, and if so, who that party was and whether it had any intention of going out to examine the wreck. Unfortunately London received no report."

He turned away as he said that. Not that he had any scruples: his tone was petulant. It had been remiss of O'Brien to fail in this most elementary of tasks and there was no excuse for clumsiness.

"Was he actually found?"

We always hope that when it comes it'll be short and sweet, a bullet in the brain or something.

"His incinerated remains were found on a rubbish heap. Some Arab boys had heard a disturbance and told the police. Despite the condition of the body there was evidence that O'Brien had been subjected to interrogation"—he turned to me quickly—"but the most exhaustive checks throughout the network have established that this was ineffective. All signal matrices are intact and codes, access facilities, safe houses, and personnel-monitoring units reveal no indication of surveillance, blowing or penetration. This aspect, at least, is satisfactory."

I went on looking at the map.

There were six of us at the Bureau with the suffix 9 to our code name: *Reliable Under Torture.* Now there were only five. That's not many. It's not many because there's only one way of earning a 9 and nobody ever sets out to get it, I mean it's not a basket of fruit or a marble clock, and they don't add it to your dossier posthumously because the whole record goes into the shredder once you've bought it. All the 9 means is that you've got yourself in a jam at some time and been grilled and got out again without blowing your cover or the mission or the whole network and with enough of you left in one piece to go on working. It also means that those bastards in London are going to pick you for the jobs where there's a high risk of the opposition treading all over your face when they want to know the time, and that sort of selection makes for a brisk mortality rate and that's why there aren't many of us. Five.

"Am I taking over from O'Brien?"

We often have to do it but we don't like it. We like to make our own mess of things, not clear up someone else's.

"No. They sent Fyson in next. He blew his cover."

"Oh for Christ sake!"

"Of course I realise—"

"You call this a mission? What kind of—"

"I wasn't directing it when these—"

"That's bloody obvious."

"Thank you."

Then we both shut up while he worked out an argument good enough to keep me in the act and I tried to decide how much it was worth shoving my head right down the barrel just because I'd accepted the mission.

He wiped the sweat off his face with a spotless linen handkerchief, not looking at me, and when I knew I couldn't do anything else about it I asked him:

"Did either of them get any info on the opposition before they folded up?"

"Very little." He was trying to keep the relief out of his voice: if I ducked this one he'd have to call someone else in and there wasn't enough time. "But at least we know that there *is* another party interested in Tango Victor and that they'd prefer we didn't go near it."

"Did Fyson see any sign of their trying to reach the wreck overland?"

"You can ask him yourself. He's here in the hotel, at your disposal."

"Is he still in the operation?"

Slight pause.

"No."

I looked at him but he was gazing at the map.

"Why not?"

"You prefer working alone. Don't you?"

The bastard was lying but I let it go. When you're working alone you can still have a dozen people manning the base or the radio or the access lines and there was some other reason why Fyson wouldn't be doing it and Loman wasn't going to tell me and I wasn't going to ask him again.

I didn't like it, anything about it, the whole thing stank, the activity killed off right in phase 1 and a cover blown without any real info coming in and the situation so desperate now that they'd had to call in a man like Loman to try holding the roof up while I ferreted around in the dark.

"You know something, Loman?" He looked up from the map. "I think you've lost me."

He didn't say anything.

I knew half a dozen first-line executives who'd turn this thing down flat—Simmons, Cockley, Foster, people like that—because you don't spend three years in training and the rest of your time working your way through the elementary intelligence-assessment fields with a Curtain embassy military-attaché cover to the major assignments at M-Classified level and then risk all your experience, all your capability, all your professional expertise on a chancy job in the dark that someone else has mucked up for you on his way in.

London knows this. It takes a long time to rear a good ferret. So I couldn't understand what the hell they were doing.

"What the hell are they doing?"

"Who?"

"Control."

"Doing?"

"Throwing us this bloody auction."

He walked about again while I stood there sweating and listening to the hot fluttering wind that was hitting the top of the atrium and shaking the sword-blade leaves, sending them rattling with a dry dead sound.

Then Loman stopped and stood neatly in front of me with his hands tucked behind him and his alert bird's head lifted to look me in the eyes and I knew he was going to keep me in this operation and work me to death if he had to, or save my skin if he had to, because there was no choice, because it was too late to call in someone else, simply because of that.

"I want you to know two things, Quiller."

Prissy, fussy voice, talked like a bloody schoolmistress.

But I knew he'd get me.

"One is that you can dismiss entirely your fears that we are engaged on a mission that has started off badly. O'Brien and Fyson were trying to pick up intelligence and pass it back to Control, and they failed. But you are not taking over from them: the original field—Sidi Ben Ali in Algeria—has been closed from operations and our base will be the oasis town of Kaifra in Tunisia. *Our* mission is to examine the wreck of Tango Victor and report on it. The operation is exclusively ours, and the task of inspecting the aeroplane exclusively yours."

Bird's eyes bright, watching me. Bloody well lecturing, Loman all over, not even trying to talk persuasively because he didn't have to, all he had to do was work on my weak point and he knew what it was. Couldn't ever stand the little tick.

"The second thing is that although our objective for the mission is a small commercial aircraft forced down in the desert, and nothing more than that, the importance of the operation is very great." He was watching for my reactions and he knew he wouldn't get any and he wasn't getting any but he went on watching. "An hour ago I was in the radio room of the British Embassy here, talking to the Prime Minister himself. He wished to inform me personally that your mission is the key to a critical situation of the highest international proportions." Head on one side, the tone informative, impersonal. "I had been told that be-

fore, of course, on the highest authority. The fact that
they were asking a director of my experience to take
charge of the operation confirmed its importance."

He turned away and took a pace and took a pace back
and stood with his feet neatly together and finished me
off.

"This task calls for the highest professional talent. I accepted it on the sole condition that I could have you,
Quiller, as my executive in the field."

Little bastard.

He was in shock.

"You mind if we don't have the lights on?"

This was why Loman had hesitated when I'd asked him
if Fyson was still in the operation.

"It was so bright down there." I suppose he meant in
Sidi Ben Ali. "It's done something to my eyes."

He went and sat down, hurrying a little to reach the
chair. He sat with his hands on his knees, as if he had to
hold his body together, looking straight in front of him.
In the dull light coming from the bathroom I could see he
was shivering.

You see them like this at the Bureau when a mission's
blown up or they've just been too long in the field, they
come in like a rag doll and Tilson says hello old horse, bit
of a rough time was it?

"Just give me the essentials," I told him, "then I'll buzz
off."

"It's all"—it sounded as if he was afraid of stutter-
ing—"I dunno." Best he could do, I suppose, for the moment. I looked interestedly round the room, print of a
fourth-century tapestry, coloured photo of a mosque, a
slight gap in the curtains so I went to fix it and he said
Don't! in a kind of sob and I left it. He thought I'd been
going to open them.

But he couldn't have been tagged here or Loman
wouldn't have let me contact him. It was just his nerves.

There was a bottle of Scotch on the bedside table and
he'd already hit it for half but it hadn't done anything, he
was ice-cold sober. I poured some out and he took it and
drank and squeezed his face shut and I got the glass before he dropped it.

"Six months' leave," I said, "marvellous, think of the
fishing."

In a minute he made a big effort, jerking a hand out, pointing to the bottle—"Drink?"

"No thanks."

I told him about London so that he'd think of home, lot of tourists in, gawping at the Guards, bloody hot when I left but nothing compared with here of course, nice in the parks, took me damned nearly half an hour before he could straighten out enough to talk properly.

"You're not going there? Sidi Ben Ali?"

"No."

"Loman said it's Kaifra, next."

"That's right."

"He wasn't directing me."

"I know."

On the sole condition that I could have you, Quiller, as my executive in the field, little bastard, working on my weak point, professional pride—vanity, if you like, what's the difference, but at least he hadn't been lying: if London picked a man like him it was strictly business and if he picked a man like me it meant this op was in the extreme-hazard classification and he'd wanted someone who was in this game for kicks and with nothing to lose.

"They got O'Brien," he said.

"I know."

"There's not much I can tell you. We didn't—"

"There's a long gun somewhere, is there?"

Because even in this light I could see there were no marks on the hands or the face and he could hold a glass and walk all right, and he'd been afraid I was going to open the curtains.

"Yes."

He'd flinched just at the mention of it.

We've all got our little ways: some of the executives can't cope with unarmed combat but they'll fiddle with a bomb till they've got the spring out; others can stand hooding for days on end but touch them with a cigarette end and they'll break. But none of us like the telescopic rifle: once you know the opposition's hired a crack shot and he's looking for you in the sights it begins to worry you because you can't walk into the street or get out of your car or move across a window and it's inhibiting. You start thinking about how to stay alive instead of how to do the job and every time a door slams you miss a breath and in the end you'll finish up like Fyson.

He'd known they were serious, because of O'Brien.

"How long did it take them," I asked him, "to blow you?"

"Three days. I know it doesn't sound—"

"Don't worry. Loman says you did bloody well."

Loman hadn't said anything of the sort.

"Pissing me about"—he managed a faint grin—"he wouldn't say a thing like that, even if I'd"—he shrugged with a hand—"but they're very active, you know. I couldn't get much sleep because we didn't even have a safe house."

"They know the plane's there?"

"They know it's in the area, the rough area."

"Because you were there? You and O'Brien? Or d'you think they've got info from the U.K.?"

From what Loman had told me about the Special Branch I thought there must have been some arrests, but the link with Algeria was plain enough because of Tango Victor's course and there could be some signal lines out.

Fyson had become quiet and I knew I was pushing him too hard.

"It doesn't—"

"No I'm okay." With another effort he said: "The Algerian Air Force did a search about a week ago. Didn't Loman tell you?"

"He hasn't briefed me yet, not fully."

Loman had made the rdv in Tunis because of the airport, I knew that. He hadn't been certain of me and it would have been quicker to bring someone else in London-Tunis direct than from down south in Kaifra where there was probably only an airstrip. Otherwise he'd have made our rdv in Kaifra straight away.

"It might have been the sandstorm," said Fyson. "It can cover things in minutes, then uncover them again."

"Loman can tell me that part of the thing." I didn't want to drain the last of his strength before I'd put the only few questions that were important. "Listen, did you get an actual sight of the opposition?"

"Nothing recognisable." He was trying to pour himself another shot and I did it for him and he bit onto it and looked better and said: "There was always that bloody gun, you see—I kept catching sunlight on it and once I just walked into range and he chipped some brickwork away. It slows you up, doesn't it?"

"D'you know if—"

Then the phone rang.

It was right next to him and after a kind of jerk he just slid off the chair and the glass smashed before I could catch him and try to prop him up and answer the damned thing at the same time, it was very awkward.

4. Kaifra

At 1915 I checked out of the Hotel Africa and went across to where the Chrysler was parked.

It had been Loman on the telephone.

"I have just talked to London and we have another directive urging us to hurry."

"The opposition's making progress?"

"That is the inference."

"Then we'll hurry."

Now that I'd let him sell me the mission I wanted to bring it off and that sand-covered wreck out there had suddenly become personal to me: Tango Victor was mine.

"It is now 1851 and I've booked you on Tunis Air Flight 916 to Jerba, depart 1945, and instructed Avis to have a car standing by for you at your ETA, 2030. I shall take the later flight at 2115 to Jerba and proceed independently to Kaifra. At Kaifra you are booked in at the Hotel Royal Sahara, Room 37, and I shall telephone you as soon as I arrive. My ETA Jerba is 2200. In this season the Jerba-Kaifra route can be driven in five hours and this will be quicker than trying for air connections to Garaa Tebout, because Tunis Air don't fly there in any case. Do you have any questions?"

"What are you doing about Fyson?"

"He's been withdrawn from the mission, as I told you."

"But I mean his nerves are shot."

"I see. Then I'll send a doctor along."

We hung up.

So at 1915 I checked out of the Hotel Africa and went across to where the Chrysler was parked and they said later at the hospital that the glass had been the worst trouble because some very small fragments had got stuck in my face and they'd been difficult to find.

There weren't any bones broken but they were worried

by various signs of physiological shock that was still hanging about, and the bruises where I'd been flung across the
pavement. I didn't remember much, but there'd been no
actual retrogressive amnesia: I checked on that right
away. I was just walking towards the Chrysler and then
the senses went partially dead through overloading: very
bright flash, a lot of noise, smell of burnt aromatic nitro
compounds and the feel of the pavement sliding round under me.

They'd made a silly mistake, that was all. They
wouldn't have risked installing an ignition detonator link-
age right outside in the street: they'd had to put something quick on board and it was probably a rocking activator and a bus had passed close and the slipstream had
rocked the Chrysler enough to trigger the thing at the
wrong time, three or four seconds too early.

Loman came as soon as I rang him and found me in
the casualty room with bowls and bandages and blood everywhere.

"Listen, get me out of here and fix another plane."

Speech sounded a bit sloppy because the mouth had got
cut up by the glass and it had begun puffing.

"Do they want to keep you under observation?"

"Yes, there's the odd bit of glass left in but it'll work itself out, they know that. And for Christ sake signal
Fyson."

He knew what I meant. There'd been no tags on me
since I'd left London—every routine check I'd made had
come up negative—but when I'd called on Fyson in his
room I'd walked right into a red sector because they'd had
him under surveillance and he didn't know and now we'd
have to tell him.

"They're established agents," Loman said.

"Of course."

Because they had a dossier on me. Fyson had blown his
cover and thought he'd got clear but they'd tagged him
from Sidi Ben Ali to Tunis and put static surveillance on
him and when I'd shown up they'd checked their data and
said yes this one's for neutralising. But they'd only had
forty-five minutes to find and fix the car and rig the bang
and that could be why they'd mucked it.

The nurse came back with another hypodermic and I
said not now and left it to Loman, it was his job, and he
was signing some kind of form accepting responsibility

when I got my flight bag and took a taxi and double-checked for ticks all the way along the Khaireddine Pacha because we didn't want any trouble down at our base and I had to get there clean.

The taxi seemed to be swerving a bit down the long perspective of the eucalyptuses, either because of the cross-wind or because the driver kept looking at me in the mirror and trying to pluck up the courage to ask me what brand of razor I used because he didn't want one, or maybe it was the hangover from the blast wave upsetting the semicircular canals: there was still some head noise.

But I could focus all right and there were no tags and the airport was negative and at 2115 I was airborne on Flight 917 with Loman's ticket and the girl was asking me what I wanted to drink.

There was a flight on the board at Jerba scheduled in at 2235 and I knew Loman would be on that one because of the hurry directive from Control: he wouldn't hang round in Tunis with his executive already homed in at base.

They had a Mercedes 220 lined up and it had an air-conditioner but I didn't switch it on: the day's heat still pressed down on the island from a stifling sky but there wouldn't be any encapsulated environment for me in the desert so I let the organism start adapting as we ran through Houmt Souk and took the causeway to Zarzis.

Starlight and the black plumage of date palms rushing overhead, the screen pocked and silvered by the death of insects and the heat coming on progressively as the road ran south until I had to start breathing consciously to keep awake.

Hit something once, a bump and the lights swinging and the wheel floating and more difficult, quite a job, much more difficult than I'd thought, than it should be, to keep traction and pull her back straight, worried me and we slowed, of course they'd been perfectly right, twenty-four hours' observation, it was just that those fidgety pimps in London wouldn't give us a break.

Through midnight at Remada and slowing again to seventy-five along the sandy track to Bj Djeneiene to avoid the turn-off at the Libyan frontier, the bruises burning now and the eyes trying to sort out the fast-incoming data without losing focus through fatigue: but the mirror was clear and if Loman didn't pick up a tag we'd have a safe base to jump from in the south.

Kaifra: 0250.

Sandy streets buried among dark massed palms, a few naked bulbs at the crossings, the headlights swinging over the humped shapes of Arabs sleeping below white walls, a mosque with a candle burning, the wind dead and the heat thick on the air and the nerves uncertain, a longing for sleep.

Royal Sahara.

Mais qu'est-ce-que vous avez m'sieu'?

Rien, un petit accident sur la route.

Il vous faut des soins?

Non, c'est fait. Du sommeil, c'est tout.

In Room 37, air-conditioning, wonderfully cool: I turned it off and opened the window and let the heat in, like opening an oven door, get used to it, be worse out there in Longitude 8°3′ Latitude 30°4′, start adapting and don't bloody well gripe.

Sleep.

Loman dragged me out of dreams of flying glass and Corinne swathed in bandages, it's the strain on the arms she was saying.

0345.

"No. Were you?"

"No."

He sounded relieved about this because it had been the tags on Fyson that had led to the bomb thing and he didn't want his executive blown from under him before he could mount the op.

"I'm speaking from base. We shall need a little more time to set up the radio, so the next rdv is for 1500 hours tomorrow at the Auberge Yasmina, rue des Singes. Please repeat."

Straight out of the bloody book, that was Loman for you.

I said I've got that and the thing went dead with a rather pettish click.

The Arab screamed, lurching backwards till he struck the wall and crouched there with his withered brown hands flung out in protection, the scarecrow body shaking under the robes, the old eyes staring in terror and the mouth fixed in the scream that was dying now, its energy exhausted.

Then hideously he began again, the sound shrilling out

of him until quick heels came tapping and a needle flashed and he collapsed like a sack of bones, whimpering.

Jbal f-al Sma, u-tēz kbīz lli khal Šams . . .

The nurse tried to lift him and I got up.

"Puis-je vous aider?"

"Okay," the big man said.

He lifted the Arab and stood with him in his arms.

"There were magnetic storms," the girl said, "it is often the way." She led the big man through the passage and into a room on the other side as footsteps neared, hurrying. The scream had woken the place up.

Mountains in the sky, and great birds darkening the heavens . . .

The driller came back and said: "Holy cats. Enough to make you knock off the booze!" He sat down, the sweat shining on his big red face and along his arms as he took a packet of Gauloise and offered me one. "Giving it up?" He scratched a match for himself. "Magnetic storms my arse—they're checking the bread supplies down at the research station, you know that? Everybody knows it's ergot. You been here long, buster?"

"Not long."

"He ain't the only case, there's others. Six months ago there was an outbreak in Mali, thousand miles south of here. You heard of ergot?"

"Grain fungus."

"That's it. There was a case in France, remember? Half a village went loco. You with the Petrocombine outfit?"

"Attached."

"I'm Bob Vickers, South 5."

"Charles Gage."

He had a hand like an earth shovel.

"We've got trouble. Smashed a core drill on a fault, four thousand deep."

The nurse came back and told him to put his cigarette out and began work on my dressings.

"Okay, dolly. You free tonight?"

Another truck drummed past the building, heading south to Camp 4. The windows vibrated and sand flew against the glass. They'd woken me at dawn, the trucks: this was the last oasis town before the drilling complex nearer the frontier.

"What happened to you, Charlie?"

"I ran off the road."

"Join the club. Mine was a horned viper—see that?"

He showed me the fang marks.

"Can you pull this sleeve off, please?"

The clinical smell of Dermo-Cuivre.

"You busters hit any oil yet down at South 4?"

"Would I tell you?"

His laugh boomed like a cannon.

"You can relax, Charlie, I'm a godless bum. If my contract ends before they get that drill out I'm moving right over to Anglo-Belge, okay? Bob Vickers works for the highest bidder."

He picked up the *Tribune* that lay on top of the pile.

"How long will this take?"

"Perhaps a little time." Her smile was quick but there was a flicker to the olive-brown eyes: the Arab had unnerved her. "There are many pieces of glass."

They'd been cutting their way out as the organism rejected them and I'd come here because I didn't want the lacerations to start opening up again later when the mission was running and the stress came on.

"How long have you got to live?"

"You mean me?"

"With a horned viper bite."

His laugh boomed again and a spoon tinkled in a beaker.

"Holy cats, that was four days ago. I'm just here for the routine blood test, so take your time."

She irrigated again and another fragment rang into the enamel bowl. The windows of the Chrysler had been given a shrapnel effect by the blast.

At 0900 this morning on Radio Tunis I'd heard that Loman had put immediate smoke out. By the sources quoted I knew he must have reached half a dozen major night desks via the Embassy signals room and his story was accepted on the principle that to a jaded night editor looking for a last-minute flash, one rumour was as good as another.

An "official enquiry" had "established" that Mr. C. W. Gage, a British geophysical consultant on business in Tunis, had narrowly escaped being the innocent victim of an error on the part of "certain political activists" when the car he was hiring exploded in the street. The enquiry led to the discovery that the man—so far unnamed—who had hired the car immediately prior to Mr. Gage was a

known member of the fanatical United Arab Front organisation, and it was therefore "confidently believed" that
this man had been the intended victim.

It was routine cover.

I don't know what the actual figures are but a big per-
centage of people in my trade finish up at the wrong end
of a bang and even the public has an idea that a law-abid-
ing citizen can get into his car quite often without being
blasted into Christendom. The classic statement to the
press is that "he didn't have an enemy in the world" and
it won't always wash with the public and it won't ever
wash with the background monitoring sections of the major intelligence networks because they automatically send
for pictures and if they recognise the face they want to
know what X was doing in Tunis or Cairo or Bonn and
there'll be a directive for someone to find out.

So today they'd pick up the radio story and tomorrow
they'd be looking at my picture in Washington and Moscow and Peking and pressing the buzzer and saying go
and see if you can find out what the London lot are doing
in North Africa.

The smoke Loman had put out wouldn't provide total
cover but it was the best he could do and he'd done it.
The only thing that worried me, by its implications, was
the fact that today he'd have to do the same thing again
because Radio Tunis had also reported that the body of
another Englishman had been found floating in the harbour late last night and that his name was Fyson.

The Auberge Yasmina was a decaying French Colonial
residence with gilded cupolas and a forecourt buried under the shade of rotting palms where I could hear rats
running. The sun's rays penetrated only in places, making
pools of light on the crumbling mosaic floor.

The door hung open and I went inside. After the glare
of the street it seemed almost dark in here but I could see
a figure, robed in white and motionless in the middle of
the hall.

"*Ahlah ou sahlan.*"

By the angle of his head I saw that he was looking
slightly away from me, and because the stranger's footstep
had worried him I answered quickly: *Saha. Ala slametek.*
In North Africa they are only just beginning to control
sandfly trachoma.

He said I should go up and I passed him and then heard Loman's voice from the stairs.

"All right, Quiller."

As we climbed, our shoes grating on chips of marble that had broken away from the mosaic, the hot afternoon light blazed through coloured glass so that rainbow patterns flowed across Loman's shoulder as he led the way up.

"They run it as a small hotel, but we're alone here except for one or two staff. The heat's too much for the tourists in Kaifra and this is the dead season."

"What's our cover?"

"Radio liaison with Petrocombine's South 4 camp for supplies and emergency signals."

By the time we reached the top floor we were sweating hard and he was wiping his face because this wasn't the Hotel Royal Sahara and there wasn't a lift and there wasn't any air-conditioning. Our weight set the passage vibrating invisibly and flakes of plaster drifted like orange blossoms from the frescoed walls.

The radio base was at the end of the building and I followed Loman in. From the size of the domed ceiling we were now underneath one of the great gilded cupolas I'd seen from the street. Faded arabesque screens, cracked mosaic floor and the minimal mod. cons. of a fifth-category package-deal hotel: bed, washbasin, curtained shower.

"This is Diane Bowman, our radio operator."

There wasn't anything in his tone.

He made it sound just like a casual introduction. But he didn't look at me: at least he had the grace to look away as he showed me how far things had gone towards perdition, how desperately he'd been driven by London to rig up this mission they'd asked for, to rig the thing up with no time for selective staffing or initial briefing and no established access facilities and not a hope in hell of doing anything more than send this whole operation staggering blindly on till it finished both of us.

Tonelessly he said: "This is Quiller, the executive in the field."

I think she came forward a pace to greet me, I don't remember, and then I suppose stopped, seeing I didn't move.

Fair hair and a young face, the mouth surprised and

the eyes waiting, uncertain of me, the stance defensive, the bare arms hanging loose but the hands tensed, a slight girl, a girl out of a fashion magazine, thin-bodied in a fisherman's vest and slacks and sandals, this summer's gear for Brighton or the Broads and all the rage and oh Christ a mission to run and this child caught in its machinery.

When I could, I looked at Loman.

There was nothing in my tone either; we'd both of us been trained, long ago, out of our bad habits; but he knew what was in my mind.

"How long has she been operating on priority missions?"

He stood with his hands tucked neatly behind him, head on one side but still not looking at me, maybe prepared for me to blow up in his face and get it over, maybe deciding on policy not to answer me till I forced him.

"Long enough," the girl said, "to know how to do it."

Her eyes were steady now, no longer uncertain of me. She stood with her arms folded and her chin lifted a fraction.

Loman spoke suddenly. I suppose the anger in her voice had encouraged him.

"When I direct a mission I choose first-class people and if this radio operator has my approval then you can have every confidence in her."

He couldn't even make it sound right.

My mind had partially blanked off and I couldn't think of anything useful to say: he and I both knew what the situation was and there wasn't anything to talk about. Professional instinct was still functioning, though, and I crossed the uneven mosaic to the window and pulled down the venetian blind and fixed the catch.

"Keep it shut."

She said:

"I like the view."

It was very quiet here: the postmeridian heat of the August sun was lying like a dead weight on the town and we were among the few people who weren't deep in a siesta. No sound came from outside this room, no sound at all.

Loman took out his damp silk handkerchief and wiped his polished face. The sweat trickled on me as the organism tried to reduce the body temperature. I didn't move. I was beginning to lose the fine-tuned sense of direction, of shape, of purpose, the thing we call mission feel that develops by infinite degrees as we go forward, step by step, into the area where we have committed ourselves to unknown tasks in the teeth of unknown hazards: the sense that tells us, at every step, that it's now too late to turn back.

This I was beginning to lose.

"Loman. It's no go."

He made an impatient gesture but said nothing.

I didn't look at the girl. It wasn't her fault.

Under the big dome my voice echoed strangely.

"You'd better signal London. Get some professional staff."

He was standing perfectly still, a listening bird, his small eyes bright and his neat head tilted. I knew there wasn't anything he could say because it was beyond him now: there wasn't time to get anyone capable from London and it wasn't his fault but I was getting fed up.

"I can get killed this way, Loman. We all can. For nothing. Just because those incompetent bastards in London have taken on a job that's got to be done so fast that we can't even hope to survive for as long as it takes to do it. This isn't an intelligence operation: it's a suicide pact."

Loman could think quite fast but he couldn't talk while he was doing it and he didn't talk now so I shut up and let him get on with it because this was his pigeon: when the director in the field sends the executive in there's got to be a professional setup. We didn't have one.

I suppose he'd thought of a dozen angles of attack in those few seconds and obviously the one he chose was the one he thought was right and he was wrong.

"I think you're showing an unreasonable bias towards—"

"Is that so?" I was really very fed up. "We've been called in by a panic directive to clear up the wreck of an operation that went off half-cocked and killed one man and blew another and by a bit of luck I missed a bomb and last night they picked Fyson out of Tunis harbour and it'd be nice to think that when they grilled him he didn't break but the last time I saw him alive his nerve had gone so they wouldn't have had any trouble. How safe's our base now, Loman? And all you can do about it is pick a kid out of school who leaves her radio in direct sight of a building at fifty yards optical range even through low-powered glasses and doesn't pull the blind down because she likes the view."

In ten seconds he looked at me and said:

"She is an efficient radio operator. Highly efficient."

When I turned she was watching me, angry because of what I'd said about her, frightened because of what I'd said about Fyson.

"All right she's an efficient radio operator but who's going to look after her if I'm in the desert and you have to leave base for five minutes?"

Before he could answer she said:

"I can look after myself."

"How?"

She drew very fast and I hit the thing before she'd finished and it spun high and chipped plaster off the wall and curved down and skittered across the mosaic.

"You have to be faster than that."

Loman said bleakly:

"I would undertake to man the base personally at all times."

"Good of you."

I went over and picked the gun up and wiped the plaster off and checked for damage and gave it back to her, a half-pound six-shot .25 standard lightweight, wouldn't stop a mouse.

"And leave the safety catch off. There's no point in a fast draw if the trigger's locked."

She took it but wouldn't look at me, her eyes were down and she was breathing fast, the heat and of course the frustration. I must have bruised her hand but she didn't let herself nurse it, a point for that but one point wasn't enough to qualify her for running the radio liaison of a mission with the death roll rising before we were even on our marks.

Loman was still thinking but he couldn't find what he wanted: an argument that could keep me with him. It was too late now for an easy trap like the one he'd used on me before.

"She was head of signals at the Embassy in Tunis and monitoring the Egyptian-Israeli frontier-incident reports direct for London. She has fluent French, Italian, and Arabic with five dialects."

I looked at the radio, its facia striped by the shadows of

the sunblind. It was a KW 2000CA single-sideband transceiver with four channels on the dial and an auto-scrambler.

"What's your frequency coverage?"

Her head came up.

"3.0 to 19 mc/s."

"Channels?"

"Four preset crystal controlled."

"Receiver sensitivity?"

"Better than one microvolt for one watt output."

"What frequencies would you use in this area?"

"7 MHz for daytime propagation conditions, 3 MHz at
night."

"How long have you worked with this type?"

"Over two years."

"Did you choose it because of that?"

"No. Because it's perfect for the conditions here."

I nodded and turned away.

Loman was watching me. I felt him watching.

She was all right on radio and she knew how the thing
worked but if I went out there a hundred miles deep into
the desert I'd be like a diver with a lifeline. My lifeline
would be the radio liaison facility and if it were put out
of action I'd fry out there like a louse. Worse: the mission would end at the same time and in the same place,
objective unaccomplished.

Loman said:

"Arrangements have been made to jump you in rather
soon."

"How soon?"

"Tonight."

This was the argument he'd been looking for.

The nearer you get to the brink of a mission the faster
you want to go: it's a kind of target attraction and you
don't want to pull out and the little bastard knew this and
now he'd thrown me the deadline and it was close. In a
matter of hours I could be out there in the silence of the
sands and alone with the objective: the broken-winged
smudge on the desert floor that no one had been closer to
than sixty-five thousand feet.

Tango Victor.

I looked at the girl.

"Did you volunteer for this kind of work?"

"Yes."

"You know it's dangerous?"

"Yes."

"What makes you want to do it?"

"The interest. And the danger."

"Would you say you had a strong sense of survival?"

"Pretty strong, yes. I'd fight like hell."

I told Loman he could brief me.

5. Mohamed

She hit the set open.

Tango to Embassy.

Loman was restive again, thinking with his feet. He'd got me to the jump-off point and there weren't any more doubts: tonight the mission would start running.

Tango to Embassy.

"What time," he asked me, "did you hear it?"

"0900 on Radio Tunis."

Embassy to Tango. Receiving you.

"No details? Just that he was found in the harbour?"

"An Englishman named Fyson. A police enquiry has begun."

Stand by, please.

She gave him the mike.

This is for London, Liaison 9. F Freddie absent believe other hand believe may pip-squeak first. No: pip-squeak. Near smoke negative please delegate. Q Quaker home on TJ-TK-S-102 repeat TJ-TK-S-102. Queries? Tango out.

I'd spread the map on the bed and he came over and began briefing me.

"I told you that after Tango Victor had taken off from the U.K. there was a suspected false signature found on a Customs and Excise declaration form. It was discovered that the pilot had knowingly taken off without proper freight inspection. Twenty-four hours later a report went in to D.I.6 in London that the Algerian Air Force was in the process of mounting a ground search by five squadrons of its desert-reconnaissance branch along this twenty-kilometre band from Oran here on the Mediterranean coast to Alouef, south of this upland here, the Plateau de Tademaït. It was described as the usual 'routine exercise.' "

"Was there any monitoring liaison at that stage?"

Customs, Special Branch, D.I.6, and the Bureau were very disparate organisations.

"No. Monitoring liaison began when a telephone call from a Frenchwoman in Tripoli was received at the airfield where Tango Victor's pilot was based—incidentally his name is Holt. The Special Branch was then called in and it was recognised that the twenty-kilometre band on the map here in fact straddled the proposed course of the freighter overland south of the Mediterranean. It seems that Holt diverted his flight to Tripoli without informing anyone, landing for an overnight stop in order to visit an acquaintance who lives there—the woman who telephoned the airfield in the evening of the next day. Evidently he had told her that he was to fly back to the U.K. after seeing her, and she phoned to make sure he'd arrived safely. It was of course only from that point in time that anyone in London knew that Holt's course across Algeria had been Tripoli-Alouef, not Oran-Alouef."

The picture was coming up and I did a visual check on the map and saw that a line drawn from Tripoli to Alouef would pass through our target area: Longitude 8°3′ by Latitude 30°4′.

"This was why the Algerian Air Force was unable to find the wreck and why the R.A.F. succeeded. The recent actions against O'Brien, Fyson, and yourself make it clear that the opposition realises that we know where the plane is and that they're anxious to reach it before we do."

"You think they're overlooking the obvious?"

He turned away from the map and walked neatly up and down. "No. I think they don't rate their chances very high."

He'd got the point but I didn't expect him to fill anything in for me: this was a briefing session at Local Control, not a planning operation in London. But there was an equation that didn't work out and it worried me: the opposition couldn't have overlooked the obvious point that if they wanted to reach Tango Victor the best thing to do would be to follow us in and make an overkill on the spot. Loman thought they weren't too sanguine about this and maybe he was right.

There was a theory I liked even less: they could have killed off O'Brien and Fyson and attempted to kill me too *because they knew where Tango Victor was lying.* And we

had to be held off while they tried to reach it. This would
explain the hurry directive from London.

"What are the chances of another desert-recco exercise?"

He stopped pacing and looked at the wall and I knew
this was something that needled him.

"That's quite impossible to deduce." He was trying to
make up his mind whether to block me off here and avoid
overloading or cover the situation for me and he couldn't
reach a decision standing still so he got into motion again.
"The opposition may conceivably include factions other
than Algerian. We shouldn't discount Libya or Egypt or
the United Arab Front organisation. Nor should we discount the effects of internecine shifts of policy. The lack
of a second search by the Algerian Air Force—this time
over the target area—does not necessarily indicate that
they know where the aeroplane came down: it could be
due to a reluctance on the part of the newly formed government in Algiers to mount an 'exercise' so close to the
Tunisian and Libyan borders. The assassination of King
Hamouda and the seizure of power by the generals has
left North African relationships rather delicate for the
time being."

I looked at the map. If we could read it properly it
could answer most of the questions.

"What made the opposition think the plane came down
near the Tunisian border?"

He looked at me with his shoulders drooping suddenly.

"O'Brien. Then Fyson."

"Then me."

"That wasn't your fault."

"I walked straight into surveillance."

"You could hardly avoid it."

"Do you think that our presence in the field is the *only*
reason why they believe Tango Victor came down within
a hundred miles of Kaifra?"

In a moment he said:

"I would like to."

I'd never seen Loman like this before: within hours of
throwing the mission into gear he was uncertain on major
aspects that London should have cleared for him before
sending either of us into the field. Everything about this
operation stank of panic and I didn't like it because I was

the ferret and the ferret's always the first to go when the whole thing blows apart.

"Who have you got lined up?"

He stopped moving about.

"Lined up?"

"If I come a mucker."

I felt the girl watching me from near the radio.

"No one," Loman said.

"With a thing as shaky as this—"

"I anticipate success." His tone had risen a fraction and he controlled it at once. "Complete success. You understand?" He was wiping his face again. "Had there been no chance of complete success I would have refused to direct the mission, regardless of pressure. I am asking you to proceed with every confidence, both in me and in the constant support we shall have from London."

I was learning something about Loman: the higher the stress the more he talked like a schoolmistress.

"All right. Tell me about access, will you?"

He began moving again at once. I'd pushed the briefing into the final phase and he wouldn't have to worry any more about the background aspects: the area where he was critically uncertain.

"You will rendezvous with a French pilot tonight as soon as he contacts me to say he's ready. His name is Gaston Chirac and he was engaged in combat flying during the Algerian war. Since then he has flown for the oil companies in desert survey work and knows the area thoroughly; he was also the world sailplane champion three years ago when he raised the altitude record to forty-six thousand feet. There is only one way of sending you into the target area without either surveillance or active obstruction and that is by glider."

"And parachute?"

"And of course parachute. Since this is a night drop, both will be dull black, to ensure that you go in unseen as well as unheard. The take-off is arranged for 2300 hours. The rock outcrop you saw on the reconnaissance photographs is approximately five hundred yards from the aeroplane and can be used as a landmark even by starlight; it may also conceivably offer partial shade during the day, though that is less certain. Your equipment will comprise the second transceiver, a 35-mm. reflex camera with flash, and of course desert-survival gear."

"What's the estimated duration?"

He'd been pacing towards me and he turned away when I said that and it needn't have meant anything but I thought it did because my nerves were getting into tune as the deadline approached and they could catch vibrations that I'd miss at other times.

"Flexible." I didn't hear anything in his tone because he'd make bloody sure of that. "Forty-eight hours at the most: you'll have rations and water for that period, plus reserves. The task itself is not exacting: we are asked for photographs of the plane and its cargo. At the same time you will be reporting in precise detail by radio on what you discover, and your report will go directly onto tape in this room."

So that if I didn't survive, all they'd lose were the photographs. That was all right.

I left the map and went over to the carved teak table and looked at the second transceiver. There was a recessed button that the other one didn't have.

"Manual destruct?"

"Yes. Ten-second fuse."

"Acid?"

"Explosive."

"Safe range?"

"Five yards."

He paused for a moment and said: "In any case it's purely a refinement: the worst you'll have to contend with in the desert will be the heat. The more difficult phase of this operation is getting you to the jump-off point without attracting surveillance or obstructive action. We must therefore take every possible care."

Near the edge of the retina an object is invisible: but movement can be seen. At the actual edge of the retina not even movement shows itself: but it triggers a reflex and the eyes will turn quickly to bring the moving object into central vision for inspection.

Static objects have no automatic interest unless their shape is significant, but to all animals movement has its own primitive significance: it may be signalling the presence of food in the form of prey or of danger in the form of a predator. In man, whose prey is killed and processed for him, the perception of movement serves as a warning alone, until the movement can be explained.

Unexplained movement is always suspect.

The rendezvous with Chirac had been fixed for 2100 hours at a *redjem* seven kilometres along the road to Garaa Tebout and I was getting into the Mercedes when the visual reflex was stimulated and I turned my head and looked away again and pulled the seat belt tight and got the engine going and thought Christ, they didn't even let Fyson die in peace.

Loman had told me he'd got here from Tunis with no tags and he couldn't have made a mistake about that because on those long straight stretches through the olive groves he would have seen a tag a mile away. I'd got here clean too and it was nothing to do with the girl because there'd been no surveillance when I'd gone to our base: that's a trip when you treble-check. So it was impossible that anyone knew I'd holed-up in Kaifra: if you forgot about Fyson.

Fyson had known I was coming here and they wouldn't have had to do very much because his nerves had been shot and he didn't carry a 9-suffix and they'd only had one question for him so it was easy and Loman wasn't being funny when he said the most difficult stage of this operation was getting me to the jump-off without someone trying to stop me.

I turned the 220 and drove under the lights of the hotel marquee and looked round to see if there were anything coming and took the east road through the tunnel of overhanging palms and checked the mirror and kept the speed steady at thirty, a little more, such a nice evening for a drive.

The slipstream didn't cool anything: it just circulated the heat. There were gnats already sticking to the windscreen and I used the wiper jets and the screen went silver and slowy dark again. The roads in Kaifra are sanded over in places: the *ghibli* blows it from the south and nobody feels like sweeping it away so it's left for the wheeled traffic to break up the drifts and scatter the sand towards the edge of the road.

I didn't like the way Loman had said the estimated duration of my work in the target area was "flexible." After two seconds he'd put it at forty-eight hours maximum but that didn't mean anything more than that I'd forced him into an obligatory answer. There are always unknown factors in any target area whether it's the office of the Cuban

Minister for Defence or the off-limits research and development section of a Japanese electronics complex under government contract or a square mile of sand in the Sahara, but the director in the field makes a point of mounting a model operation on paper before he sets the real one running: and people like Loman and Egerton and Mildmay do it with a slide rule and a stop watch and a blueprint of the area.

That word "flexible" simply meant that on this operation the director in the field didn't know how long it should take me to do the work once I'd gained access and it pointed to the same thing that all the other features pointed to: those bastards in London were sending me in with almost no preparation and once I was there I'd have to carry the whole of the load. The "constant support from London" he'd talked about was strict cock because there'd be nothing London could do if I mucked it right in the middle of the job.

Yes, of course I must try not to muck it but in a panic directive like this one the chances were a bloody sight higher.

A lovely night, with clear stars and soft shadows. The thing was to do it without bending a wing or anything because of police enquiries later. I didn't want to leave any paint.

He wasn't using his dipped heads but the sidelights were quite bright enough for me: they kept floating into the mirror and out again as we left the avenue of palms and got onto the wide sandy road bordering the desert.

Dark 404, nothing exceptional.

And he was alone. Wearing a fez, someone local. But quite professional, the way he hung back a long way and took a short cut now and then, crossing my bows a hundred yards ahead as if he were someone else. He knew the roads here, the intersections, and after ten minutes I got fed up because he was so showy: it wasn't going to be easy with this one. So I did a U-turn and took three rights with the lights out and caught him at an intersection and he had the grace to swerve and look worried but it didn't make things any better because he began hanging on much closer so the only thing it proved was that I'd done it on my own doorstep.

He was only a tag: there wouldn't be any action unless

I did something busy. If they'd wanted to neutralise me
they'd have used two men: one with the wheel, one with
the gun, the rear tyres first to slow me and then the rear
window, picking at the bottom left-hand corner while I
couldn't duck any lower without losing sight of the road.

He only wanted to know where I was going.

The rdv was twelve minutes from now and I didn't
want to turn up late for Chirac so I started a slow routine,
using the sand to slide on and flicking the lights out at the
fast end of a right-angle turn and doubling in the dark
and slipping him twice before he worked out the score
and decided to keep so close that I could see his eyes in
the mirror. No go.

Kaifra isn't a big place and it's surrounded by desert
and that made it difficult for me: there wasn't much
choice of terrain. I suppose he'd got his air-conditioning
on and that made me fed up again so I thought I should
go and stare him out somewhere along the desert road to
South 4.

I've only done it twice before and I don't like it because
there's a touch of Russian roulette about it and that's inconsistent: in order to complete a mission you have to
stay alive.

If Loman had known what I was going to do he would
have had the shits and I tried not to let this reinforce my
decision to do it. He would have argued that it was the
duty of an executive not only to protect himself against
obstructive action by the opposition but also to avoid
resorting to tactics that could hazard the mission, so forth.

On the other hand my chances of getting out of the
present situation alive weren't too high either: the man in
the 404 realised that I was going somewhere exclusive because I'd been trying to throw him off. We could keep
this up for half the night and if we went anywhere near
his base he might decide to bring in some support to finish
me off and if you start running with one on the tail and
another one closing in from ahead of you the chances get
progressively disappointing until they move in for the kill.

So I turned left twice and then right and found the
road that ran through fifteen miles of dunes to the South
4 camp. The massed palms blocked most of the starlight
but we didn't go onto heads and he kept coming up very
close every time I jabbed the brakes and when he got used

to the rhythm of the thing I broke it and started drifting across his bows and he didn't like that either because we couldn't see much with parking lights and I suppose he didn't want to switch his heads on because it would have looked so amateur.

Brakes: drift. Another drift and sand flew as the tyres scattered it. Brakes: oh very close and I cleared it because I didn't want to leave any paint on him.

Drift. Brake—drift and he got nervous and hit something, trunk of a palm and then I gunned up and he spun a lot and I lost him and swung into the long desert road and went all the way up through the gears on the automatic and crossed the hundred mark with the power still coming on, no lights yet in the mirror but they'd be there soon.

Ravines both sides.

Not deep ones but the engineers had followed the natural lie of a bedrock *gassi* and then raised the roadway high enough to stop the south-blowing *ghibli* from burying it under permanent drifts of sand.

Coming now, yes.

Faint lights in the mirror. Headlights, faint.

It would be all right out here. The setting was classic: sand, stars, and the highway leaning across the desert to the horizon, a fallen column. There was nothing complicated.

You can do it by first putting a critical amount of distance between your own car and theirs. You can do this either by relying on superior acceleration and maximum speed to take care of the distance-factor or by taking them through a series of feints and passes to slow them up before you go out for the kill.

The 220 had the edge on the 404 but it would have taken twenty miles to build up the degree of distance needed and I didn't have the time and that was why I'd made a point of slowing him in phase 1: it had brought the time-factor right down with a bang and the whole thing would now be over within the next thirty seconds and if I were still all right I could go back and keep the Chirac rdv more or less on time.

It was very important not to touch him. Loman could do quite a lot to keep me out of official trouble because his cover provided him with the required diplomatic immunity and the Embassy had been asked to give immedi-

ate support in the event of a signal, but things could get
tricky despite precautions and two years ago when Proctor
had just finished setting up final penetration for a first-
class cipher break in a Curtain state consulate he blew the
mission because he'd left his car parked on a pedestrian
crossing and London got very upset.

Tonight there was going to be an accident and if it was
the 404's and not mine I wasn't going to report it and everything would be all right so long as there weren't any
marks on the Mercedes.

The power was full on and I left it for five seconds
while I worked out the odds. It depended on the kind of
man he was: it depended totally on that. And I didn't
know him. He could drive all right and didn't chuck it in
when things got rough but it didn't tell me much about
the one factor that would finally decide the issue: his
breaking point.

No data.

It raised the risk but it was a calculated risk and the
odds looked fair so I kicked the brakes and watched the
needle because in the starlight the swinging parallax of
the dunes didn't make for a good enough reference and it
was safer to drive on instruments. Patch of sand and we
lost traction and I got it back and wrapped the friction
round again, slowing through ninety, seventy, fifty with the
lights in the mirror getting brighter as the distance closed.

Fabric getting hot: normal. Maximum deceleration
curve right out of the book and very effective but now I
began wondering if I'd allowed the correct distance: all
I'd had for a reference was the time he'd taken to come
back into the mirror and the brightness of his headlights
when he'd turned them on.

Twenty.

Ten.

Zero and I used the last of the momentum to swing the
220 into a fast U that brought us facing the way we'd
come and then I gunned up by leaving my foot just where
it was and letting the automatic send the needle up progressively.

His headlights seemed rather bright even allowing for
the fact that I was now facing them and I started wondering again whether I'd judged things right but there was a
rising fifty on the clock by now and everything was

shaping up well enough; I think it was only the primitive
animal brain starting to worry: the organism didn't like
the look of this at all, up on its back legs and bloody well
whining.

Ignore.

Speed now 70.

His estimated speed: 80 plus.

Minimum impact figure if things went wrong: 150.

I didn't put the heads on yet because I wanted to save
that till later: three or four seconds from now. At the moment he wouldn't be absolutely sure what I was doing: he
would have lost my rear lamps but that could mean I'd
simply turned them off; he would have picked up my
parking lights but he wouldn't necessarily identify them:
with an eye-level horizon the big North African stars
seemed to be floating on the dunes and this would confuse
him.

I had to wait for the instant when he realised that I'd
turned round and was coming at him on a very fast collision course: then I'd start making him nervous in the final few seconds in the hope that he'd see the point.

Bloody well whining. Brain-think had partially gone and
the organism was snivelling about the risk: we wouldn't
be here tomorrow, no more women, no more anything, so
forth. His headlights very bright in my eyes, almost blinding. The dunes streaming past, the warm air rushing at
the windows. Clock: 85.

Running it close.

Certain areas of the forebrain still functioning: the
paramount factor was his threshold of fear and that was
established by personal characteristics: the degree to
which he valued life, the extent of his subservience to the
idea of Allah, the measure of his willingness or otherwise
to be beaten in a dare, other things, many other things.
Not at all certain this was in fact forebrain activity: point
now reached when self-critical capacity very much dimin-
ished, sounded more like the organism panicking again,
trying desperately to raise doubts and scare me into
chucking it.

No go.

It was quite a narrow road. It had been designed to
take the width of two trucks with enough space between
to let them pass. This meant that if you were driving a car

the size of the Mercedes 220 and kept right in the middle of the road there wouldn't be room for anyone else.

Headlights dazzling now and no means of judging distance any more, the gap closing at a rising 165 mph and too risky to leave it later than this so I hit the switch and flooded him with light and hit the horns to bring in the scare factor of the karate yell and sat there staring him out.

I wondered what his name was.

Ahmed Somebody. Mohamed Somebody.

Thirty-four missions and only a few scars and then I met a man named Mohamed, unlikely name for an epitaph, why not Blenkinsop? My own, yes, my own fault. Not fault exactly. Whole thing was calculated. Miscalculated, thought he'd break first.

Light fierce and sight gone, driving blind, eyes shut and the retinas burning. Sound coming in explosively fast from the desert night, he'd been so far away, now so close.

Dark.

Dark and the wind rocking as the slipstreams hit and dragged and set up turbulence, a great cough of sound then silence.

Brakes.

Eyes watering badly, the road swimming. Dark only comparative after the blinding light, silence relative to that unpleasant explosive cough, be interesting one day to try estimating how close he'd passed, how late he'd left it, how far he'd been airborne over the ravine before gravity overcame momentum, slide rules, and stop watches, but really only one of those things you think are still going to be interesting later. They're not. Christ sake more brakes.

Slowing.

Nearside tyres nibbling at the edge of the road, important not to go over, anything could happen if you hit ground at a bad angle and started rolling. Don't spoil it now.

Brakes. Slowing and locking and sliding and bringing it down through fifty, forty, with the ribs pressing into the seat belt. Acid in the stomach, various glands performing, a lot of adrenalin, a certain degree of weakness along the forearms, general feeling of lassitude as the organism tried to break the tension down, all right you snivelling little tick, I won't do it again.

When the speed was low enough I swung the wheel over and turned back. There was an orange glow against the sky about a mile away and by the time I got there most of the petrol had burnt out. I went close enough to make sure what had happened and then got back into the car.

6. Chirac

"*C'est bien le numéro 136 que vous m'avez demandé, m'sieur?*"

"*Oui, Auberge Yasmina.*"

"*Ça ne répond pas.*"

"*Insistez un peu.*"

"*Mais il ne sonne même pas, m'sieur.*"

"*Pourquoi pas?*"

"*Eh b'en, il est en dérangement. Je vais—*"

"*Vous êtes certaine?*"

"*Absolument. Je vias le signler. Je regrette, m'sieur.*"

The cabin was stifling.

I hung up.

There was still the odd flash, the afterimage of his headlights: the retinas kept registering the glare. My hands weren't perfectly steady yet: when you do something like that the organism thinks more about the consequences after you've done it than before, because the tension has gone and there's time for nightmares.

Disregard.

Outside the cabin the terrace of the Oasis Bar was crowded, mostly with oil men in transit to and from Petrocombine's South 4 camp. Light from amber lanterns threw shadows from the trellis screens and the tendrils of tropical creepers; a Malouf Tunisien from overhead speakers was half-drowned by the voices of the drillers; three young prostitutes were going the rounds, formally shaking hands.

Check. Double-check. Negative.

Because I didn't like the thing about the telephone not working at the Auberge Yasmina: she'd said it didn't even ring. It's not terribly comfortable to lose communication with your base two hours before a jump-off. It doesn't steady the hands.

It was essential that Loman should know about the 404
in case we needed local smoke out: there'd be a police
enquiry because the accident had been fatal and someone
might have seen a Mercedes 220 on the South 4 highway
about the time there'd been a glow in the ravine. We
don't like police enquiries because it means a lot of questions and it can hold things up.

Bloody thing didn't even ring and I didn't have any
means of knowing if it were just a routine breakdown, the
heat buckling a conduit, a rat nibbling the cables, or if
someone had cut the lines before they'd gone in for Loman and the girl with a submachine gun. No means of
knowing, at this moment, whether the mission was still vi-
able or whether in the arabesque room beneath the gilded
dome of the Auberge Yasmina it had been blown to hell.

The whole town had become a red sector: the whole of
Kaifra, not just the Yasmina and the Royal Sahara and
the Oasis Bar. Because they wouldn't just throw some
flowers over that burnt-out wreck in the ravine: they were
professionals and they had my dossier and they'd know I
wouldn't neutralise a tag unless I were running close to
some kind of deadline.

I left the cabin and went through the terrace and out to
the Mercedes and checked and got negative and noted the
trip and took the road northeast to Garaa Tebout and
drove for seven kilometres until I came to the pile of
stones.

He broke a pack of Gauloise and lit up.

"Excuse me, do you—"

"No."

"I am trying to give it up, you know?"

"You won't do it that way."

He laughed and squinted at me through the smoke, a
small wiry close-knit man with a hooked nose and stubble
and weathered skin, his eyes permanently narrowed
against glare even here in the starlight.

A Renault stood on the far side of the *redjem* and he
led me across to it and turned on the interior lamps, getting a torch from the glove pocket. A map was already
spread on the rear seat, the same Sheet NH-32 of the
Hassi Messaoud area that Loman had briefed me with.

"We shall take off an hour late. There was a delay because of the work—they have to make hinges on the front

edge of the cockpit hood, you know? And they have to make the *trappe* underneath so I can drop the supplies."

"We take off at 2400 hours?"

"C'est ça." He clicked the torch on. "You know the Sahara?"

"I know the desert."

"Okay, *c'est la même chose. Alors*—these red marks are the drilling camps in our area: Petrocombine South 4, South 5, and South 6, the Anglo-Belge group Roches Brunes A, B and Roches Vertes I and II. The circle here is round the platinum-prospecting complex set up by the Algerians, okay? These we shall use for our bearings." He looked up at me. "Of course nothing is certain, you know? It will depend on the winds. If they are right, I can drop you from the *planeur*, but if they are wrong we must come back and I take you out by the airplane—you were told of this?"

"Yes."

But not precisely. On the second run through the briefing at the Yasmina the subject had only been touched on: Loman knew there were quite enough doubts in my mind without adding to them. He'd just said that Chirac was "confident."

"Maybe I can do it, *comprenez?* But only maybe. The winds here are very strange, with freak upcurrents from this range here and dead pockets to the southeast; also the air is cooling very quick after sundown, which is bad. The desert is different from other places, *mon ami*. You know how I learned about the air over this region? From watching the vultures—they are *planeurs*, the vultures, and they smell out the winds. I have watched them. Now I do like them."

Ash fell and he blew it off the map.

"What are the chances, Chirac?"

"Hein?" He flattened his hand, rocking it. "I cannot say easily. Maybe it is better than fifty-fifty, about that. We will know when we slip the cable and start smelling for the winds, like those birds."

He moved the torch again. "These blue marks show the three beacons of the Philips radio relay network that crosses the area where we will go. They carry red warning lamps so we use them too, for our bearings. The drilling rigs also have lamps at night—there are more airstrips than oases in this region, because everyone looks for the black gold, you see? For the oil. So we have enough land-marks, I think. After we will slip the cable it is different, a little, because then we are alone and we have to make a straight line southwest of the radio tower here. There is nothing else we shall see after this tower." He shrugged with his hands. "But maybe it is okay, we will find the winds that we will need."

I looked at the pattern he'd traced with his torch.

"You mean you're making the final run-in from this tower by dead reckoning?"

"It is the only way, you see. There are not any more landmarks. But I know the terrain quite well—I fly the geologists all the time and we make aerial survey."

"Are you familiar with the actual target?"

"*Hein?* Sure I am. It's this outcrop here at 8°3′ by 30°4′, *n'est-ce pas?*"

Note: Loman hadn't told him about the aeroplane.

"Yes."

"I do not know the actual rocks, of course—they're very small, and we won't see them anyway in the darkness. But our target is ninety-seven kilometres south-west of the Philips tower, so we have a fix."

"What's your airspeed going to be?"

"Maybe a hundred, but not more than that, because I must keep the angle of glide at two degrees, or we will not make the distance."

Fifty-eight minutes for the whole trip, tower to target.

"Will you want me to compute your mean airspeed?"

He laughed and dropped ash on the map again.

"How did you know? I will lend you my Sony."

He chain-lit another Gauloise, his eagle's face squeezed into a frown over the glow.

"You normally use a pack a minute, Chirac?"

He looked up at me quickly and started to laugh again and then let it go because I obviously knew the score and he didn't think it was worth trying to make it sound funny.

"You know how much I am getting for this trip, *mon ami?*" He stamped the butt into the sand. "A hundred thousand francs in cash, if I can drop you from the *planeur* successfully. And insurance in the amount of five hundred thousand—that's half a million new francs, okay? If I don't get back, my family will be comfortable for quite a few years." He looked away, thinking for a couple of seconds about what he was saying. He was the kind of man who would keep a photograph of his wife and children on him wherever he went, the gloss of the surface dulling and the corners curling until its very shabbiness told not of neglect but of constancy. "Anyway I try to get back, *hein?* I am not a fool."

"How far," I said, "will you push it?"

He raised the palms of his hands. "Listen to me, please. It is nice money, okay, but you know what they say—you can't take it with you. So I will not push it too far, you un'erstand? When I tell you what they pay me, it is just telling you how much is the risk, when they will pay me so high for a few hours' work." He blew out smoke. "In a way it is easier for you, my friend, if I can drop you right on the target—because then they will know where you are, and where to find you. But when I turn back for Kaifra, the nearest oasis, I might lose the wind, you see, and I can come down anywhere on the sand, anywhere at all, maybe halfway, that's eighty kilometres from you and from Kaifra—from anywhere, and you know what that means? It means the same as if I have come down in the sea, eighty kilometres from the nearest shore, and try to swim there, you un'erstand?"

Carefully I said: "But you'll be carrying flares."

"No." He squinted at me through the smoke. "No, *mon ami,* I will not be carrying flares. That is in the contract too, as well as the half-million-franc insurance. If I go down on the sand, I will make no signals to bring people near to your target. I must not do that—I must try to walk out by myself. And like I say, they will be comfortable for a few years."

A point of light showed in the distance and I watched it.

"And I will keep to my contract," he said, apparently wanting me to know what kind of a man he was. "Listen to me, after the Algerian affair I was a mercenary for certain people who I will not mention, some private armies, you know? And I fought like hell, I earned what they pay me. Also I have been forced down in the desert sometimes when there are sandstorms or the motor gives out, so I know what it feels like when you think your life is going, when you have to think about what it is better to do—to shoot yourself or let the thirst send you mad. Oh yes, I have done this. So I know I can keep to my contract if that happens." He tapped me slowly on the arm. "The thing is, whatever happens, to remain a man. Do you not think so? Only in such a way can you die in peace."

They were the lights of a truck coming south from Garaa Tebout. I could hear it now.

"Of course," I said.

"You do not think so?"

"Well, actually I'm a bit wary of last thoughts—it can spoil your concentration when you're trying to duck. Would you say it's normal for a truck to be coming south on this road about this hour?"

"*Hien?*" He frowned into the distance. "Oh sure. The airfield at Garaa Tebout takes bigger planes than Kaifra." He dragged smoke in and it began fluttering out on his breath as he talked. "Anyway, we shall try to come back, you and I, from the desert."

"Yes fine. Can you douse these lights a minute?"

"Okay."

He leaned over and turned them off, the torch as well, and I sensed him watching me in the gloom.

"You are expecting some trouble?"

"Not really."

It was just that the *redjem* wasn't much good as visual cover: a long time ago it had marked a crossing in the paths of herdsmen, and near it there was the ruin of a gypsum and mudbrick shelter; this area had once been grazing land for sheep, I supposed, before the wind from the desert had smothered it with sand. Chirac had put his Renault on the far side of the shelter but there hadn't been room for the 220 and it wasn't concealed from the road.

It wasn't instinct alone that made me want the lights off: we were a hundred and fifty minutes from take-off and London was sending us panic directives and the base phone was dead and this whole region was a red sector and all Chirac could do was add up his life insurance and if there'd ever been a time when I didn't mind being seen making rdv contact along a lonely road it wasn't now.

His face turned silver and our shadows lifted and swung under the roof of the Renault as the light came flooding from the road.

Heavy diesel. Canvas sides: PETROCOMBINE S-5.

Fine sand falling as the dark came down.

"That is a bum outfit, you know? They don't pay so good and the air-conditioning is always *en panne,* you should hear the drillers talk about that!" He turned the lamps on again. "When I quit mercenary work I fly mostly for the big American companies here, looking for oil. That is how I come to know the desert, every square kilometre from Oran to Ghadamis, and that is why they choose me, your—*associés.* You want an *aviateur* who knows the Sahara, you send for Chirac."

He dropped the butt of his Gauloise and heeled it out.

"I start giving it up now, *hein?*" Without changing his tone he said: "You are looking for oil in that place?"

"That's right."

He laughed amiably.

"You will be there for maybe three days?"

"Maybe."

He'd been told how much water he'd have to take on board.

"That is not long, if you are careful." He drew the map off the seat and folded it. "I will brief you on the actual flight when we rendezvous with the pilot of the aeroplane. Is there anything you would like to know right now?"

"Just one thing: Where can I get a gun?"

"*Hein?* You don't have one?"

"No."

He leaned into the Renault and slid the map into the glove pocket, slamming it shut and reaching underneath.

"You can borrow this, *mon ami.*"

I took it and found it heavy, a couple of pounds or more, a Colt Official Police .38 six-shot with a six-inch barrel and chequered grips.

"When do you want it back?"

"When you come back from the desert."

The twin dark lines were drawn finely across the firmament from Andromeda through Cygnus to Vega, then they struck into the black cloud of palm leaves above my head.

The night was soundless.

Diffused light glowed against the cupolas on the far side of the trees but I couldn't be sure where it came from. On this side there was nothing and I moved again, disturbing the flight of insects below the rotting leaves and moving on as far as the wall, looking up.

There was no need to examine their whole length, but only those sections where they could be reached easily and cut. The hall was unlit and when I passed inside I waited for the blind man's voice but he wasn't here: that was certain because he would have challenged me.

I used the pen torch and found the junction board with the connections exposed and thick with dust, the knurled knobs green with oxidisation, one of them missing and the wire held with a paper clip. I cleaned the end and the thread of the terminal and reconnected it. *Mais il ne sonne même pas, m'sieur, il est en dérangement.* You don't say.

A sound and I held still and counted a hundred seconds but it didn't come again, one of those unpleasant sounds that had no particular feature so that you had to identify it according to your fancy: contracting timber or a door in the draught or a distant shot.

A group of wires ran horizontally and then upwards, ending in a hole where loose plaster was plugged. I crossed in the dark to the stairs and used the torch and saw the right ones, tracing them higher and stopping to listen and climbing again until I came to the top floor. They hadn't been cut.

She was pointing the bloody thing at me and I said don't do that and she put it down and I shut the door.

—*Hi pry Q Quaker dation minim*—

—*Hold on, Embassy.*

"All right," I told her.

Repeat please from "big flash."

Hi pry Q Quaker dation minim lady point ops one hundred proxy point all red vigil out. Do you want to reply?

She looked at me and I said: "Tell them to stop belly-aching."

Please send: Understumble point willing relay. Tango out.

She cut the switch and stopped the tape and pushed her hair back from her face: it was like an oven in here and she looked beat.

"Where's Loman?"

"At the hotel."

"The Royal Sahara?"

"Yes."

"Why?"

"He wanted to talk to you, but the phone doesn't work."

"Try it now."

Acetone on the air, been doing her nails.

The venetian blind was still down and they'd put the base transceiver on the other side of the room where it couldn't be seen from any of the windows even if they weren't covered.

"*Je'n' veux pas de numéro. On était en panne ici, mais maintenant ça marche.*"

I played the tape back to catch the first bit they'd sent but it was only another hurry directive: I'd never known London get so hysterical, what the hell did they think we were doing all this time if it wasn't trying to get me to the destination with the minimum delay?

I gave her the .38 and she nearly dropped it because compared with her own it weighed a ton.

"Have you had any small-arms training?"

"No. There wasn't time to—"

"D'you know what the phrase means, 'to stop a man'?"

"Not exactly."

"It means to stop him coming towards you. If a man were running towards you and you fired that gun of yours at him he'd just keep on coming, and unless you'd hit him in the brain or the heart there'd be time for him to kill you or smash up the radio, or both. But if you use this one you'll stop him short, and at the range from here to the doorway you'd actually throw him back."

"I see."

God, it was awful: the thing was nearly bigger than she was.

"Hold it with both hands if you want to, and be ready for the recoil and the noise. Safety catch here, load like this, fire, the usual thing, all right?"

"Yes."

"It gives you six shots, and don't forget to count."

"All right."

"Have you got enough drinking water here?"

"Yes."

"Salt tablets?"

"Yes."

I went over to the telephone and picked it up and listened for bugs, all red vigil yes but we knew that, al-

though I suppose it was encouraging to know also that
Control was obviously monitoring the opposition's movements rather closely. Say that for London: they were warning us that the heat was on down here before we'd had
time to report it.

"*J'écoute.*"

Negative bugs.

The line's perfectly okay now so will you cancel that
request for repairs, and I'd like 113.

Be awkward if Loman were smack in the thick of a hot
signals exchange on the 2000CA and a man called to
mend the telephone.

"Yes?"

He'd taken my key and gone up.

"Tango."

"Quaker, yes?"

I listened for bugs again.

"There was a tag tonight."

"What happened?"

"He had an accident."

"Where are you?"

"That's right."

"I'll see you."

"No. Things are getting difficult. I'll spell it out for you,
all right? And leave there now, can you?"

He thought about it.

"Very well." Then he said: "We'll synchronise."

"1017."

"Thank you."

I hung up.

It was too dangerous even for us to be seen at the
Royal Sahara at the same time, even if we weren't together, because I wouldn't be able to check him for surveillance when he left there without exposing myself:
they'd put one onto me at the hotel already so they knew
that part of my travel pattern.

I could have waited for him here but he only wanted to
go over the briefing again because he'd got the twitters
and there wasn't enough time left. If there'd been anything urgent to tell me he would have insisted on a meeting and he hadn't done that.

"Tape me, will you?"

She pressed for start.

Quiller to Loman. The tag was in a Peugeot 404 and I

*got him into a ravine about five kilometres along the road
to the Petrocombine South camps. He burned out. I was
in the Mercedes 220 so you'll need to monitor the enquiry
and decide if there's any smoke wanted. Further: I'm
keeping a rendezvous with Chirac at the Mosque
Hamouda Pasha at 1050 and he'll be taking me to the airstrip. I did this because I want to change the 220 image
before I leave the town. Further: if the telephone here
packs up again, check the junction board in the entrance
hall. Further: I recommend that you remain at base until
end of mission if this is possible. London confirms opposition in closest proximity. Quiller out.*

She pressed for stop and said:

"You're bleeding."

"Have you got anything?"

"Yes."

Since this morning I'd taken off most of the dressings
because it was bad image security at a time when I was
being hunted, but there were still a few places where co-
agulation wasn't complete. My right shoulder had been
stiffening up all day but there was nothing I could do
about that except hope to Christ I could do the jump
without getting the harness fouled up or anything.

"There's no need to swab it. Haven't you got any plaster?"

I watched her cutting it and wondered who she was,
what had happened at home to make her break loose and
work abroad and get hijacked into a hit-and-miss under-
taking that hadn't proved anything so far except that life
was cheap.

"Was it the bomb?"

"That's right."

Her eyes were serious, concentrating on fixing the thing
straight, a fine dew of sweat above her tender mouth, a
strand of light hair lying curled in the hollow of her
shoulder, the nearness of her reminding me of all I stood
to lose if tonight I walked into shadows without watching,
or made a sound when silence held the only hope of life.

"Were they trying to kill you?"

"Not very hard."

Her warm fingers pressed, smoothing it flat.

"Don't you find it odd, to be still alive?"

"I find it quite comfortable."

She stood back and looked at me steadily, her quiet

eyes preoccupied with working something out for herself, maybe the feeling of oddness she expected me to have, because she didn't know that in my trade the risk of extinction carries its own anodyne: familiarity. There's always of course the question suddenly in the mind when the glass comes fluting through the nitro fumes or the headlights burn in your skull while you sit there staring them out: *Is this the one?* But afterwards, when the shrill of the nerves has quietened, the only answer is *no, it wasn't the one.*

She looked away and put the reel of Elastoplast back into the tin, seeing my blood on her fingertips and for a moment considering it and then doing nothing about it, shutting the tin and putting it back on the shelf, her movements slow, reflective.

"Where's my gear?"

She turned.

"Your what?"

"The radio and the camera."

"Oh yes. We had it picked up at a rendezvous. It should be on board by now."

The time gap closed with a bang and the mission was there in front of me, ready to run.

7. Magnum

I waited for him.

The street was silent and nothing moved.

Naked bulbs stuck out here and there from the corners of walls, their yellow light defining the perspective of the street and the turnings from it. The curved fronds of the palms hung piled against the minarets and the filigree of window grilles, their tips burned brown by the heat of never-ending noons; in them I could hear rats rustling.

1025.

This is the moment, in the last phase of premission activity, when we wonder why we do the things we do: psychologically the brakes are coming off and we are gathering speed and soon we shall be pitching headlong into the dark and it's unnerving and we try to busy ourselves while the deadline closes on us, so that we don't have to think too much. So it's uncomfortable to have to sit in a car and do nothing, while the last minutes run out. It's not a good time to think.

There was a handbasin in the corner so why the hell didn't she rinse them there, I didn't like it, the way she'd looked at them, what was she saying, that it was here on her fingers by grace of whatever gods had decreed that I shouldn't be too close when the thing went off, bloody nonsense, they'd cocked it up that was all, tuned the rocking mechanism till it was too sensitive and then a bus had made a draught or something like that. It doesn't do, at a time like this, to think you're being looked after by some kind of providence: start walking round ladders and you'll only get run over because survival begins in the brain, not the navel.

Soft-eyed little philosopher with her downy arms, two hands to hold the bloody thing and no training for priority ops, Loman ought to be shot.

The street was narrow, running thinly into the dark of trees at its very end. That was where I would be going soon, accelerating through the perspective of the known dark into the unknown dark.

I would wait here another two minutes and then I'd have to take the first of the risks that I must run between now and the rendezvous. He was very good of course but he wasn't an executive in the field and therefore didn't have the training or even the experience: it's a weak point and we think it's dangerous and we're always asking the Bureau to do something about it but you might just as well try selling a jockstrap to a eunuch.

The scent of mimosa was on the air, adrift in the starlight from blossom I couldn't see from here, and the sky dripped diamonds, Andromeda and Cygnus and Vega and a million more, their reflection ablaze in the gilded cupola where she was, we'll miss a lot of things, oh a lot of things, if we're not careful.

Sweating like a pig and cursing him now for not coming, checking too often—1029—1029.15—1029.30—time you learned to count without looking all the time at the dial, risk it anyway and if the whole thing blows up you can say it was his fault, didn't leave me enough time to check him for ticks.

Front-end configuration amorphous, colour dark blue or dark green in this light, coming rather fast but that was normal, Capri, no, Taunus, no, Chrysler 160, the lights

dipping over the sandy hollows, driver alone, the dust
flying up in his wake—1030.15—give him a minute and
then go, running it close blast his eyes.

He passed the Yasmina and did a square loop and
parked in the side street and walked, short neat steps like
a bird's, looking from side to side in case he missed anything, the last time I'd be seeing him for a while or forever if I didn't watch out: and then I found myself admir-
ing the little bastard just for still being on his feet because
this time they'd really blown an egg all over him and for
the last forty-eight hours he'd been busting a gut to set up
an op and he'd done it and we were ninety minutes to the
off and I suppose you could say that was something, you
could rank him among the élite: the professionals.

Negative.

Distant throb of a truck on the highway south, somewhere a starved dog baying. No other sound but the rats
among the leaves, no movement anywhere along the
street's narrowing channel.

1031.15 and still negative.

I got the engine going and the nerves quietened a bit
because he was a director, not an executive, and he could
have picked up a tag and led him to base without knowing
and that would have blown it, the lot. But it was all right
and whatever happened now I'd have the comfort of
knowing that base had been intact at the moment when
the brakes came off.

The lids of the bins banging back and the tumble of
empty melon skins and the bones of birds, steam rising
and swirling into the air-conditioning vents, the boys in
bow ties and the trays volplaning on their raised hands,
the din of cutlery in the metal sinks.

"Je m'excuse—je suis trompé de porte!"

"Comment?"

"Je cherche le restaurant!"

"Passez par ici, m'sieur—allez-y!"

The doors swinging and the trays coming back loaded
with the detritus of *Melon Glacé, Canard à l'Orange,* the
drillers dining late so as to get some drinking done first.

The restaurant full, the lobby empty except for a few
staff. Check, double check. Negative.

"M'sieur?"

"Trente-sept."

Door boy, desk clerk, telephonist, a man from Hertz.

I used the main stairs. It was possible that I could now be seen through the glass façade above the entrance but the panels were solar-tinted and it had to be risked and in any case there was no alternative route. I'd gone through the kitchens because they were nearer where I'd left the car, below the third lamp from the group of yuccas where I could see it from my room, and if they were watching the main entrance for me they'd draw blank.

1037.

The estimated schedule was ninety seconds from locking the 220 to reaching the windows of Room 37 and that didn't give them time enough to rig anything.

Loman would have left the shutters closed and the curtains drawn but they wouldn't necessarily be lightproof so I stopped halfway along the corridor and took a bulb out and dropped a 100-millime piece across the contacts and blew the lot and went into 37 without swinging the door too wide.

Total dark, hit a chair, touched the curtains.

The slats of the shutters were angled at forty-five degrees and I couldn't see anything above the horizontal and this was the first floor of a five-floor building so I opened a shutter, taking a full minute to swing it wide enough to let me through onto the balcony.

Check 220: negative.

Above the wax cascade of the yucca blooms the balconies of the east wing were ranged in unbroken lines. Most of the outside lamps were burning but the rooms were dark: the restaurant was full. The building was in the tourist-Moorish style, an elongated complex of arches and carved screens with two arabesque lamps and a tubbed *orangier* on each balcony and creeper climbing from the lawns below, and he was observing me from the third floor, seventh room from the left.

The lamps were lit on the two balconies on each side of mine but it didn't help because he was using binoculars and their lens hoods would be cutting out the peripheral glare. There was almost no glint on the lenses and I might have missed them except that he'd forgotten to mask the chrome thumbscrew on the tripod.

It was difficult to judge how much light I was reflecting but the likelihood that he was able to identify me at this range was critically high. Despite this there was a chance that he hadn't seen me so I moved my head and not my eyes because the reflective capacity of the whites is greater than that of the iris and pupil by a factor of more than double and in certain lights it can make the difference between being seen or overlooked, shot dead or only winged.

I was now directly facing the Mercedes 220 and computing the angle and the thing I didn't like was that there was no visual obstruction between the car and his balcony: he'd watched me arrive and unless I could do anything about it he would watch me leave.

Time probably 1038.30 couldn't look.

It was difficult because I was scheduled to leave here in a minute and a half from now and there wouldn't be time to call up a taxi and I couldn't commandeer the nearest private car I found outside because those drip-nosed Agathas in London have got the whole thing written out under *Public Involvement* (Standing Orders) and if you blot your copybook they'll suspend you from missions and for the next twelve months you'll pass the time breaking hieroglyphs in Codes and Ciphers or standing-in for a sandbag at the thousand-yard range in Norfolk.

He wasn't doing anything, not moving about or anything. I couldn't see a barrel coming up but of course there could be two of them and the other one could be inside the room where there was no light to pick up surfaces and my skin began crawling because at this range I wouldn't hear the detonation before the skull was blown.

They were being inconsistent.

Inconsistency is dangerous because it brings in the unpredictable: if you don't know which way the opposition's going to jump you can't tell where they'll land.

They grilled O'Brien and then they killed him.

They surveyed Fyson and then they broke his nerve across a telescopic rifle without firing a shot and they didn't wipe him out before they'd finished with him as a contact control that led to my own exposure.

With me they went straight in for the kill and when they fouled it up they didn't try again: they changed their minds and decided that since I was still alive I was worth tagging and that was so bloody inconsistent that it brought out the sweat on me because at any minute they could change their minds again and I could be standing here against the wall with my forehead coming slowly into the centre of a 3X scope while his finger took up the tension on the spring.

I'd seen all I wanted to out here but I didn't hurry because speed can be fatal if it isn't dictated totally by brain-think and this was stomach-think, this sweat on me and the crawling of the skin, I knew what Fyson had meant, the threat of a long gun can bring you to the pitch when all you can think about is the sudden air rush, wherever you are, walking in a street or coming down some steps, the silence of the small bright beautifully turned object as it nears you so fast that the fine tune of its passage is outstripped so that you never hear it, or driving along a road where the buildings are strange to you, their windows open, while the little cylindrical stub of lead and copper-zinc alloy spins towards you, intimately to invade the consciousness and turn it into mindless chemicals, bringing an end to all you ever were.

Slowly, my fingers behind me, finding the varnished wood of the shutter, guiding my feet until the shadow of the terrace screen came to fall across my eyes and I passed inside the room and stood filling the lungs with oxygen for the nerves while the telephone began ringing and I let it go on until I was ready to answer it.

"I am leaving now," he said.

"All right."

I hung up.

1040.

He'd been punctual. It was a help. It is a help, *mon ami*, when you are in a spot and someone demonstrates his reliability. It gives you hope.

I left the shutter as it was, half open: there wasn't any technical advantage in closing it; on the contrary he'd pick up the movement because I didn't have the time to do it slowly. There was a slight advantage in leaving it half open because psychologically it suggested presence: you normally shut things when you leave a place. I left the curtains drawn.

Sound and I froze. Corridor: voices.

The lights, oh yes, they were wondering why they'd fused.

I picked up my flight bag and went out. It wouldn't be a good idea to go through the kitchens again so I took the swing door to the gardens, going past the swimming pool on the far side where there was shadow and thinking as fast as I could because the place was a trap: they wouldn't put surveillance on me from that direction alone——they'd cover the whole scene.

The hurry wasn't at this end: Chirac would wait for takeoff until I was ready to go. But London wanted me to reach Tango Victor soonest possible and that pulled the whole schedule tight and I wasn't going to accept his midnight ETD because with a bit of luck they might finish slapping the dope on before then and we could get off the ground while it was drying.

The path turned left and I took it and kept to the shadow of the oleanders until I was within thirty yards of the 220 and then I stopped because at this point I'd be moving into the surveyed area and even if he didn't recognise me from behind and above he'd know who I was when I got into the car.

I didn't want to do a thing like this without being quite certain there was no other way. Technically it looked like suicide but sometimes it has to be done: we have to move deliberately into known surveyance even when it isn't done to deceive. We have to do it for various reasons: because the schedule of the mission has become critical to the point of jeopardising it by delay or because the threat to life is so immediate as to justify a lesser risk or because there's a fair chance of dodging mobile surveyance once we've left the immediate area.

Two of these reasons were valid for me now: if I didn't reach the wreck on the sand before anyone else got there the mission would come to nothing and it was therefore at this moment jeopardised and London would agree. There would be mobile surveyance taking over from the man on the balcony because tonight they wanted to know where I was going and the fact that one of them had got killed trying to find out wouldn't deter them since it was now obvious that I was going somewhere interesting, and I had a fair chance of dodging a mobile tag because it was something I'd learned how to do.

1042.

So I broke cover and the skin began crawling again because it was reasonably certain that on the balcony of the seventh room on the third floor the hooded lenses were now swinging down on the tripod swivel and steadying.

Ignore.

Range sixty yards, angle of fire thirty-five degrees low, target centred.

Ignore and keep on walking and think of other things.

Chirac was rather good material: he'd got the point. After all he was only helping us out: he wasn't a professional spook and he didn't possess the bruised lopsided sense of loyalty to the Bureau that's always there like a scarecrow wherever we go. Kaifra tonight was a red sector and he was in it and if they got a fix on him and managed to take him and grill him I'd be walking straight into an ambush when I kept the rendezvous at the Mosque Hamouda Pasha.

They knew how to conduct interrogation: they'd operated on O'Brien and got enough out of him to blow a five-star field executive like Fyson as soon as he'd arrived in Sidi Ben Ali and they'd finished him off in Tunis and got the name of Kaifra out of him or they wouldn't be here now because Loman and I had got here clean. If they did it to Chirac we wouldn't expect him to protect me or the Bureau or his own mother because they were experts so I'd thrown him the stock alert and told him to phone me at the Royal Sahara at exactly 1040 and use four words and those four words precisely unless he was under duress and then he could use any variation he liked: *I am on my way* or *I am starting out now*, so forth.

It would give him total protection because it allowed him to keep to the truth: I have arranged to rendezvous with him at the Mosque Hamouda Pasha but he won't go there unless I telephone him to say when I am leaving.

They couldn't blame him if I didn't turn up: I could have caught a cold or something.

Fiat 850, Volkswagen, Peugeot 504, Toyota Land Cruiser with spades strapped on, Citroën DS, nobody in them and nothing else in sight of the 220 so they must have put him round a corner or somewhere in total shadow. He'd move off when I did but this insistence on concealment at the beginning of our run seemed a bit pointless because he couldn't get on my tail without spreading himself all over the mirror and they knew that. It was another nasty little inconsistency and I didn't like it.

Oleanders, tamarisk, deep cover ten feet from the Mercedes on the other side and I slowed as I walked towards it because they might not like using a rifle in the hotel

building—it would make a lot of noise and people would
get inquisitive—so the best thing would be for the man up
there to have signalled my arrival so they could put someone in cover here where the noise wouldn't be so loud.

I walked towards it.

If they let me get as far as the car I could stop worrying: they hadn't had time to rig a bang because I'd kept it
under observation except for the ninety-second period
when I'd gone into the hotel through the kitchens. The
timing from Room 37 to the swing door I'd used as an
exit wasn't much more than half a minute.

Five paces and I reached the 220 and got in and started
up, not looking at the hotel but checking the Vauxhall
and the hardtop GT-6 that had now come into sight from
where I sat, nobody in them, nobody anywhere. No sound
of a starter and I was waiting for it and it didn't happen
and I thought blast their eyes for not playing it by the
book: they'd let me get as far as the car but I still
couldn't stop worrying because they wouldn't just put one
isolated observer up there to log my arrival and departure
times at the Royal Sahara. They knew I was pushing the
deadline because they'd already had a mobile tag on me
tonight and now they ought to be hooking a new one onto
me, or a dozen, and they weren't.

There was the bare possibility they were holding off,
letting me run while they could do it without any risk of
losing me: the road from the hotel to the town centre and
the main intersection was approximately 1.5 kilometres
and it was the only route you could take if you wanted to
link up with the major highway north to Garaa Tebout or
south to the complex of drilling camps so they'd be virtu-
ally certain I'd be using that stretch. The awkward thing
was that I couldn't avoid it. The Mosque Hamoud Pasha
was half a kilometre from the oasis road and Chirac was
on his way there so I shifted the stick and got rolling because it was the only thing left to do.

The coloured lights of the marquee sent rainbows flowing across the bonnet of the 220 as I swung past the steps
and took the east road between the overhanging palms,
mirror-check negative.

High degree of cognitive dissonance, most unpleasant. I
was expecting lights to come into the mirror and they
didn't and it threw me. Something was missing from the
equation and I couldn't see what it was unless it could

simply be that they were so monumentally disorganised
that they didn't know how to operate. It would be nice to
think that.

Forty on the clock and I left it there: the road was
sandy in places and the crown finished in a ragged edge of
macadam within a foot of the palm trunks. The mirror
was hazed over now with the dust I was sending up but if
lights moved into it I would see them.

There were buildings at intervals standing back from
the road, the small white-domed winter residences of re-
tired merchants and date farmers, and they vanished as
the windscreen went and I smashed the flat of my hand
against the crazed glass and broke a hole in it but I'd been
driving blind for two seconds and in those forty yards the
Mercedes had drifted off-course and the nearside tyres
were over the edge of the macadam and I had to let her
go another foot and then bring the wheel round to force
the front tyre back across the edge before I could get any
kind of stability.

I was slumped low by now and the second shot hit the
roof and it banged like a tin drum and I knew the trunks
of the palms were getting in his way but there were a lot
of gaps in them so I kept low and sighted through the
wheel and the hole in the granulated screen but it was
very awkward and we began swinging wide again and I
suddenly felt cold because if the drifting got worse and I
hit a tree and finished up stationary he'd take his time and
pick me off when I tried to get out and if I stayed where I
was he'd come up close and make it a certainty.

The speed had risen a fraction but it didn't affect things
very much: it was just a question of how steady the target
was when he lined up the next shot and I didn't like this
because if I tried to jazz the thing around to spoil his aim
I increased the risk of crashing it and giving him a sitter.

Very close and glass flew and I felt the sudden air-rush
from the hole in the windscreen so it was the rear side
window he'd smashed. The two windows on the other side
were still all right so he was firing from a position well
above the horizontal and the explosive shattering of the
glass had covered the noise of the secondry impact on
the inside panel of the door.

Almost certain the observer at the Royal Sahara had
picked up the telephone when he'd seen me getting back
into the 220 but this ambush must have been set up be-

fore tonight because it carried communications and it
wouldn't have been any use without them: this marksman
had been installed as soon as they'd established that my
travel pattern included the only road between the hotel
and the major intersection in the town centre, but they'd
waited for tonight.

I'd used this route six times since I'd arrived in Kaifra
and they'd waited for the seventh and given him the signal
that I was just leaving the hotel and he'd gone up to the
roof and checked his magazine and the 220 was rocking
again as the third smashed into the door pillar and pain
stabbed into my scalp but there was no concussion: it was
a group of metal splinters and not a ricochet of the shell
itself.

This would be the long gun they'd used for the breaking of Fyson's nerve and this time they wanted to kill with
it and there wasn't anything I could do except keep all
four wheels on the road and hope to survive.

He wasn't an international. He was trained and experienced because the target was now traversing at right angles at twenty feet per second and the only lighting was
backglare from the headlamps and there were trees at intervals across his field of fire but if he'd been an international the first shot would have neutralised: there's a con-
ceit among the top-flight professionals like Molinari and
Kuo and Tomlinson that they only ever use one bullet for
each assignment.

This man's *forte* was fast use of the automatic reloader:
by the dull thump of the last shell after the ricochet had
left it almost inert I'd say he was using something like a
.44 Magnum, a brush-country weapon with enough power
to drive its ammunition through a six-inch pine tree in full
sap, and he'd been firing with a controlled rhythm that
had kept him on the target throughout the period of three
or four seconds following his first shot. I couldn't tell how
long he'd be able to maintain fire and I didn't want to give
myself any false hopes because it could be anything up to
a twelve-shot rotary magazine and he was working at
roughly one per second and if he had nine shells left he'd
be using the last one while I was still in murderously close
range at a hundred and eighty feet.

A hole appeared in the scuttle three inches forward of
the windscreen and both the aural and visual effects re-

sembled those from a blow with a pickaxe and it confirmed what I'd thought about the size of this gun: it was really quite big. He'd overcorrected but this time the error was dangerously narrow: the third shell had hit the rear window approximately forty-eight inches from my head and this one had drilled the hole in the scuttle eighteen inches in front of me and it would have worried me but there were so many factors in play and one of them was the possibility that he hadn't seen where the shell had gone in because it hadn't made so much of a mess as the one that had smashed the window.

I could feel him thinking.

We were very close, he and I. Not close friends but close enemies. The total energy of his brain was devoted to the intricate equations governing our shared situation: speed of target in traverse, speed and extent of movement laterally as the target wavered, horizontal angle of fire, vertical angle of fire and the incomputable factors presented by the configuration of the palm trees and the movement of the light from the headlamps, so forth. And the result of this mental energy was being expressed by the flight of the cylindrical objects whose accuracy was linking us closer and closer together, moving us nearer the point at which there would come profound personal involvement as the intention of this man's brain exploded in my own.

The more difficult phase of this operation is getting you to the jump-off point without attracting surveillance or obstructive action.

Put it like a schoolmistress but when it came to the crunch the terms were simpler: flesh and blood and a bullet, the will to live and the urge to kill, the moment of truth.

Oh Christ he was close and I felt the air wave across my eyes and the force smashed the facia and sent splinters whining past my face as we drifted badly because of the shock and I tried to pull her straight and for the first time cursed him, being afraid and needing to diminish him by names. The trees swung and the lights sent their shadows lurching as the tyres lost their hold on the sandy surface and the back end broke away and I brought it straight and used the throttle for traction and got it and piled it on.

Five.

He'd brought down the error from forty-eight inches to
less than one and he'd done it in two shots and I sat waiting for it, listening to the whistle of the wind through the
gap in the screen and watching the dips and hollows of
the road as the lights pooled shadows there and then
swept them away, his image in my mind, a dark face
pressed to the gun, its eye brilliant in the light on the road
ahead of me that was gathered by the telescopic lens and
focussed on the pupil, thrown on the screen of the retina
for interpretation by the brain: *higher and to the right—
fire.*

Six and the impact and a ricochet and fine glass fragments shivering in the air from the instruments and then a
shoulder blow as the shell doubled and I took the last of
its inertia and the wheel jerked and I lost it, the lot, spinning once over the loose sand and rocking across the edge
of the macadam with the vibration shaking the granules
from the frame of the screen and the windrush sending
them past me in a stream of flying hail as the flank of the
220 struck across a tree trunk and we pitched the other
way and found the road and bounced there with a tyre
bursting and a headlight blacking out.

Lost it again and we spun with the last of the screen
fragments shaking away and falling across me while I
dragged the manual into low to kill off the rest of the
speed but the front end wouldn't respond and a palm
trunk ripped a wheel panel off and left the front fender
creased backwards and howling on the tyre with its shrill
note rising as I got traction in low and brought her back
onto the road and shifted the lever and took the speed up
again through the early range with the stink of heated
rubber fouling the air.

The howling noise was very loud, marking my passage
through the night, but if I slowed he'd take his time and
set up the final shot and I kept up the speed, drifting
crabwise with the burst tyre dragging and the one headlight slanting away from the road. Something important
was trying to get my attention but brain-think was at a
discount and the oasis road came up before I realised that
it was a six-shot and he was changing magazines.

Half a kilometre from the Mosque Hamoud Pasha the
front tyre melted through and burst and a lot of the howling stopped but the steering was very awkward now and

it was really a question of how long it would take him to get into his car and come up on me with a full magazine.

The dark oblong shape of the Renault was standing under the palms, glow of a Gauloise, threw my flight bag in and pulled the door shut.

"Go very fast, will you?"

8. Airborne

I set the door lock and got the belt adjusted.

He glanced at me.

"*Ça va?*"

"*Ça va.*"

I suppose I was bleeding again.

He swung through the main intersection and accelerated hard along the South 4 highway and I pulled down the passenger visor and angled it to line up the mirror, negative.

Chirac flicked the stub through the window.

"I heard some shots just now."

"So did I."

He laughed cannily and shut the window and pushed the vents open and there wasn't so much noise.

"Do you expect we shall be followed?"

"It's on the cards."

"*Comment?*"

"*C'est possible.*"

Two of the stars on the south horizon were beginning to glow red and I watched them.

"Do I go fast enough?"

"Not if you can go any faster." There was 140 kph on the clock and the engine was running at peak with valve bounce creeping in. "How long will it take to reach the airstrip?"

"Maybe ten minutes, a little more."

London was panicking but I didn't have to try cutting actual seconds off the schedule: it was just that if the man with the gun had got into his car he might have seen the Renault when we'd left the Mosque.

Mirror negative.

I could see now that the two red lights were stationary ahead of us and if it was some kind of breakdown I hoped it wasn't blocking the road because we wanted a clear run. There were three lights now and when I'd considered all the other possible explanations I voted for the idea that there were two vehicles halted on the road about a mile in front of us: a few seconds ago I'd felt my weight shifting slightly to one side and my elbow had been pressed gently against the door panel so we must have taken an almost indefinable curve and the visual effect had been to reveal one of the second vehicle's rear lamps by parallax.

"Is that a truck?"

"I would expect so, yes."

"If it's a breakdown, just keep on going."

"Okay."

We were coming up on the lights very fast and he began flickering the heads as a warning and I wondered whether he'd be able to judge how much room there was to go past at this speed before it was too late to do anything about it. Chirac was all right but there was a bit too much garlic-and-Gauloise philosophy about him, the thing is to die like a man, so forth, absolute balls because whether you die like a man or the back end of a pantomime horse you're going to stop breathing when it happens.

There were some other lights, white ones, moving around in the ravine below the road and then I got it and stopped worrying and sat back and watched him put the Renault through the gap between the edge of the road and the police car and ambulance standing on the other side. Nobody tried to slow us: they were all busy down in the ravine, two of them carrying a stretcher.

"There was an accident," Chirac said.

"It looks like it."

He reached for the blue packet and manoeuvred a cigarette out one-handed. "Some people drive too fast, *mon ami*."

It looked like a false sunrise as we topped the dunes a mile from South 4 camp, the brilliance of the derrick lamps lifting into the sky and flaring there among the stars.

We were already running parallel with a wire guard fence hung at intervals with notices: DÉFENSE D'ENTRER

. . . Défense de Fumer . . . Danger de Mort. Trucks moved beyond the fence, unloading sections of piping, and the derrick lamps shone down on storage tanks and a fleet of jeeps and half-tracks.

"The drill is down to four thousand metres," Chirac said as we began slowing, "and last week they make a core drilling and bring up oil in the sandstone, so it will be not long now before they strike. But like I tell you, they are a lousy outfit, so maybe the oil will be lousy too."

The two guards checked our papers with the gates still closed, then gave us passes and let us through and Chirac drove at the regulation 20 kph past the living quarters to the south end of the airstrip where the windsock was hanging limp a hundred yards from the hangar. From here the immediate skyline was a freize of pumping units, rigs, hutments, and vehicles, with the towering derrick and radio masts rising behind them. The steady drone of the diesels sounded from the rotary table half a mile away but here it was relatively quiet and I could hear voices from inside the security zone where the first stages of the pipeline were being set up.

The hangar was a single-span stressed-iron unit, an item of ex-war stock with the original camouflage design showing faintly through the silver heat-reflecting paint. There weren't many lamps burning inside and for a moment I didn't see the glider because its matte night-blue finish gave it the same tone as the shadows on the corrugated walls.

Chirac put his hands on his hips.

"Et voilà! Mais quelle vache, hein? What a cow! But it will fly very well, and that is what we need."

Much bigger than I'd expected: a three-seater pod and boom design, shoulder-wing, straight dihedral, very large chord, ugly to look at because of the lump at the front end and the almost black paint.

"Have you flown this type?"

"Mon Dieu, there isn't another like this! The Algerians used it for radio-observer drops during the war, then the Météo converted it for research on thermal currents, then Anglo-Belge put different mainplanes on it for low-altitude surveys, and now look what we do, we make the trappe beneath the cabin and paint it like this! Tout sim-

plement, he is a cow! But I can fly anything, *mon ami*, even a cow, so we shall go well up there, don't worry please."

He fished for his Gauloise and lit up and remembered the fire risk and said *merde* and scuffed the thing out. I wished he were a degree less nervy.

I'd expected a lot of interest from the drilling crews but the only people in the hangar were the three riggers doping the fabric of the new trap door and a man in flying gear coming across to us from the far end.

"What's our cover story for this flight, Chirac?"

"Comment?"

"What's the official reason for our using this glider?"

"Oh yes, I will tell you that. It was being flown for Anglo-Belge on a magnetic-rock survey a few days before, but the wind becomes too low, you see, so it was force-landed on the nearest airstrip, which was this place. Now we are going to take it back to Anglo."

"Why at night?"

"The wind is good right now."

"Why the blue paint?"

"Écoutez, mon ami, who the hell asks to know a thing like this?" He jerked a thumb towards the main camp. "That drill does not stop, never, day and night, you see, unless it breaks or it strikes oil, and then they are even more busy than always, you unnerstand? When they work they have no time to think of different things, and when they stop work they are too damn *fatigué* to do anything but sleep. They do not wish to ask about the *planeur*." He turned as the man in the flying gear came up. *"Pierre, je te présente Monsieur Gage, l' anglais dont je t'ai parlé.* This is Pierre Batagnier, who will fly the aeroplane that will tow us."

Small compact man, more flesh on him than Chirac, much less nervy about the eyes. We shook hands and he went over to the riggers.

"Alors Michel, tu es prêt?"

Ten minutes, the man said, and it would take longer than that to warm his engines.

Chirac got the map and spread it across a crate and the pilot joined us. "Okay, now listen please. Pierre will tow us to the northeast of here until three thousand metres of altitude, and that will bring us somewhere by the third

Philips radio beacon at this blue mark here. This is because it is a normal route made by aeroplanes across the drilling complex from South 4 to the Anglo-Belge Roches Vertes II, so nobody will think it strange to hear us go that way, you see? After this point we will slip the cable, and Pierre will return here alone."

I kept thinking of base.

"Now we shall be for ourselves, and we will make a circle to bring us east of the Algerian platinum-prospecting camp right here, and then we will go down maybe a hundred metres at a fifteen-degree angle of glide to make a good speed for our final run to the target area, you unnerstand?"

Kept thinking of the arabesque room below the dome, some kind of association, mustn't ignore, think later.

"And now we will cross the No. 2 Philips radio tower, the blue mark here, at maybe a hundred kph of airspeed, using these red marks for our bearings. They are Petrocombine South 5, South 6, and the Anglo Roches Brunes B drilling camps, and we shall see their lights on the derricks. We will gain the target area maybe sixty minutes from when we have begun, here at the radio tower. So it is at this place you must start to make the figures for dead-reckoning on the *ordinateur* Sony, you unnerstand?"

"What's this distance here: Philips tower to target?"

"Ninety-seven kilometres. Of course we will go a little more far than this in actual air distance, because of our angle of glide, but that will depend on the winds we will find as we make our approach."

The arabesque room and the way she'd been holding the gun at me when I'd gone in. Some kind of association. Important? Something overlooked?

"Now please tell me if there is anything you will wish me to repeat, about this thing."

"You've made it clear enough. The wind factor governs the situation at both ends of the flight, is that it?"

Cellulose. Dope—nail varnish. Sense of smell strongly associative. Dismiss.

"*C'est ça*. If there is no wind when we will make the circle over this complex here, we must make a less big angle of glide, not to lose too much altitude. And if there is no wind near the end of our approach to the target area, I must stay much higher so that I have my chance to get back here, or anyway so that I come down somewhere not far

from any water and people, you know?" He began folding
the map. "Of course when I tell you 'no wind' like that, I
mean any wind that is not good enough to go higher. *B'en,
je crois que c'est tout.*"

Batagnier straightened up.

"*Allons-y?*"

"*Allons-y.*"

The pilot went back through the hangar, shouting for
some ground staff, and one of the riggers trotted after
him. A minute later a Koffman starter banged and the engine took over, then the second one fired.

I checked the time: 2351.

"My stuff's already on board?"

"You can see it from inside the cabin, not through the
trappe."

I climbed in and checked the setup. They'd taken out
the centrally disposed third seat and made the drop trap
in the floor below it, accommodating the 'chute immediately forward of the polyester container to keep the loads
balanced: I would be sitting beside the pilot and the
weight of a third man was transferred to the supplies and
transceiver. The ripcord was linked to the fuselage by a
tension breakaway for automatic opening and release, so
that all the pilot had to do was drop the trap and the rest
of the operation would go into sequence.

The hangar had begun drumming and I saw a tow
truck moving across and turning and backing up. Chirac
was calling to me above the noise and I pulled the hook-
release ring to let them link up the cable.

I climbed out and they tilted the mainplane horizontal
and began towing. The pod design formed a sound box
and the noise was like an empty crate being trundled on
roller skates, and the whole structure flexed so badly that
Chirac had to keep shouting orders to the driver of the
truck to break up the periodicity. A gust of sand stung
our faces as Batagnier's twin-engined Fauconnet gunned
up and swung its tail, rolling towards the airstrip. The tow
truck made a diagonal line across its wake and left the
glider in position fifty yards behind it.

Watching Chirac as he directed the preliminaries to
take-off it occurred to me that he was the key man in the
Bureau's attempt to have Tango Victor's cargo examined
at first hand: and to a certain extent Loman had been jus-
tified in persuading me that we weren't taking over a

wrecked operation with orders to clear up the mess, but were setting up our own mission with a specified objective.

Someone in London had said: we want a mercenary flyer to do us a night drop in the Sahara, someone who'll keep to his contract, a man who doesn't mind risking a stray shot if the money's right.

It wouldn't have been difficult to find a man like Chirac in a region where there were more airstrips than oases and where working conditions were tough and the pay commensurate, but when they saw his record and learned that he was an ex-champion sailplane pilot they saw the chance and refined the mission and bumped up his insurance to half a million francs to cover the increased risk and told him to get himself a glider.

The access had been revamped in a big way and the fact that the Minister had decided to sting the Treasury for that amount of loot made it clear that the Bureau had told him it had a chance of paying off. From this data I was certain of two things: the opposition was monitoring all aircraft movement in this area by every means including listening posts, and they were doing it in the hope of tracking me in to the target area and neutralising me at the site of the objective.

Priority requirement: silence. The silence of these wings across the starlit dunes, our passage leaving no trace on the screens of the acoustic scanners dispersed among the oases between Sidi Ben Ali and Kaifra and the complex of drilling camps.

Strict hush.

The sand blew back from the Fauconnet as Batagnier ran up the revs and tested for mag drop and the ground crews by the glider turned their backs to it, hanging onto the wingtips. Then the roaring died and the props idled and I saw Chirac turn and look in my direction, lifting a hand.

Give it to London then, give them a bit of credit. They'd been prepared to drop someone in from a powered aircraft and risk the opposition picking it up and going in for a kill in the final phase of the penetration: a crude and bloody business that always costs more lives for fewer results whenever they're driven to mounting this kind of operation with the opposition already in the field. They do it on the principle that when the objective is high priority and there's even a ten per cent chance of the executive's coming out alive with the stuff they want it's worth this brand of brute frontal attack on the target that might offer a chance of knocking out the opposition in the target area itself. They do it when they're desperate.

They'd been desperate but they'd seen Chirac as the key to something more controlled and they'd worked on it and come up with a design that at least made sense on paper and the delay in planning had brought them right up against the clock and they'd had to shake the whole network with panic directives but give them this: they'd got a bit of elegance into the mission at last, a bit of class, sent for a top kick like Loman and told him to pick his own executive for the field and set the thing up and make it succeed, bring off a classic.

I anticipate success. Complete success. You understand?

All right you little bastard we'll give it a go.

They'd turned the glider to line up with the runway and I walked into the carbon-monoxide airstream that was coming from the Fauconnet. Chirac was getting into his parachute and one of the ground crew was holding mine ready for me and when I was settled into it Chirac passed me some goggles.

"You will need these, if there will be a sandstorm."

I slung them round my neck. The rigger was helping me to adjust the 'chute harness and we pulled it too tight and a flash of pain burned in the nerves of my shoulder where the ricochet of the sixth bullet had left bruising.

"*Ça va, mon ami?*"

"*Oui.*"

I dropped my flight bag into the cabin and climbed aboard and buckled the restraint belt. Chirac called something to the ground crew, I didn't catch what, then he followed me in and settled his feet on the rudder bar and checked the four instruments: airspeed indicator, spirit cross level, compass, and variometer.

He raised his hand.

"*Allons-y!*"

The rigger stood away and lifted both arms in a signal to Batagnier and then walked to the wingtip, waiting. The revs went up and the airstream began fluttering at the hood of the glider as the Fauconnet rolled cautiously, taking up the slack in the towline. A jerk came as it tautened.

Chirac was peeling some silver paper.

"You want some gum?"

I shook my head and he put the strip into his mouth and flicked the paper into the air current and slid the hood shut as the Fauconnet gunned up and we began rolling. A haze of sand came flying against the perspex and the man at the wingtip broke his run and fell away as the speed rose and the vibration hammered under our seats and Chirac felt the resistance coming into the controls and brought the stick back gently, feeling his way, gently again until the vibration died out and the sand haze cleared and the mission was airborne.

The first derrick light came into view on the starboard side. Chirac couldn't see it from his seat but he noticed me watching the light and said above the windrush:

"South 5."

He'd clipped a chart on the facia but never looked at it.

When the light came abreast of us northeast I checked the time at 0013 hours. The silver-painted storage tanks were distinct and I could see a truck on the move.

Ahead of us we could see the navigation lights of the Fauconnet and the short bright flames from its exhaust stubs. Its engine noise was steady, drumming at the hood above us, and the smell of exhaust gas had seeped into the cabin.

South 6.

0027.

Altitude 1300 metres.

The detail was less distinct: the ash-grey sheen to the west of the drilling tower could have been storage tanks or the semidomed roofs of the living quarters. We were now picking up No. 2 Philips radio beacon, its red warning lamp shifting slowly across the desert floor as we overflew it.

The air was cool.

Monoxide and spearmint and above our heads the stars in their millions flowing peacefully across the curve of the perspex. Course northeast.

Overflying the Roches Vertes drilling camp at two thousand metres I thought I heard a change in the Fauconnet's engine noise: a slight increase in volume and pitch. I waited for Chirac to remark on it but he said nothing and I looked at the instruments.

Air speed unchanged at 110.

Angle of climb unchanged at 18°.

They were the only two that would reflect the altered note of the Fauconnet ahead of us but they remained constant. Batagnier hadn't increased his speed and he hadn't pushed up his angle of climb and I didn't like it.

Red light moving below, very distant on the starboard side.

No. 3 Philips tower.

Impossible to tell whether a new sound had come into the immediate area. There should only be one source: the 100CV twin-engined Fauconnet.

No mirrors, either inside the cabin or outrigged in nacelles.

The blind spot rearwards of this pod-and-boom design was rather large. The air was cold now but I was beginning to sweat because London had done their best but it might not be good enough, not quite good enough. If their decision to charter a glider for final access to the target area meant that the opposition had set up listening posts to monitor aircraft movement in this region then the sound of the Fauconnet was at this moment being registered on their scanners. There hadn't been anything we could do about that: Chirac had ordered this course northeast from South 4 because it was an established airlane across the drilling complex and if we'd made any kind of circuit to avoid the camps our sound would still have been picked up and we would have been immediately suspect.

The probability that they were picking us up now was all right because they wouldn't investigate every aircraft movement across this region provided it followed a routine pattern: what they were listening for was unusual traffic and especially an unscheduled flight from any of the strips near Kaifra in the direction of the open desert. Each post would essentially have its own facility for the immediate investigation of suspect aircraft movement: a machine standing by with its engine warmed and a pilot ready for take-off.

The danger wasn't there. It was in the possibility that our own operation had been penetrated without our knowledge. It had been necessary to engage people outside our own cell and although Chirac and Batagnier must have been screened it wouldn't have been advisable to let the ground staff at South 4 know that this flight had a clandestine aspect, even though there had been no secrecy about the take-off.

London had done its best but if the change in the engine note of the tow plane was in fact an illusion created by the additional noise of another aircraft flying behind us the mission would end here, two thousand metres above the desert and a hundred kilometres from the target: Tango Victor.

The aft structure of the glider provided a blind spot big enough to conceal a bomber. The glider itself provided a blind spot for the Fauconnet even if it carried outside mirrors. If there were a third aircraft now flying a northeast course towards No. 3 Philips tower only the pilot of that aircraft would know.

"Chirac."

"J'écoute."

"Have you noticed any change in the engine note?"

"When?"

"A minute ago."

"Oh yes—he went into coarser pitch."

"He's got variable props?"

"But yes. And we are quite high now."

"I see. Have you got any spare gum?"

Altitude 3000.

Chirac watched the instruments.

Thirty seconds later the Fauconnet began levelling off.

I couldn't see the No. 3 tower light any more from starboard: over the past ten minutes it had been drifting slowly out of sight towards our midline as Batagnier changed course to overfly it directly.

The engine noise was flattening to a steady drone as he throttled back to compensate for the increase of speed at level flight.

It was now very cold in the cockpit.

"You will please check your seat belt."

He went on watching the instruments.

I checked and reported.

"Very well."

He pulled the release and the cable snaked away and the force of the deceleration thrust me hard against the belt as the nose went down. I caught sight of the tow

plane once more, quite small as it wheeled against the horizon to retrace its course, then we were drifting, alone in
the night sky.

9. Drop

There was only the wind's sound.

Sometimes it changed, subtly or grossly, as Chirac
searched the heights for their currents. The air rushed in-
audibly over the wings and the sound was not from there
but from imperfections in the streamlining of the cabin:
the landing gear housing, the flanges of the hood-runners,
the edge of the drop trap.

A sibilance came from them, a whistling through the
teeth, then as we swung to meet the wind and headed into
it the sound changed to a low fluting, eerie and musical,
then died to a whisper as we drifted across the current,
the long wings lying against it.

"Southwest," said Chirac, listening to the sounds.
"Maybe ten knots."

A head wind for our flight path. That was why we'd
come here. But he could have been wrong about the pre-
vailing air movement and it was reassuring to have his
forecast confirmed.

"We can go straight in?"

"Not yet. In a little time. I want to know more."

He sat listening, touching the controls a degree and
bringing them back, feeling the air as sensitively as if his
hands were spread open against it, his fingers sifting it for
information. Below us the landmarks turned slowly, the
lights of the three camps revolving inside the greater orbit
of the radio tower.

0046.

Nerves all right but a thought insisting, a reminder of
the margin of error that no one had wanted to talk about,
neither Loman nor Chirac nor I myself.

I'd asked Loman about the duration and he'd said flexible and I'd asked Chirac what the chances were and he'd
said fifty-fifty and it meant the same thing: with the target
at this distance and the run-in made by dead-reckoning
the margin of error for dropping me with accuracy was

critically wide and the break-off point was anywhere on the invisible circle drawn around the mission objective where I couldn't survive long enough to do any good.

Ignore.

The wind whispered past the perspex hood and above us the starfields turned, their vastness diminishing us, making of us a mote of dust adrift in the dark.

Altitude 2900, must keep to facts.

Keep to the facts, in any case, that don't add up to despair: it's too soon for that.

The starboard wing lifting and our weight shifting and the air desolate in its crying, the sound the winter wind makes under the doors. The nose going down and a scream coming into the sky, dying away as we climb suddenly, the squab seat pressing up and the harness creaking, a shelf of air where we hover and then slide away, circling, the wind plaintive, its voice the voice of the mad Arab, whimpering . . . *mountains in the sky . . . and great birds darkening the heavens . . .*

The air cold, a blade of it cutting across my face from the crack in the hood-runner. My whole body cold, and stiff with its bruises and in no mood shortly to be hurled from its minuscule shelter among the stars.

"Very well."

A certain philosophy in his tone, a note of fatalism, no time left for the little Gallic ironies, none of the *mon ami* as we swung through the figures on the compass scale towards the southwest, our final flight line.

"Are you going in?"

He said yes and I unzipped the case of the Sony.

Weight shifting as he began flattening the curve.

Still visible: No. 3 tower. Coming into view: No. 2 tower and the white light markers of South 5, South 6, and the Roches Brunes camps.

"You will begin to compute when we will pass over the No. 2 radio beacon, you know?"

"Understood. I want your value for the head wind."

"Eight knots."

Noted.

Also noted: eight knots estimated average and not reassuring to spell it out like that but this was the main factor in the margin of error, his inability to know to what extent our airspeed would be true and to what extent it

would be expressed by the wind in the pilot head. From
his experience of this region he could say that in this season and at this hour a ten-knot wind at three thousand
metres above the platinum camps would indicate a wind
of eight knots average along our course to the target area
but what he couldn't say was that this indication was reliable enough to let him drop me within the prescribed lim-
its of the objective.

If we flew into this precise degree of head wind he
would drop me right in the centre of the ring but if there
were an error of two kph on either side he'd drop me so
wide that there wouldn't be a hope of locating Tango Victor before my supplies ran out.

The harness creaked as he moved the control-column
and I watched the angle of glide go down to fifteen degrees. The soft rushing of the air rose until the sound was
like the hissing of a steam valve and the whole of the airframe began shivering as the stringers took the strain.

Altitude 2850—2840—2830.

Airspeed 95—105—115.

Time 0051.

No. 2 beacon dead ahead of us, a crimson glow.

I turned my watch to the underside of my wrist and
used the left hand to steady the Sony on my knees, the
right hand to operate it.

Speed still rising through 140—145—150.

Airstream very loud, a lot of vibration.

The light on the tower was moving slowly towards the
edge of the blind spot below us and he couldn't leave it
much longer.

"Be ready, please."

"Ready."

Angle of glide fourteen degrees: he was anticipating
and realised it and corrected to fifteen.

"Listen now, please. I am going to trim the angle to
two degrees in a few seconds. Then I will tell you when
we will pass over the tower. It is then you must begin
computing."

"Understood."

He brought the column back and the red light vanished.

Quite a lot of pressure from the seat.

Wind noise decreased.

Angle 2°.

Compass: 225°.
"Begin computing."

"Her name is Monique."
"I expect she's pretty."
"Oh yes, I think."
The inconsistency still on my mind.

In Tunis they'd rigged a bang and got it wrong and didn't try again. In Kaifra they'd set up observation and put a tag on me to find out where I was going and that was all they'd wanted to do because if they'd meant to neutralise they'd have used two men instead of one. To this extent I could penetrate their thinking because they had my dossier and therefore they were professionals and would follow procedures known to me. Then they'd tried to kill again, this time with a long gun, and that was inconsistent.

"Also I have two children, you know? They are boys."
"How old are they?"
"Jean-Paul has five year old, and Georges has seven."

I hadn't been able to give it to Loman to work out so I'd have to tell him as soon as I called up base. He didn't know I'd been shot up but someone might have found the Mercedes by now and half the town would know about it and he'd pick it up before very long and then I suppose he'd just wet himself and assume they'd junked my cadaver and he wouldn't be able to phone the airstrip staff at South 4 because of the strict hush conditions so now he'd be hopping up and down in front of the base transceiver desperate for a signal and crossing himself at thirty-second intervals.

"I have got a snapshot, you know, of those three, that I made a long time before. But I can not fetch it now."

He couldn't move, couldn't move even a hand to get to his pocket, hadn't moved for twenty-nine minutes, just sat with the control-column watching the angle of glide and the compass while I punched the Sony for him every time the second hand passed the top of the dial.

Airstream steady.

"Sixty-four."
"Okay."

Two theories: the opposition had an undisciplined cell or their signals were inefficient and the inconsistency was by accident and not design, or there were two cells operating and they were in conflict on the question of policy. In either case it indicated pressure: their Controls were putting out panic directives as fast as London.

0131.

Dropping in nineteen minutes.

"I will tell you of something quite amusing. It was on the same day when I make the altitude record that Georges is born, you know that? The flight for my *planeur* had been arranged, and I went up after I come from the hospital to see my new son. I feel so light, you know, so happy, that I always think it is that fact which helps me go so high up."

"You felt inspired."

"C'est exactement ça! I find the thunder cloud at one thousand metres and I fly up with it until twelve thousand, and then find the wave lift waiting for me, and the sky is the limit! The feeling was quite like anoxia, you know, but of course I had the mask on a long time before. So I wanted to have him christened 'Icare,' you see, but my wife says 'Georges' is more convenient, because she has an uncle of this name."

0142.

Eight minutes to the drop.

Of course it was just conceivable that Control had picked up a trace of the marksman. There was a ten-tenths flap on in London so they'd have alerted the whole network for data monitoring and there must have been signals coming in from both hemispheres for analysis.

There aren't many telescopic rifles among the European intelligence networks because it's a device used specifically for assassination and there's not nearly so much fuss caused with a little cyanide in the toothpaste. The long gun demands a relatively sophisticated setup and a couple of years ago when Parkis had directed the *modus operandi* of a neutralisation thing it had taken him three weeks to line it all up including requisition of premises, covert communication channels, access and egress, target movement monitoring and the technical demands of the gun itself in terms of range, angles of fire, appropriate ammunition, so forth. But if it's a special case and there's enough time for these preliminaries and the eye at the scope has been trained into the international class there's an overwhelming advantage because the terminal act can be performed impersonally and without the risk of retaliation: once the instructions have been confirmed by Control or even Local Control the target has only to pass through the selected point in his travel pattern and he knows nothing more.

Parkis had used Tomlinson for that one, winkled him out of a duck shoot on Lord Kenfield's estate and put him into an executive jet at Gatwick with a Remington .410 across his knees and a street map of Kronshatadt to read. He had a rotten cold but it didn't affect his performance, just the one shot, and it broke up a cell we'd been trying to get at for nearly three years.

0145.

Five minutes.

The thing was that if our overseas units picked up anything about a known marksman last seen with a ticket for Tunis or Jerba and passed it for routine analysis in London there'd be an immediate hit when Loman told them I'd been under a gun. They'd know it was almost certainly the same one that had worried Fyson in Sidi Ben Ali but even a random signal with some new information in it could link up with existing data and put a name to the man and there's a saying at the Bureau that stands up rather well: *once you can blow the man you can blow the cell.*

Four.

Airstream variable and therefore unpleasant because windspeed variation could make a mess of what I was doing on the Sony and I could come down anywhere.

"Now, please?"

"Seventy-six."

He wanted to count up for distance and I wanted to count down for time which was a bit more logical but he'd stuck his heels in about it and said he didn't feel comfortable "working backwards" so I let it go.

Three.

"Ninety-one point eighty-five."

He watched the instruments.

"Repeat the briefing, please."

His voice had gone dull suddenly.

"Free the belt. Slide back the hood. Wait for the order. Jump and look out for the leading edge."

"Very well."

Didn't really seem necessary but he'd dropped people before and he knew his onions: at the last minute when you're thinking about the imminent free fall you can cock the whole thing up by getting your feet caught in the belt or bashing your head on the hood you forgot to open, do it by numbers and it's foolproof.

"Where shall I put this thing?"

"Leave it on the seat."

Dull, toneless, because she was pretty and one was five, the other seven.

0148.

"Ninety-three point six five kilometres."

"Bien."

Two minutes.

I didn't have anyone, *nothing of value, no next of kin,* but that kind of comfort's really an intellectual pursuit because we've all got a skin and that's what the organism says we've got to save, yelling its bloody head off, couldn't care less about the insurance.

"Ninety-five point six seven."

"Okay."

One minute.

The night seemed vast.

The stars gave a sense of orientation but only in one plane and all they did was show which way was down and that was where I was going, down through the dark to the endless night-lying waves of sand, of silence.

The 8 looks so like a 9 and they're side by side.

Slipshod maintenance, dead flies in the pitot-head.

A change in the wind.

Ignore.

"Ninety-six point two."

"Very well."

Twenty-eight seconds.

The odd feeling that we were arriving somewhere. Difficult, here where the night was as vast as it had been before and the dark as featureless, to understand that our journey together was over. No control tower or platform or jetty or gates, nothing to mark a junction or a terminal, only the dark and the delicate pointer going its rounds.

Tick-tick-tick.

"Ninety-six point five."

"So. Be ready then."

He brought the column back just a little.

Level flight.

Ten seconds.

We had agreed that at this point I would stop computing. Ten seconds represented a quarter of a kilometre and that much distance could be critical if I dropped wide but if I went on computing to zero as a refinement it wouldn't allow for the time I needed for getting out.

Tick-tick-tick.

French keen on shaking hands, frustrating for him, control-column too sensitive, no go the niceties.

I hit the belt clip.

Tick-tick.

Hood back and a blast of air, roaring.

Leave the Sony on the seat.

Altitude 75 metres.

Tick.

Good luck, Chirac.

Adieu!

Free fall.

10. Tango

One, two, three.

Blood in the head and the stars swinging below me.

Less horizontal buffeting, more vertical.

Four, five, six.

Free fall velocity rising very fast.

Air less cold.

Seven, eight, nine.

Pull it.

Crack of the pilot 'chute.

Then the jerk and the drag and oh Christ—

Blackout.

Swinging gently.

Couldn't quite relate anything yet.

Nearly did it again and thought I'm not going to and the pain didn't stop but at least I stayed conscious. It had been the shoulders, that was all, the bruising on the pavement in Tunis and then the ricochet of the .44 tonight and then the awful wrenching from the harness because I'd

been more or less upside down when the main canopy had
filled and the fall velocity had been braked from more
than a hundred kph to less than fifteen and the pain had
overcharged the nerve channels and that was that.

Still very uncomfortable, feeling of being on fire, inability to concentrate on other things but the forebrain functioning well enough to alert the organism and I began
looking downwards so that I'd see the sand coming up
and have a chance of relaxing the muscles because if I hit
it the wrong way I'd pass out again and I had a lot to do.

No particular visual definition yet: a certain lightness
below, with darker areas, but could be illusory.

I could make out the figures on the dial of my watch
without needing the phosphorescence, not much point in
wanting to know the time but it helped me to feel I was
getting back into some kind of control over things. Time
was important: ask London.

There was something I ought to be checking on but it
didn't matter for the moment, couldn't be expected to
look after everything when there was this Godawful sensation across my shoulders. Be easier when the harness was
off. Swinging gently, the rhythm soothing, the night air
soft against my face.

It does matter.

Bloody well wake up and have a look, can't see it, don't
panic, use your suspension lines, pivot full circle, none too
easy, monkey on a string, now keep looking because it's
very important indeed.

Couldn't see the bloody thing anywhere.

Rest. Relax. Watch the ground.

The whisper of wind in the shrouds.

He couldn't have forgotten to pull the release. You
think of such extraordinary things when your life's on the
teeter, of course he'd pulled it, he was an experienced
flyer and he'd dropped people before. But he'd had to give
me five seconds to get clear so that the 'chutes wouldn't
foul each other and I couldn't see it because it would be
above me and the canopy was in the way, thirty feet
across and right over my head, what the hell would you
expect.

A lot of pain, it wouldn't go.

Then bloody well shut up about it.

Nothing below with any definition: it just didn't look
like empty sky, that was all, the desert was there all right.

If I hadn't punched an 8 instead of a 9 and if some slip-shod instrument-basher hadn't left enough dead flies in the pitot-head to affect the airspeed reading and if the wind hadn't changed I was now floating above the only point on the surface of the earth describable as Long. 8°3' by Lat. 30°4' and it was less than forty-eight hours since they'd put on the show for me.

Run it back, will you?

Stop.

Back another fraction.

Stop.

Yes, that's the one. I've got it now.

An ash-grey smudge on the photograph.

Tango Victor.

Somewhere below me now but very difficult to believe because Loman had said flexible and Chirac had said fifty-fifty and that meant the margin of error was horribly wide and although the wreck of the twin-prop short-haul freighter was certainly within a few kilometres of the point where I was due to come down I might never reach it, never see it, because this was the desert.

Look, they don't do this to you without thinking about it first: even those arthritic old tarts in London aren't as bad as that. When they send a ferret down the hole they don't tell him much but they've done it with me so often that I've managed to pick up the odd clue about the way they think. It wasn't lack of planning in the advanced pre-briefing phases that had left us with a critical margin of error at the access point, and it wasn't indifference to the question of my survival or otherwise that had let them send me out here where the chance of life was small. They just had to do what they could.

This was the *best* they could do, not the worst. This was *all* they could do, instead of nothing.

They hadn't been able to turn this one down. I think they'd probably tried but the pressure had been too great and they'd been forced to set up the op. I'd only known it to happen twice before since I'd been at the Bureau and in each case the decision-making had been at Prime Minister level.

He wished to inform me personally that your mission is the key to a critical situation of the highest international proportions.

If he didn't talk like a bloody schoolmistress he could

have put it rather more concisely: *This one's shit-or-bust*.

We call it a one-shot mission and it means if you don't pull it off the first time you don't get another go. You can refuse it if you like but if you accept it you've got to play it their way and put up with panic directives and dodgy communications and makeshift access lines and do what you can with what you've got and somehow get in there and do the job and bring back the goods. It means more than just the increased risk of your losing your life: it means that if you can't complete the mission it's the last chance anyone's going to get. There are various factors governing this but the most common one is time.

Time governed the Tango mission. In London they'd been pushed for time but they'd set it running as best they could and provided superlative access lines right into the target area: my final approach to the objective was being made invisibly and in perfect silence. The margin of error was deadly but if they'd narrowed it the invisibility and the silence would have had to go: we would have brought a powered aircraft and searched the area with flares and landing lights and made a direct drop onto the target but I wouldn't have had five minutes to work in before the opposition arrived.

The margin of error had been unavoidable. That didn't make it any narrower: but it made it more acceptable.

Air spilling from the canopy. Its dark fabric was spread above me, filling half the sky. I couldn't see the supply 'chute but I believed it was there, following me down, had to believe it was there because if it weren't I would already have begun to die.

The senses were coming back and I had the impression that each swing was taking me more and more to one side: the canopy was restless and I could hear the rising sibilance of the airstream through the suspension lines. There was a lateral force operating and this must be the south wind, the *ghibli*, that Chirac said he hoped to find blowing when he made his attempt to reach the South 4 strip. It didn't feel very strong; I wished for him that it would be enough.

Warmth was touching my face and I looked down. The heat of the sands was rising and I reached for the lines and held them, waiting, seeing nothing but knowing that land was near.

Important to remain conscious.

The chances were that I'd hit sand and the impact would be cushioned but if Chirac's dead-reckoning had been accurate enough to bring me down on a radius of five hundred yards from the centre of the target area I could hit the rock outcrop and if a spur caught one of my shoulders I'd flake out again and that would be dangerous.

The canopy above me had been blocking my view and when I hit ground and the nylon collapsed I must get an immediate visual fix on the supply 'chute. I would be able to see it while it was still airborne because when I'd bailed out the airspeed had been 99 kph and Chirac was going to wait five seconds before he released and with a wind factor common to both drops the supply 'chute would come down approximately a hundred and fifty metres from where I landed. But if I didn't see it before it struck ground and the canopy collapsed it would be hidden by the dunes: and I wouldn't know its direction.

With our bearing of 225° from the radio tower we'd flown with Pegasus directly ahead and I could see the constellation now but Chirac had made a right-hand bank when I'd jumped and I didn't know if he'd resumed his course before levelling up to make the second drop or if he'd simply pulled out of the turn and levelled at a tangent. If I didn't see where the supply 'chute came down it would mean a search in the dark among the dunes with no certainty of ever finding it.

Warm air against my skin.

The lines whispering: I could feel their fine vibration.

Sudden inundation of optical stimuli and the world filled with contrasts—the far horizon line where the stars met the rim of the earth and the rising undulations of the dunes blotting it out as I pulled on the lines to break the impact and then went limp and rolled once on my shoulder with the harness wrenching, dragged the release and tried to get up, couldn't.

Everything kaleidoscopic and the pain like a furnace roaring in my bones, try to see where it is, most important, the high stars sliding down the wall of night and sand in my mouth, *get up,* not really important yes *very,* spitting the sand out, a dark shape moving over there where there's nothing, nothing to mark it, the canopy lowering, lowering, yes *got* it, the roaring and the red of stars flying, fall this way then, *this* way, fall with your head towards it and remember, remember when you wake, your *head* is *towards* it, the black sand bursting against my face.

Pale fire.

Blue, pale blue fire before my eyes.

A ring of it, a rosary, an annulus of luminescent blue.

The two pointers at right angles, their blue, it doesn't take, their blue light trisecting the ring of fire, take long for the brain to seize when it wakes on what it can find, familiar things to facilitate recall, twelve and three, the underside of my wrist lying turned towards my eyes, three o'clock.

Your head is towards it.

Over there. It came down over there.

Three o'clock and all's well, we have the means to survive.

Got up and it happened again and I became very frustrated and spat out the sand, hanging on all fours like a dog and thinking this won't do at all, where's your dignity, now get up and stay there and *don't turn.*

Over there.

Note carefully. The high dune to the left, curving to the unequal-sided V where it joins the next, the lower one, and the bright star five degrees above it to the right. Observe and absorb.

I had a reference. The gap in the dunes and a star. It was the only known shape here where I was a stranger: it was a kind of temporary home.

It took time to get there. Over an hour. It was more like three hundred metres instead of a hundred and fifty and the directional error was ten degrees and the dunes were dark. I took the parachute with me because later it would make extra shade and I couldn't leave it behind, the idea wasn't actually to litter the desert with landmarks, but it took a bit of dragging, I couldn't fold it and the sand kept getting in it but it did a good enough job wiping out my tracks.

There was a light wind blowing, blowing from Diphda in the south, is it enough for your needs, *mon ami?* It had blown sand already against the container on that side and the 'chute was almost covered. The desert hid things from you: beware.

A rip-string and I pulled it, opening the polyester like a sardine tin, putting the lid on its back and scooping sand in before the wind could lift it. The 2000CA was on top and I took it out and stood it on the lid and pulled up the telescopic aerial, not hurrying, just a routine movement of the hands and perfectly confident, Loman was experienced and the only time he'd ever lost a base was in Bangkok and we weren't there when it was blown and besides she had a gun, the big Colt that Chirac had lent me, hold it with both hands if you want to and be ready for the recoil. And anyway I'd asked Loman not to leave base because one gun wouldn't be enough if she were alone and they raided the place, feet on the stairs and the door kicked open and the first one going down but after that she'd lose her head and just go on pumping the thing wild with her eyes shut and they'd reach her before the sixth.

Chrome of the aerial shining, the low wind moving its tip.

3 MHz.

Channel 2.

Mike.

Tango.

It sounded strange, a human voice in so desolate a place.

Tango. Tango.

The same stars, these same stars, would be there above the gilded cupolas where the rats ran among the rotting palms. The town would be asleep.

Eyes closing and I opened them again quickly and took a breath, steadying. Fifty-six hours ago I'd got off the plane from Tokyo and the metabolic clock was still trying to get the time right, a feeling of not quite being here, of not being anywhere, just afloat on some kind of tide.

Tango. Tango.

A domed ceiling and a cracked mosaic floor, three faded arabesque screens and the shabby appurtenances of a fifth-class hotel.

The other end of the lifeline.

What frequencies would you use in this area?

7 MHz for daytime propagation conditions, 3 MHz at night.

Tango. Tango.

The sand blown by the wind, its fine grains hitting the side of the polyester box with a dry whispering, the only answer.

Already in the past hour the sand had almost covered the spread of nylon: in the starlight I could just make out the few dark folds that remained. Soon it would cover the harness, then the box, and then if I went on sitting here like this, like a man in prayer, it would cover me as well, a desiccated mendicant forgotten by his gods as he intoned for their deaf ears the mystic word, until he was buried, grain upon grain, beneath his sins.

Tango.

One of them would be there. Loman might have had to leave base to contact Chirac or use a phone if the wire had come adrift again on the junction board or he could have gone down there to the hall to fix it but in that case Diane would be manning the transceiver, and would answer.

The wind gusted, scattering the sand.

A faint gleam on the aerial and the chrome rims of the dials. It was a good-looking set: a matte-black case with a neutral grille and the controls tapered and finely knurled, the on-off switch recessed so that a chance movement wouldn't activate it. The illuminated dials were dark.

No adequate excuses. Flight disorientation, the blast wave, the general wear and tear of getting here alive. Not really adequate.

I put the switch to the "on" position and checked the frequency again at 3 MHz.

Tango.

Tango. Base receiving.

A good signal, loud and clear.

I'm down.

Are you in the target area?

I don't know.

He waited and I didn't say anything so he came in again.

Do you have any problem?

Not really.

He waited again.

I wasn't being very communicative. You're supposed to volunteer a bit of information, not leave your director to tease it out of you. Thing was, I wanted to go to sleep now.

Was the drop made successfully as concerns bearings?

Oh yes. Put the little bastard out of his misery or he'll keep you talking all bloody night. *On Chirac's reckoning I'm somewhere near the target, but it's too dark here to see anything. There aren't any rocks on the skyline. Going to take a dekko in the morning.*

Silence again.

Are you perfectly fit?

What?

Are you in a fit physical condition?

Of course I am.

Bloody sauce. Resented that. I told him:

Listen: there's a telescopic rifle in Kaifra. Christ sake watch out for it. And the Mercedes is a write-off.

He was thinking about this.

We heard some shots.

Kaifra was a small oasis town and you'd hear the stuff coming out of a .44 Magnum wherever you were.

They were the ones.

You are not wounded?

No. Another thing is that I think there's more than one network trying to penetrate our operation. Been working a few things out and there's one or two inconsistencies.

He considered this.

You're talking about their apparent indecisiveness during the pre-jump phase?

Their inconsistency.

Yes. This has already been the subject of signals with Control but we're glad to have you confirm.

A pat on the head for a good little ferret, dear Lord you banish me unto the wilderness and the only company you can find for me is Loman's.

One star, the bright star that had guided me here, was going on and off at intervals and I took note of it.

When will you start looking for the objective?

At dawn.

Not before?

Rather quick.

It's too dark. Instructions?

On, off. On, off.

It wasn't the star doing it. I was doing it myself. The star was lying exactly on the horizon and my head kept going down, fatigue, reaction setting in, so the star looked as if it were going on and off.

Silence. He was sulking.

No instructions.

Tango out.

Quick fade of the image: the dome and the arabesque screens.

Mike back into the recessed clip and the switch down and next time don't forget to turn the bloody thing on when you want to call up base, save a lot of worry, I thought they'd had it, both of them, thought we'd all had it.

Loman could do the worrying now. He'd got his executive into the field but the bearings were all to hell and we'd got to cool our heels for another three hours before we could get moving again and in three hours the opposition could make up a lot of ground. There'd been no security blackout for the take-off from the South 4 strip: London could have sent in a unit of screened ground staff with a prearranged access to facilities but even then there would have been people at South 4 who knew that a glider had gone up, and short of requesting Petrocombine's cooperation in treating the event as a paramilitary secret it would have been impossible to keep the thing hush. The opposition cells would be routinely combing the area for items of intelligence and if they picked up the news that a glider had been towed airborne they'd want to know where it had landed and if they drew blank at all the local airstrips they'd assume there'd been a desert drop and they'd send for a direction-finding unit, fully urgent, because radio would be the only means of communication between the field and base.

Once the opposition set up a D/fing operation in a town as small as Kaifra I'd give our base twenty-four hours before it was blown.

There was a sleeping bag in the container and I unrolled it and threw it down but it was no go: I'd have to make an effort, some kind of effort, to find out if I'd come down anywhere near the target. This before I could sleep.

Even if there were only a thin chance of locating the freighter's wreckage before first light it was worth having a go because in the night's cool the sweat loss and water intake would be less than a tenth of the quantities produced by the day's heat.

There was another thing: psychologically I'd been homing-in on the target since they'd shown me the picture of it in London. The smudge on the photograph had become the subject of intellectual attraction and I felt its influence on me now, stronger than before because it was closer.

It was impossible to judge how far I stood from the nearest dune: I could only see it in two dimensions, its dark spine humped against the stars and breaking the distant skyline. It was less than a thousand yards away but the desert is like the ocean: the chance of death by isolation is immeasurably greater, and values become changed. Go a thousand yards in the dark and you may never come back.

There was a torch among the supplies, with some spare batteries, but I wouldn't use light for a marker: you learn to conserve, to know the sudden pricelessness of ordinary things. There was a tin mug and I put it upside-down on the tip of the aerial and waited for the wind to send it ringing; then I walked to the dune and climbed it.

In the photographs, taken from the near-vertical, the definition of the shale upthrust had been vague, but I would expect a stratified configuration at ground level in this region, like the rocks near Kaifra, sharp and broken and sloping, distinct from the curvilinear dunes. But I saw nothing like that, though I twice turned full circle. The skyline was uniformly smooth.

Then I began shouting and turned again, my voice going into the distant dark and dying there. Twenty or thirty feet high, the squadron-leader had said, so there'd be an echo from them if they weren't too far away.

Tang-o . . . Tang-o Vic-tor . . .

My feet burying deeper as I turned.

My eyes closed so that I could listen better.

Shouting, turning under the dome of stars.

Tang-o . . . Victor . . .

Dying away.

All I could see from the height where I stood, all I could hear, was the margin of error, wide as the endless dunes.

11. Signal

A sense of frightening exposure.

Last night there had been the stars, their names known and their order long ago established by the ancients. Now there was nothing. A map had been replaced by a blank sheet of paper. In the dark it had been possible to believe that when morning came I might see familiar shapes, however far away: buildings or trees. Morning had come and I saw nothing.

For another minute I lay with my eyes open, pinned to the earth's surface in infinite solitude. It was the sameness of this terrain that appalled: if there had been a range of higher dunes within sight, or a rock or a tree, any kind of feature to break the facelessness here, I could have related with it and arrived at some kind of orientation: I could have noted that it was on my left or on my right, in front of me or behind; and there could have been the idea that if I set out to reach it I might find other features becoming visible beyond it as I approached.

There was nothing.

Nothing to see, nothing to hear: the silence was absolute.

During the night the low wind had died, and my sleeping bag was only half covered by drifts of sand; but my tracks to and from the high dune had disappeared. This was the desert, and if a man chose to disturb the perfection of these primeval sands, let it be shown that his passing shall leave no trace.

I drank from one of the five-litre *bidons* and pressed the sides before screwing the cap on. The sun was a diameter above the horizon and I thought of opening for reception but Loman would only order a change of frequency for daytime conditions and ask if I'd sighted the objective and that wasn't a question I wanted to hear put into words.

I hadn't been delaying things since first light but there was a marked reluctance to go and find out the worst: and I could do that by going to the dune over there and climbing it. We don't mind if London's policy is to send us in with only a minimum of data but we always know that at any stage of an operation it can take us beyond the point of no return: and that point could already be behind me now.

Edwards had been in this position eighteen months ago in Yugoslavia: in the thick of a direct Control-to-field signals exchange in the final phase of the mission he'd found out by accident that if he failed to reach the objective he'd automatically become expendable—and he'd kicked. We didn't expect to see him back in London for at least ten years if he were lucky but he'd infiltrated a CIA courier line and did a fast deal with a batch of strict shut documentation and got a flight out of Zagreb with a party of chess players on a cultural exchange and asked to see Parkis the minute he reached the Bureau and Parkis had flayed him alive and then fired him.

The point Edwards had been trying to make was that it's all right if an executive fouls up a job and Control throws him to the dogs before he can do any more damage, but it's not all right for the Bureau to send him out on a Curtain thing without telling him there's a high risk of his becoming expendable *automatically* because the mission's been planned like that.

There's no middle line we can take on this one. The complexities of an intelligence operation don't even have a static design: its pattern shifts as the mission progresses, and values are changed hourly. Control can put a man in the field on a routine bugging stint at a presummit convention and the whole thing can suddenly hot up and he's out there trying to handle something so big that if he drops it he won't survive and all you can blame the Bureau for is not pulling him out for the sake of his own skin.

But that isn't what the Bureau is for.

Parkis had given us the picture after he'd fired Edwards: Parkis doesn't like unrest among the ferrets. During the end phase of the mission it had been decided that the only way to get Edwards right through to the objective was by cutting him off from most of his escape lines and letting the opposition think that no one would attempt this brand of the impossible unless he were a lunatic. To an extent it came off because they withdrew a lot of surveillance and Edwards got through to the signals room of the Hungarian Embassy and was closing on the objective—his actual mission was a cipher-bust near the centre of the Yugoslavian network—when he'd seen what London had done to his escape lines and panicked and got out.

We don't like Parkis but we thought he was right. All we ask is that the Bureau doesn't plan a mission that *depends* on an expendable executive. That, in certain cases, would amount to murder.

In my case there was a fact among the unknown background data that I knew must exist and that I had tacitly accepted when Loman had given me final briefing at the

Yasmina. It was obvious, and it was this: if I failed to reach Tango Victor I couldn't expect to be pulled out of the area. The entry in the book wouldn't read *Mission Failed* but *Executive Deceased*. In most cases it comes to the same thing but there's a technical *nuance* because the failure of a big operation creates a lot of depression at the Bureau and it makes the whole thing look a bit better if it can be shown that the executive lost his life in the attempt: it means that no one can say he wasn't trying hard enough.

London wanted me to find an aeroplane and examine its cargo and if I couldn't do it they'd want to make it very difficult for anyone else to do it. They'd taken great pains to put me down here in strict hush and if I couldn't find the objective they wouldn't allow Loman to make any noise pulling me out.

Understood and accepted.

But it seemed a long way to the top of the dune.

They were Zeiss 22-50s but I didn't use them until I'd turned full circle and looked for the freighter with the naked eye because if I had to use a 22 magnification to pick it up it would mean it was a day's march distant and the sun was already hot on my skin.

From the low area among the dunes I had looked and seen nothing and from this height I looked and saw nothing but it was infinitely worse: down there the piled waves of sand had limited my range of vision but from here I could see for fifty miles in every direction and *still* there was nothing. It was a dun-brown seascape, an area so vast that it had no end until it met the sky itself. The silence of it alone was diminishing to the spirit, adding lifelessness to endlessness: the semblance of a seascape, because of this, was only partial; there was no sound here of the wave's leap or the hiss of spindrift. Silence and stillness together cast the mind beyond the thought of death and held it in awe of this place where life itself had never been.

My shadow alone moved, turning as I turned, its giant pointer lying curved across the dunes.

An instant's hesitation of the hands, fear of confirming the negative findings of the naked eye, then I raised the binoculars and adjusted the focus to infinity. The red of the spectrum refracted at the edge of the field to leave a glowing ring, and through it passed the flow of images, repeated until they became meaningless: one sand dune looked like another, and here they were spread in their millions.

After two minutes I had to lower the glasses, mesmerised. The agoraphobia still played in my senses, a hovering dread of exposure that I couldn't quite keep away as I stood here in the middle of the empty earth beneath the empty sky, a goose-flesh feeling of vulnerability: I was a creature without shelter, without a hiding place, caught in a trap where the vastness of freedom itself imprisoned me.

I prefer the more natural haunts of my kind, the sooty warrens of the city streets, to this cosmic waste where the grains of sand are unimaginably many.

I turned twice more, full circle.

At least there would be no more effort needed, now that this point was reached. The reckoning had been wrong, that was all. Somewhere between the Philips tower and the zeros lining up on the computer there had been a mistake made in the figures. The margin of error, *mon ami,* is even larger than we'd thought.

There was no point in organising a day's march: by the law of averages I would be as likely to move away from the wreck of the freighter as towards it. I had a compass but I didn't know the bearing. If I set off at random the odds against success were precisely three hundred and sixty to one.

Onset of lassitude, euphoria almost. Pain coming back, normal reaction, nothing important to do, can concentrate on the discomfort, crouched on the sand with my back to the heat and the light, here endeth the mission, you can't win them all. A vague sense of wonder that the sun was perfectly silent, sending this degree of heat over so much distance, you'd expect to hear a roaring, however faint, here where silence could be broken by a grain of sand hitting the side of a box.

My shadow humped before me, an insubstantial buddha.

Try again I've tried then bloody well try again.

Lurching about, it's the sand, you can't ever get your balance. The red ring flaring at the edge of the field and the dunes flowing through, full circle. Negative. Take a rest.

A kind of sleep, timeless and with no dream element re-called, teeming images but so disconnected as to have no significance, then on my feet again and wandering about feeling stronger physically but not really determined about anything, the organism taking care of itself, getting the wind up because the box down there wasn't very big, forty-eight hours plus reserves and that's our lot.

Kept bumping my forehead against the eyepieces, sweat running down, awareness of sand in the boots and a thirst beginning, a certain amount of cerebration continuing: the parallax factor critically important because a near dune could block medium-field gaps, be an interesting thing to work out—given a man of certain height standing upon a dune of a certain height and given a million dunes, the nearest of them concealing the gaps between those more distant, what proportion is hidden from him?

Hell with academic problems: concentrate on the one thing that could just conceivably drag the mission back on its feet and yes you snivelling little perisher, save our skin.

Parallax.

By lateral movement the observer exposes to view the gaps between distant dunes hitherto concealed by those in the foreground. By bodily rotation he increases this exten-sion of view a hundredfold. Put it like that and it looks fair enough but the wreck isn't necessarily visible in one of the gaps, it can be lying low on its belly full square be-hind the highest dune of them all and you can practise your lateral movement and bodily rotation till the heat knocks you flat on your face.

The red ring flaring, the sand flowing through. The shadows changing as I turned from the sun through the south to the west. The sun hanging there in its roaring silence and pouring the sky ablaze across the eastern wastes of the earth until its tide lapped about me, burning.

They are there, the gaps you couldn't see before: you're looking at them now but can you tell which they are? You expect to find any difference between one thing and an-other in this region of the damned where the sun and the wind have driven away identity?

Turn. Keep turning.

Of course this wasn't the only dune in the Sahara and I got off it and tried another one because a kind of madness was setting in and although I knew about it I decided to ignore it because the organism had taken over a long time ago but it was going to be hard work: it was saying if we don't find the wreck and finish this job they won't ever pull us out and we'll die here so we're going to climb every dune in the desert till we see it, come on.

Climbed one of them twice, found my own tracks still there, getting rather dodgy, four times down there for a drink of water, not very slaking because it was warm.

The sands flowing like opaque flood water through the vision field, the gaps dipping like the lines on an electro-cardiograph.

Turn. Keep turning.

Stop.

21°.

Now go down, go down and drink. And open up.

Tango.

Tango receiving.

I want to confirm that I am in fact in the target area.

You've seen the plane?

No. But I've sighted a rock. It should be the shale outcrop. According to the R.A.F. people there's no other rock visible within seven miles of the objective and even on dead-reckoning Chirac couldn't have dropped me so wide.

He considered.

I would agree. How far away are you?

It's difficult to tell because the air's so clear. I'd say about two miles: it looks like one but I've doubled it.

What bearing has it?

Twenty-one degrees.

He was looking at the photograph and its annotations.

Then you should find the aeroplane almost directly in your path when you head for the outcrop. Its bearing from there is two hundred degrees.

I'll make my heading twenty. Change frequency?

Yes, to 7 MHz. Please repeat.

I repeated and asked for time-synchro and we ended.

Then I did what I knew I would do: I went to the top of the dune and put up the Zeiss and looked again at the distant tip of rock. My life had depended on sighting this single landmark, and I wanted to be sure I hadn't dreamed up a mirage.

Their mass had been thrust upwards from the earth's crust to leave them standing reared and angular against the sky, their strata sloping at twenty or so degrees from the horizontal and their base littered with brittle fragments that had broken off. In several places a whole shoulder of rock had foundered, making an angled arch and giving shade, and under one of these I made my camp.

The flooring was the canopy of the supply 'chute and the roof was provided by my own, propped and draped with the help of the telescopic tubing that was part of the survival gear.

Lizards had run from the area of shade, skittering so fast across the sand that they seemed to float on its surface. I watched them, encouraged by the evidence of life in this region where I'd thought that nothing could hope to live.

For an hour I slept, in the heat of the noon. The distance had been nearer two miles than one and I'd had to make two trips, each time bringing a parachute and half the gear and provisions: four hours' work including rests in the shade of the rocks before I set up the camp. Earlier, even when it had been cooler, this degree of effort would have been beyond me: it had been the sight of the tip of rock, the knowledge that it was there, that had given me the strength.

At 1234 hours I made a signal.

He had to be told, before I decided what kind of effort was needed. Effort used up water and it used it up very fast. He had to be told, although there wasn't much he could do about it. The first thing was to get him to believe it.

Can I have that bearing again, from the rocks to the freighter?

Two hundred.

I checked the compass. The bearing was lined up directly with the tracks I'd left.

What's the distance from the rocks to the plane?

Four hundred and eighty-five yards.

He wasn't going to like it.

Loman, I'm at the rock outcrop now. I've pitched camp.

I had to wait for him to recheck the annotations on the photograph. No change of tone.

Your heading was twenty degrees?

Yes.

You must have passed close to the aeroplane.

Not close enough to see it.

Then the poor bastard shut up for a bit.

I looked across the blazing sands to the point where my tracks vanished. There were big areas between the dunes and they didn't have the regular formation I'd seen at the point of drop: the rocks would deflect the wind here, setting up turbulence. But I had a clear view for more than five hundred yards and the bearing was correct and I ought to be looking straight at the wreck of the freighter. I was looking at an unbroken waste of sand.

Loman came in.

Quiller.

Hear you.

Do those rocks show any signs of ferrous oxidisation?

He was dead scared but he didn't show it in his voice. He showed it in his thinking: he'd got the blown-up photograph in front of him with the distances marked and he should have worked this one out for himself and instead of that he was panicking. I told him:

No. And it wouldn't make any difference, Loman. The compass could be affected up to fifteen degrees and I'd still be able to see a twin-engined freighter less than five hundred yards away.

Pause.

You are quite sure.

Christ, d'you think I'm just guessing?

I was bloody annoyed because they'd said it was a picture of a plane that had crash-landed at Longitude 8°3′ by Latitude 30°4′ and now I was here on the spot and I couldn't help thinking how much effort we'd all made just to prove they were wrong.

Even Loman was thrown.

I don't understand.

Join the club.

After a while he said: *How was the drop?*

Routine.

I knew what he was driving at but I wasn't in the mood to give him any help: let him stay on this tack and I'd blast his head off, that was all.

Did you bring all your provisions with you from the point of drop?

Yes.

And both parachutes?

Yes.

It was exhausting work.

A bit thirst-making.

There's been no kind of accident? No water spillage?

No.

He saw I wasn't going to cooperate so he just put it on the line, didn't like having to do it, wasn't his way.

How would you describe your general condition, physical and mental?

Not too bad. Bit of sunburn.

His tone went dull: overcorrection.

I would appreciate a more precise answer.

So I thought he ought to have one.

Listen, Loman, the drop was a right bastard and I've just shifted a hundred and seventy kilos through two miles of soft sand in the direct sun but if you think I'm too far gone to be able to see a whole bloody aeroplane against a neutral background at five hundred yards you're wasting your time. Who was the executive you were running last—Dewhurst or someone?

Quite a long time went by. I don't think he was sulking or anything: he'd got a damn' sight too much on his plate and he was going to have a lot more unless he could do something about it and that didn't leave any time for making mental notes to the Bureau to the effect that certain executives appeared to require supplementary refresher courses in Norfolk.

Quiller.

Hear you.

Can you give me an approximate configuration?

Of these rocks?

Yes.

Stand by.

I switched off to save the batteries.

He'd begun thinking straight but it was going to be a nasty five minutes because there weren't many answers to the question and this was the one with the built-in dead end to the mission.

The compass gave 14°-194° for the elongation and I noted it and took the pad with me and it was like walking out of the shade into a molten gold wall. This was the eastern face and a lot of heat was coming off it because of seven or eight hours' prezenith absorption. I could feel the sweat drying on me as fast as it came through the pores: there was no moisture when I passed a hand across my face.

I made my way clockwise.

Lizards scuttled across the broken shale on the ground: they were quite big, a foot long, one of the Iguanidae, and they didn't go far from where I passed, but froze with their angular heads lifted to watch me. Possibly they had never seen man before and their caution was primitively learned, the mistrust of an alien creature so large that it blotted out the sun.

South face and turning west.

The general configuration was oblong and the angles were clearly defined: the material was so hard that erosion hadn't rounded it. The sun and the night frosts had loosened the strata into laminations and the wind had worked at the result; in places the weathering force had left horizontal necks and the weight of the unsupported rock had brought it down so that now it leaned on the main structure in irregular buttresses, making shade. In these areas there were more lizards than nearer the open and I supposed their one enemy was the vulture.

No. 2 Fighter Reconnaissance had said there weren't any other rocks within seven miles of this group. I thought about that for a minute and then gave it up.

West to north.

They watched me with their gold-ringed eyes. A pair of them turned their heads slowly as I passed, only one of them flashing into the crevice behind them with its long tail scattering the group of snail shells in the hollow where they fed. At night there would sometimes be moisture here.

Seven miles.

If Loman got the precise bearing from the R.A.F. we might work out the chances but they were almost nil: from this morning's trek the immediate reckoning was a minimum of fourteen hours by day, leaving out the factor of diminishing energy in terms of progressive fatigue. And the thing was self-cancelling because the more water I carried the more I'd use up.

North to camp.

My hand reached for the beaker and I stopped it and led it to the transceiver switch.

Tango.
Tango receiving.
Pencil ready?
Yes.

Over-all shape: oblong. Elongation 14°-194°. Direction clockwise. Five paces. Right-angle to left. Seven paces. Right-angle to right.

Pauses while he drew the shape.

Could you, mon ami, have made an error of seven miles?

Twenty-one paces. Oblique angle right: one-four-oh degrees. Six paces.

Two bastions of rock seven miles apart. Near one of them, a crashed plane.

Oblique angle right: one-two-oh degrees. Sixteen paces. Angle eight-oh. Fourteen paces.

A crashed plane confidently assumed to be visible at a distance of four hundred and eighty-five yards in a direction precisely established by air photograph.

Angle left: one-six-oh. Ten paces. Angle right: one-five-oh. Six paces.

Question: why is the plane not visible?

Make a straight-line return to the starting-point.

Bit of bad luck, *mon ami*. We not only missed the target by seven miles but we made the drop so close to the wrong group of rocks that I naturally thought they—

Six paces?

What? I made it seven.

All right. The join isn't precise but no matter.

He loved things on paper. Loman loved things on paper. Also he loved things being precise. He loved to get things exact and it tended to blind him to reality and he didn't even give a thought to the fact that if you have to pace out a rock configuration with your boots kicking through rubble and the heat trying to knock you down and the sand giving way when you need to measure your paces correctly you won't finish up exactly where you started. You'd do it here all right, but you wouldn't necessarily do it on paper. And that was where it really counted. Bloody Loman would tell you that.

Steady. Anger—heat—sweat—thirst. Don't forget where you are.

Not his fault. I was having to wait, that was all. He was looking at the photograph now, looking at the sketch and then at the photograph. Taking his time.

Christ I can't go seven miles.

Fourteen hours minimum through that blinding furnace and finish up delirious and the last drop gone.

The definition on the air photograph wasn't too clear because they'd blown it up to the point where the grain would start fogging so he probably wouldn't be able to match the narrow end of the formation where the pacing went six and six and five, all short runs, but the over-all shape ought to give him an answer.

Sweat in my eyes. In the shade here it wasn't evaporating so fast. Pronounced heartbeat: quite regular and perfectly normal in these conditions. *Thud-thud-thud.*

Looking at the photograph, then at the sketch. The girl watching him. I didn't know if he'd got juxtaposed stills of the terrain surrounding the target area and I wasn't going to ask him because that'd be another nasty one if both outcrops had much the same shape at this degree of blow-up. The girl watching him.

You there, Diane?

Yes.

How's tricks?

All right.

Lovely day, isn't it?

Yes.

Tried to say it with a smile, couldn't make it. Nerves in her voice, nothing explicit, just a tenseness. I suppose she knew the score, worked out what we were doing, didn't like it, none of us did. Rotten having to wait.

He said:

Those are the right ones.

Shut my eyes and said:

Oh that's good.

I'm going to ask those people to confirm everything for us, the scale, orientation, and particularly the distance and bearing of Tango Victor from the rocks. Someone might have made a slip.

Just what we need.

It's a possibility we have to consider.

How long will it take, Loman?

Perhaps thirty minutes.

Kaifra—Tunis—Crowborough—London. No delay at all from Kaifra to the Embassy because he'd use the radio and the signals room in Tunis would use their own. Crowborough—London was the slow bit, by normal telephone.

I want to be out there longer than that.

He still hadn't told me to get moving and I didn't like it: he sounded too bloody relaxed. The panic had gone

because we knew now that we were at least in the target
area but he still ought to be worried because the aeroplane
had disappeared.

You're camped in the shade at present?

Yes.

*I want you to stay there for the moment. I'm in signals
and London is monitoring.*

Didn't like it at all and the sweat was running into my
eyes, what was he in signals for at this phase?

For Christ sake fill me in, Loman.

*I just want you to stay at your base so that I can call
you immediately if I need to. I take it you'd prefer not to
carry the transceiver about in the full sun.*

I know that bit.

Five-second pause.

Chirac has reported.

He all right?

*Oh yes. But he didn't find the wind he needed, so he
had to circle for several hours to gain enough height to
make a final run-in through dead air. He came down in a
gassi twenty kilometres from South 5 and they picked him
up in a half-track.*

Oh Christ there'd been some kind of security leak,
smell it a mile off. He wasn't relaxed at all, he was just
overcorrecting again.

Did he report by phone?

*Yes. He hadn't been able to begin his final run-in until
shortly after dawn, and he says he was observed by an aircraft at considerably higher altitude.*

Worse than I'd thought.

What area, Loman?

Quite a long pause. Didn't want to worry his executive.
All the worrying was meant to be done at Local Control.

*Not far from the point of drop. He puts it at something
like fifteen kilometres from there. He was flying in the
dark for most of the time and couldn't even see the No. 1
Philips tower or the Roches Brunes derrick.*

I couldn't see why Loman had to get into signals with
Control. And I was beginning to think I didn't want to
know. You don't bring in London on a local security leak
unless the whole thing's been bust wide open.

What was the aircraft registration?

He couldn't read it.

Too high?

Yes.

I had to think how exactly to say it.

Loman, have we still got a mission?

It was a bloody awful thing to ask your director in the field and I knew that but I wanted the answer.

Let us hope so.

There was a faint crackling noise somewhere. Not from the set. I looked past the edge of the canopy.

Quiller.

Hear you.

What is that noise?

Lizard, cracking a snail open.

He didn't bother to answer.

I looked out from the canopy across the blaze of sand, for an instant seeing it, then seeing it vanish.

Loman, I want to go out there.

Not yet.

While I'm fresh. Let me go and look for the bloody thing. It must be there somewhere.

Certainly it must. But we have to wait for London.

Bloody London, get on your tits.

Switching off transmit.

Very well, but stay open to receive.

Had to drink some water, then I lay on my back and decided not to think about the aircraft that had been observing Chirac only fifteen kilometres from the point of drop, Loman's headache, not mine, though of course when the crunch came I'd be right in it, like that poor bloody snail.

Slept.

Tango.

Check: 1319. Switch.

Tango receiving.

I have London's signal. Monitoring liaison with Algiers informs that five squadrons of desert-reconnaissance helicopters are to search a prescribed area of which your own position is approximately the centre.

I watched the lizard. It had found another one and the crackling noise began.

When do they start?

They are already airborne.

12. Sandstorm

I stood watching them.

They were quite high, about five hundred feet, but their shape and their flight were unmistakable: they drifted in circles, their wings held like black hoods to trap the air. From this distance I couldn't see their heads but they were watching me: despite their feigned disinterest I was the focal point of their circling.

I hadn't noticed them before but they'd probably been somewhere overhead since early this morning, attracted by the movement of the dot that had been making its laborious way among the dunes towards the rock outcrop. Their patient observation heightened my feeling of vulnerability and I had the urge to go back to the refuge that thirty minutes ago I'd been sharing with the lizards.

Nobody likes being watched, and this was particularly unpleasant because I was being assessed as potential carrion.

I moved on again, trying not to drag my feet and leave tracks. The heat of the sun was like a weight on my back, pushing me down rather than forward, and its light struck upwards against my face, reflecting from the sand. I knew that the water flask was still a quarter full and was tempted to drink, but when I'd broken camp and pushed everything into the shade I'd noticed that one of the *bidons* was already empty. In the last ten hours I'd used half the water suply, pouring it into my body as you pour water on a fire.

The desert is not like other places. The slaking of the increased thirst puts back only fifty per cent of the water lost in the cooling process, and in this degree of heat my cooling process was breaking down because the sweat was being evaporated the instant it reached the skin. In one hour I was generating seven or eight hundred calories and my sweat was ridding me of less than five.

Sometimes their shadows drifted near me as they crossed the sun.

At the four hundred and eighty-fifth pace I stopped.

Long. 8°3′ by Lat. 30°4′.

The sands were smooth.

Loman hadn't received confirmation from No. 2
Fighter-Reconnaissance before I'd left camp: I'd told him
I wanted a last chance to find Tango Victor before the helicopters got here. But I knew now that I should have
waited, because give or take a few yards I was standing
where the smudge had been on the photograph. Somewhere
they'd made an error: the scale had lost a nought or the
gearing had been inverted and this wasn't where the
smudge was at all.

The wreck of Tango Victor was across the dunes there,
or a thousand yards the other side of the rocks, not far
away, ten minutes on foot in normal conditions. Here the
conditions weren't normal and it could take me an hour
or five hours to find it because the dunes were higher than
I was and in some places I couldn't see more than a hundred yards: I was moving through a maze.

A bird's-eye view was the only way and five squadrons
had been mustered and refuelled at the nearest airfield to
these rocks: Fort Thiriet was a hundred and thirty kilometres distant and the helicopters had been deployed in a
sweep formation of sixty aircraft on a twenty-five kilometre front to the immediate north of the Areg Tinrhalès
and they were heading this way while I stood and cursed
some stupid bloody clerk in uniform who'd finished the
mission for us before it began.

The pressure was finally on and there was nothing I
could do about it. There was data streaming in so fast that
I couldn't deal with it: the over-all picture they never like
giving us was coming up under the hypo. The Chirac security leak had been bad luck and not his fault but it had
revealed the importance of the objective in the eyes of the
opposition: all they'd been informed was that a camou-
flaged sailplane had been observed over the open desert at
dawn today, but an entire arm of the Algerian Air Force
had been assembled across the country and deployed from
Fort Thiriet, an airfield right on the Libyan border.

There'd been no time to put out even a token an-
nouncement of a "routine exercise" and this fact alone
meant either that Libyan Intelligence was fully aware of
the situation or that the Algerian government was so anxious to locate Tango Victor that it had risked embarrassment at high level between the two countries.

In addition to this was the indication that it was their
last throw and that they were confident of locating the ob-

jective before anyone else: because if they failed, and if
an opposing network succeeded, they would have made it
obvious that their search had been for the crashed
freighter, whose cargo was so politically explosive that the
armed forces of two countries had been called in to assist
the intelligence services.

The Bureau itself was intensely active and within a matter of days had brought its support communications to the
pitch where half an hour ago Local Control could give me
full details on the desert-reconnaissance operation including the precise area and width of sweep. At the same time
the entire network was under general monitoring and if
Analysis Section thought I'd be interested to know that an
attempt had been made to assassinate General Chen Piao
or that a missile-to-missile device had just come off the
drawing boards in Smolensk or that the Brazilian Minister
for the Interior had handed in his resignation three weeks
after accepting the post they'd pass it to Control for Local
Control and the execuitve in the field and I'd get it almost
as fast as a phone call from London to Crowborough on
the priority line.

I wouldn't get it in so many words. The original data
would go through filters until the essence was extracted
and made available. Even if support communications
hadn't been energised then general monitoring would have
reported sudden air movement in Algeria by desert-reconnaissance units and Analysis would have jumped on it
straight away because they had Algeria as the *locale* of
one of the listed ops currently running.

Behind me, as I stood here isolated in the desert wastes,
was an organisation striving to inform, direct and support
me as I went deeper into the mission and closer to the target area; but now that I was here there was nothing they
could do for me, and nothing I could do for them.

Loman had predicted a forty-five-minute deadline for
the arrival of the Algerian squadrons in this area and
there were fifteen minutes to go in terms of their ETA. In
terms of the actual mission my time ran out to zero as I
stood here listening for their rotors, because even if I
climbed the nearest dune and saw Tango Victor dead in
front of me it was no go. London wanted photographs
and a full radioed report of the freighter's cargo and fifteen minutes wasn't long enough for me to go back for
the transceiver and bring it here.

The sands were quiet.

My shadow lay prone, a spirit felled by the heat.

Something in my mind was trying to attract my attention and I was aware of it but unable to read its significance: it was like a sound heard but not identified. I let all thought subside, leaving the way open, while my body and its senses remained where they were as my mind ranged, released, finding images for me: the low wind and the pattering of the sand on the side of the box, the folds of the parachute half covered, and the unexpected word in my head—*beware*—without either reason or coherence.

Drawn blank.

I turned back towards the rock outcrop and the sand hissed faintly across my boots. Halfway there I stopped and drank the rest of the water and left the cap of the flask dangling on its lanyard. Then the sky became gradually filled with infinitesimal vibrations, so faint that I thought the sound was only in my head, but as it strengthened I began moving faster and when I was certain what it was I broke into a clumsy run through the sand's obstructive softness, worried now that I'd left it too late to reach shelter before they came.

There seemed to be no particular direction to the sound: it was a steady thrumming under the sky as if the air itself had started to vibrate, to shake with some kind of cosmic disturbance. The vultures had broken their circling flight and were drifting southwards, driven away by the noise. It was loudening quickly now and for a moment I didn't see the helicopters because I'd been looking for them too high. They were detaching themselves from the skyline and growing bigger and I went into the niche I'd made for myself among the stowed 'chute canopies and lay flat with my legs drawn up, and waited.

Once they'd seen the freighter and landed near it I wouldn't be so exposed, but while they were still airborne they'd be checking this outcrop and for the moment I wanted to remain unseen. I didn't know what kind of orders Loman would give me when our mission ended a few minutes from now: it was just possible he'd ask me to observe the activities of the opposition at the site of the objective in case there was anything we could usefully tell London.

He would probably leave it to me, when the time came, to decide whether I should expose my presence and hope

to live as long as the first implemented interrogation or
crawl from here to the open desert and cut a vein. All
London would require was that the opposition shouldn't
learn anything from me and that was easy enough to ar-
range.

The noise was very loud now and the rocks were trap-
ping the echoes. I pulled my legs up a bit more and managed to crawl another inch into the narrowing gap.
Something was in here with me but I didn't know what:
something alive and I suppose sheltering as I was from the
throbbing sky outside. Telepathy at its lowest level is emo-
tional and I was aware of fear, not my own but another
creature's. There wasn't anything more for me to fear because neither I nor the mission were any longer under attack.

The camouflage was highly developed and only the glint
of a gold-ringed eye gave it away. It was about two feet in
front of me and almost on a level with my face: probably
I'd driven it in here unknowingly when I'd stowed the
canopes and provisions and it had been afraid to clamber
across the strange terrain they'd formed on the rocky
floor. Its forefeet were splayed on each side of the scaly
bulk of its body and its head was lifted to watch me, the
black iris glistening within the ring of gold. It kept utterly
still, afraid of me because visually I menaced it giganti-
cally, almost filling the niche, and possibly afraid of the
helicopters: it had no sense of hearing but it was probably
picking up the vibrations in the rock.

I had positioned the transceiver so that I could use it if
I wanted to, and I ought to tell Loman the situation even
though he couldn't do anything about it.

Tango.

The form of the pointed head was prehistoric: it was a
descendant of the lizards that had been here before man.

Tango. Tango.

The rotors chopped heavily at the air and I was tempted to move my head and take a look but there wasn't any
point: they were military desert-reconnaissance aircraft
making an area sweep at low altitude and there wouldn't
be anything in their shape or colour that could tell us anything we didn't already know. The chance of their
catching the movement if I turned my head was one in a
thousand but I might just as well not risk it.

Teach me, my small and ancient friend, how to keep still.

I didn't call up base again because it was obvious now that Loman had decided to keep radio silence. I got a lot of squawk and tried two channels and came back and found them quite close at 6 MHz.

113: *ihtafidou bi kasdikoum i-la mitine oua sabrina degré.*

The volume of sound from their rotors was making the frame of the transceiver vibrate and I could feel it under my fingers. Shadows swept across the mouth of the niche where I was lying, and the lizard appeared to move slightly but I knew it hadn't: it was just the shift of the light contrasts as the shadow passed over us.

120—121—122: *an-zi-lou mina oulou-ouikoum hata miyate mitra.*

They obviously had a group captain above and to the rear of the line keeping them in order. It occurred to me that I was being gratuitously masochistic about this because at any moment the observer in the machine nearest these rocks and the site of Tango Victor was going to call up and report seeing the freighter. That would be the precise instant, if we wanted to be particular about it, when the mission would end. But I couldn't resist listening in because I always like to know what people are doing.

Ali: ha-l'-laka a-ne toufahissa hadihi a sokhr mini djhatika?

Ta-ya-b.

Dust began blowing in: their rotors were creating a wave of turbulence across a twenty-five kilometre front, whirling a cloud of pulverised quartz into the air and letting it fall as they passed. The light became amber-tinted and the colours of the lizard deepened.

104: *sahihou al kasd.*

The stink of kerosene.

Head lifted, a golden eye staring.

If the vultures eat the lizards and the lizards eat the snails, what do the snails eat?

The note of their engines held steady.

I waited for one of them to break the line and land near the freighter. The others would follow, gathering in a swarm. It was going to be very noisy here.

It had been the weather that had beaten us: the wind.

There hadn't been enough for Chirac so he'd been forced
to circle for height till after dawn and they'd seen him
and it wasn't anyone's fault and for a moment I felt sorry
for Loman because the little bastard had done his best,
put his ferret into the field and set up a makeshift base
with an operator to man the set even though the poor little bitch couldn't hold a gun and he'd seen me through the
access lines and kept me in touch with London, done all
he could and now the whole bloody thing had gone grinding into the dust and he wasn't a man to take a failed
mission in his stride, not Loman.

The note of their engines was steady.

And quieter now.

Kerosene.

Kerosene and the dust settling and the brightness coming back into the light while I lay prone watching the reflections in the dark unwinking eye, while I lay surprised
and not quite understanding, listening to the thrum of the
rotors passing towards the west, while I lay with weakness
flooding into me as the tension came off and the nerves
lost their tone, the sound from the sky dying away until,
as I lay listening, silence came.

Switch.

Tango.

Can get quite worked up when your base won't answer
then I remembered and span it back to 7 and called him
again. Still wouldn't bloody well answer. They've been off
the air for over two minutes now well don't panic there's
no action needed but why don't they answer they're my
base and this is my lifeline.

Tango—Tango.

It was her voice, soft and precise.

I said:

Where the hell have you been?

Loman hates that: he likes you to make a point of re-
plying with the code for the mission, not his day today,
the sweat running into my eyes because we'd confirmed
these were the right rocks and the freighter must be near
them and they'd put sixty choppers across the area and
they hadn't seen it so it couldn't be here after all.

I'm sorry. We were monitoring the helicopters.

So was I.

Then Loman came on.

Tone rather tight, rather correct.

Quiller.

Hear you.

Where are the aircraft at present?

They've gone.

They overflew your position?

It wasn't really a question. Diane spoke Arabic and she'd monitored their frequency so she'd heard them telling each other to "check those rocks" and she would have told Loman so he knew bloody well they'd overflown my position. He just didn't understand it and I knew what that meant: he'd got confirmation from London.

I was still lying prone and there wasn't any more need so I crawled backwards out of the niche but stayed in the shade, my shoulders against the rockface. There was a scuttling sound and I turned my head and saw it had gone. Then I shut my eyes because the panic was over and I wanted to think.

Did they overfly your position?

I ought to be helping the poor little sod.

Yes. Slow speed, low altitude, took their time, couldn't miss it. You've had confirmation from No. 2 Fighter-Recco, is that it?

Pause.

Yes. There has been no error of any kind.

Didn't make sense.

There must have been, Loman.

You and I have confirmed that the rock outcrop where you are now is in fact the rock outcrop in the photograph. The R.A.F. has just confirmed by signal that the object in the photograph is a crashed aeroplane and that it is lying on the sand at a distance of four hundred and eighty-five yards—four eight five—from the outcrop with a bearing of two hundred degrees—two double-oh.

Vaguely I thought no wonder he's been worrying about my mental condition but he can think again now because a hundred and twenty men of the Algerian Air Force couldn't see the thing either.

You do it for me then, Loman. You work it out. That's what you're for.

After a bit he said:

Stay on receive.

I shut my eyes again.

There wasn't anything he could do anyway. Get a pencil and paper but there weren't any figures, no way of checking. Talk to the girl but what could she do? Any of us do?

Beware.

Not quite a word: the shape of a thought. The fine grains hitting the side of the box in the low wind. More scuttling now, maybe I was stuck right outside one of their dens and they couldn't get home. It had sounded like the sand when it had pattered against the polyester box in the low wind, with the folds of the 'chute-canopy still showing where the sand hadn't yet drifted, I'd made a mental note at the time, warning myself that the desert wasn't like other places.

Of course he'd go straight into signals again with London and ten minutes from now they'd have a full-scale emergency meeting in session at the Bureau and I hoped it'd keep fine for them.

No one else could have got here first. We knew there were at least two other networks with a crash-priority interest in Tango Victor but there hadn't been time for them to get here and anyway we'd have had a flash about it from Control: if the opposition beats another cell to the post in the end phase of a mission then everyone gets to know about it, don't worry. And they couldn't have taken the wreck away, even by a concerted chopper lift, without making so much noise and leaving so much mess that the rest of us would have just taken a look and gone off home.

Scuttering. They were quite big things, heavy when they ran although they ran like a flash. They bothered me, wouldn't let me alone, the sound of the sand pattering against the side of the box, the low wind slowly covering the nylon 'chute, a mental note, the desert hides things, beware.

Someone was saying oh . . . my . . . Christ . . . in a kind of measured tone, perhaps not aloud, just inside my head, and I opened my eyes and looked through the scratched sunglasses to the blaze of the dunes out there. Then I hit the transmit.

Tango.

She answered straight away so I knew he couldn't be in signals with London and I suppose it made sense because this problem wasn't for Control, it was strictly local. He'd been using his time thinking.

He came on and I said:

Can you get hold of a met.-record for this area covering the last three days?

He didn't ask why, so perhaps he'd been thinking on much the same lines as I had. He just said he'd contact the airfield at Kaifra. The phone was obviously working now because he was back in a few minutes and said yes, there'd been a sandstorm two days ago, particularly severe.

13. Objective

The tube went in and I pushed, leaning on it.

When I pulled it out the sand ran into the hole it had made, filling it. There wasn't anything pointed I could use: the end of the tube was blunt and therefore not very efficient as a boring tool but it was all I had. It was one of the sections of telescopic tubing among the survival gear, meant to hold up fabric and make a shelter.

I pushed it in again, six feet away, and leaned on it.

Skin perfectly dry. Cooling had stopped.

I'd have to watch that because heat stroke develops quite rapidly: the body temperature starts rising soon after the stage where the sweat evaporates without having time to cool the skin. Quickened pulse, coma, death.

I drank again to replace some of the sweat but the water was hot and gave no sensation of quenching the thirst: it was just liquid going into the organism. I was having to calculate now and we were running it close: one more litre was left for working with, and one reserve litre for staying alive during sleep. I could go another ninety minutes at this rate on a litre but that didn't have anything to do with it because the heat explosion would begin a long time before then unless I could take some rest.

They'd come back and their shadows drifted across the flank of the dune as I pushed the tube in and struck nothing.

Pull it out. Two paces and try again.

It must be this one, this dune, or the one on the far side

of my No. 2 camp. I'd brought a canopy and three lengths of tubing to make shade, and the 2000CA had been left on receive. In the last two hours I'd taken four equally spaced rest periods of fifteen minutes. Loman had come on the air twice to tell me (1) that the Algerian squadrons would refuel west of here and disperse to their home stations without making a return sweep and (2) that Chirac had confirmed that even a medium sandstorm could bury an aircraft the size of Tango Victor.

Chirac had pointed out that the freighter had probably hit the sand with the undercarriage up to avoid flipping over and in any case would have gouged a deep trough until the aerofoil had started planing. This would leave the tip of the rudder only two metres or so from the ground and the main structure considerably lower. The 35-mm. Nikons hadn't been able to register this because they'd been almost vertically above, but from ground level it couldn't have been easy to see even before the sandstorm had blotted it out.

Probe and try again, two paces.

The chance of hitting the rudder or the aerial mast was remote. According to Chirac's reckoning the wings, tailplane, and fuselage would be at least two metres from the surface. I'd once been in Arizona when the wind had reached seventy and the whole desert had got up and blown across the sky and it had taken us a day to dig out the half-tracks.

Push and lean and pull out.

I didn't know anything about falling over till my shoulder began blazing. I couldn't seem to get up because the whole weight of the sky was pressing on me. Heart hammering a lot, throbbing behind the eyes, get in the shade, crawl there if it's all you can do, but get there.

Sand in the teeth, gritty, and my hands burning, using them as forefeet, clumsy, going too slow, have to hurry, pool of shade, prone.

He called up at 1631 hours, waking me.

No, I said.

Slight moisture on the skin and the pulse back to normal but I knew it'd start again within ten minutes of gong back into that furnace.

He wanted details.

I'm using a metal probe, area focus the same as before.

It seemed to have taken me a long time to say it and now I as out of breath. He didn't answer straight away.

How much longer can you go on working there?

I don't know.

My hand just reached for the flask: I hadn't actually decided to drink.

I am only asking for an approximate idea, of course.

He had to say it again before I registered.

There's water for about an hour's work. But I'm starting get—starting to get—heat stroke symptoms.

Quite a long pause.

Would you be able to remain under shade until nightfall?

My head swung up suddenly and my eyes opened.

You mean you could drop more provisions?

No.

The pulse had quickened and there was an almost immediate increase in sweating. But he'd said no and it was the first time it had actually been admitted that this was a strictly shut-ended mission unless I could find the objective.

I propped the mike on my knee, heavy to hold, cost water.

Take all—it'd take all the water I've got, waiting till dark.

It would be cooler then. You could work—

No go. Thing is to press on. Tango out.

Only way to shut him up. Not a thing he could do, not even drop more water. He'd have to signal Control and tell them the score: the executive in the field has a limited number of hours to live, am I to abandon?

I got up and went out and the slam of the direct heat nearly knocked me down and I staggered a bit and then got some kind of rhythm going. The tube was stuck in the sand where I'd left it, too hot now, blister your hand, so I kicked it over and got hold of the other end and began walking to the part of the dune where I'd halted operations. About half-way there I tripped over his foot.

It took a little time because he might be able to tell me things by the way he was lying, face down and with his feet towards the end of the dune. I worked slowly, trying to get all the data the situation could provide. My tracks

had a slight curve in them: I'd made a detour on my way
from the canopy without meaning to, and this was why I
hadn't tripped over him when I'd gone in to rest. I turned
him over.

He had died in terror.

The hands flung out as he'd fallen, perhaps running too
hard, running like hell away from the wreck of the
freighter, running in terror. His face showed that much.
He had died screaming.

Not far away there was something black showing in the
sand: my feet had brought it to the surface; it lay at the
edge of my tracks. It was plumage and as I pulled it upwards the wing rose, scattering sand, and then the gross
black body with its bald head dangling, the hooked beak
agape. The bird, like the man, had died screaming.

There was another, so near the man that in moving his
body, turning it over, I had exposed part of its wing. The
heat didn't seem so bad now and I was moving more
quickly, a sense of purpose reviving the organism. I made
a direct line to the end of the dune where his feet had
pointed, and tripped again, dislodging a peaked cap from
a man's head. His body was in the same attitude: he'd
been running away from the freighter. His face had the
same expression.

A third vulture was lying at the foot of the dune: I was
kicking into the thing before I knew it. I didn't stop to examine it because the renewed strength in me was pushing
me onwards and the fourth time I drove the tube into the
sand it struck metal.

Distance 485 yards. Bearing 200°. Longitude 8°3′ by
Latitude 30°4′.

Tango Victor.

I used the tubing like an oar, bringing the sand away
but only enough to guide me. This was the leading edge
of the tailplane and I moved across the flank of the dune
and began probing again. It was already clear that the
bodies had been lying only just below the surface because
they were to the north of the freighter, in the lee of the
dune: it had been the south wind that had done this, the
ghibli.

The sand fell away as I worked at the area aft of the
trailing edge, port mainplane. It was where the door of
the cabin was likely to be. For a while I missed it because
it had been left wide open and I was actually digging

through the drift of sand that had formed in the cabin itself between the pilot's compartment and the freight section. The heat was intense because the fuselage had
become a quartz-coated oven and I gave it a couple of
minutes and came away.

It seemed twice as far to the canopy and I drank some
water and dropped prone and let the muscles go but the
hammering didn't stop, must do better than this, body had
to keep going because there was work for the mind, still
had a mission running and we'd found the objective, not
long now. The hammering shook me, colours throbbing
behind the eyes and the skin perfectly dry, rather worrying, the bout of renewed energy had been dangerous, keep
still, just keep still.

Tango.

I didn't answer, didn't move, you want to live, you've
got to keep still. Breathing difficult, the weight of the
shoulders compressing the lungs, roll over, over and lie
still, a thin cackling from somewhere, unearthly sound,
coming again, a high cackling above the canopy, they'd
seen the two bodies.

Tango.

Don't move. Don't even think, brain function heat-pro-
ductive.

The spread nylon bluish above me and motionless, the
air totally calm, my arms melting into the sand, my legs
dissolving, the nerves inert, the pain of the bruises ebbing,
the body cradled in euphoria, control it, stay just this side
of unconsciousness, the hammering fainter and less insistent, the lungs filling of their own accord, the healing process taking over from the stress syndrome, lie still and all
will be well.

Moisture gathering on the skin, the skin cooling, the
heart rhythm slowing, the colours receding from the optic
nerve, order restored.

Tango.

I opened up the transmit.

Hear you.

A sound from someone farther away, obviously Diane,
a soft intake of breath. I suppose they'd been getting edgy
because I hadn't answered for a while.

Loman asked:

Have you a problem?

Not now. I've found the plane.

Three or four seconds.

Congratulations.

Poor little bastard, saved by the bell, the whole bloody mission back in his hands, quite overcome. He was asking me for a report.

I can't tell you much yet, I've only just started. Thing's covered with sand. Both crew were running away from it when they died.

Please take photographs.

I'm going to. Oh you mean of the crew?

Yes.

I thought for a bit.

I've moved them.

That doesn't matter. Photograph their faces.

I didn't like it at all.

Loman, have you any idea what's inside that plane?

No. I am merely passing on instructions from London.

I believed him because there couldn't be any reason for him to withhold information at this stage: his executive was going into a hazardous area and wanted all the help he could get. The blackout on this cargo was so total that Control wouldn't even tell the director in the field, a man of Loman's status.

Play it by the book for a change and consider demanding information from London before proceeding. Loman would have to signal if I asked him: executive requests details as to type of hazard, so forth. It wouldn't be unreasonable because commerical aircrews are not timorous men and these two had run clear of Tango Victor with the fear of Christ in them and I was expected to go in there and find out why.

Loman.

Hear you.

Have you any idea of the risk, I mean how big?

He thought about that.

No. You say the crew were running away from the aeroplane when they died. Do they look as if they were frightened?

Terrified.

It was perfectly clear to us both that London had an idea what had killed Holt and his navigator: the instructions had been for me to take photographs of their expressions.

Do you want me to signal Control about this?

I thought that was rather civil of him.

Because he didn't fancy it at all. He'd got his ferret right up against the quarry and ready for the kill and he didn't want to disturb it. The moment I went off the air he'd switch channels and send to London through the Embassy in Tunis: *Q Quaker now destin objiv point.* It's the one signal that makes any kind of bang throughout the departments concerned with the specific mission and it would give Loman a lot of joy to send it. To ask for additional information would just cause delay and he knew we couldn't afford it but he was still ready to do it if I insisted.

From here I could see the dark hole in the dune and all I had to do was walk over there and go inside and complete the mission: all they wanted was a batch of pictures and a taped report on Tango Victor's cargo and it probably wouldn't take more than half an hour and then Loman could pull me out and we'd all go home, a crash-priority operation at PM level completed inside seventy-two hours of Tilson's briefing me in London.

Not really the time to tell them the executive in the field had got goose flesh.

Loman.

Hear you.

They realise this cargo could be dangerous.

Yes.

They probably know what it is.

Yes.

Why would they decide to keep us uninformed on this, even though it's going to wreck the whole mission if I'm killed?

He answered almost at once and I knew he'd been waiting for this question and had prepared the reply.

I can only think that the area is so sensitive that the risk might be greater if their knowledge were passed on to us.

I'd expected that.

You're talking about implemented interrogation.

Yes.

At any phase?

At every phase, including this one.

I was going to ask him how he worked that one out but

it was simple enough when I gave it a second thought and I was suitably warned: brain function wasn't satisfactory, the heat and everything, and the worry about what was inside that black hole over there. What he meant was that in Kaifra he was exposed to the risk of capture and interrogation by an opposition cell and that if it was implemented by the usual pain-stimulus methods he would probably give them information. The info he already possessed was lethal if it got into the wrong hands but without it he couldn't have taken over as director: it was just that London was scared of adding to it unless they had to.

They'd know, as soon as he told them, that I was now within minutes of going into the freighter and if they could signal me direct there wouldn't be any problem: out here in isolation there was no risk of anyone raiding me and since I was on the point of moving into hazard they'd be prepared to warn me on the type of difficulties I'd be faced with. But they couldn't do it.

They'd have to advise me through Crowborough, Tunis, and Kaifra, exposing the signal to switchboard, staff, cipher clerks and people in the same room with them. They could throw out a preliminary signal carrying a selected code structure and then follow up with the encoded material for me to break up but it still wouldn't be safe because the clerks in the Embassy cipher room could read it for themselves.

Bloody nuisance but there it was.

They were cackling again and my scalp got up. Bad sign, bag of nerves just when there was something important to do.

All right Loman. Tell London they can go and stuff themselves. I'm going in.

Quite a long pause.

Very well. Please take all precautions.

How the hell can I when I don't know what's in there?

Not at all good, nasty show of nerves. Couldn't look away from the hole in the dune, getting obsessive, best thing would be to finish the job quickly.

Loman, what stage are you going to start running the tape?

As soon as you enter the aircraft.

They give you an auto-destruct?

Of course.

They'd had to. They're not entirely witless in London: they'd narrowed the risk down to a matter of minutes. They couldn't signal me any advice because nobody had to know about this cargo, not even Loman, but in a few minutes from now I'd be telling him and in precise detail and they'd covered the situation in the only way they could: the moment my report was finished he'd be putting the tape into an auto-destruct container and once he'd shut it and set the fuse the risk would be over because if anyone else tried to open it they'd just blow it up.

The precisely detailed information on Tango Victor's cargo would remain only in Loman's head, and until now I hadn't realised that in one respect this was a shut-ended mission for him too. For her own sake he'd send Diane out of the room when I started reporting: she couldn't reveal what she didn't know, and most trained interrogators can tell whether you're lying or not when you say you've no information for them. But Loman would remain at risk and if the opposition located the base and raided it and went to work on him the auto-destruct thing wouldn't be a lot of use.

So this was a 6-K mission.

Not many of them are. It's mostly left to the discretion of the director and executive in the field because they're placed better than anyone else to decide what ought to be done, but sometimes an operation comes up where the area's so sensitive that they like you to sign one of their buff-coloured forms before they brief you. Of course you can refuse, just as you can refuse any specific mission for any of a dozen reasons, but once you've agreed to sign Form 6-K you're issued with a set of capsules and it's up to you to make sure they're dispersed among your gear so that if you've put one in your flight bag and you leave the thing on a bus you've still got a spare in your pocket.

They can't force you to do what you've signed for: it's just that your professional pride has been brought into things and as far as I know they've never had anyone let them down. What gives us a giggle is that these capsules are issued to us in Firearms, it seems so bloody appropriate.

Some of us have pulled in a 9 suffix to our code name and they don't bother to make us sign anything: we've proved we can't be broken this side of unconsciousness, so we don't carry capsules on this kind of mission unless we've actually asked for some, to avoid possible unpleasantness during the operation. Not many directors have the 9 because they're far less exposed in the field than their executives and I knew Loman hadn't got one because there's a list and we know who's on it.

So he must have signed the form on this trip. There'd be no point in ordering him to put the tape in a bang box if he was liable to get snatched and grilled. They're usually brightly coloured with a distinctive pattern, so people don't confuse them with indigestion pills or anything.

Perhaps that was why he'd been so nervous. We all get a bit ragged towards the end phase and this time we were having to cope with the heat as well.

The sweat was coming freely now and the pulse was about right so I told him I was ready to go.

Very well. We shall be off the air for a few minutes.

Going to signal Control, tell them we'd found the plane, three jolly cheers. I picked up the set and the camera and walked into the sun.

The first one had a thin moustache, rather well trimmed, bit of a lady's man and hardly the type who'd want to go into the album looking like this. Three shots from three angles and don't ask me why they wanted actual pictures, there was something important I was missing but there wasn't time to worry it out. The second one had either been pecked or caught his face on something sharp when he'd flung himself out of the cabin. A couple of close-ups of the dead vultures and one shot of the doorway making a hole in the dune.

A lot of dry cackling again, I supposed they were frustrated because I wouldn't let them get at the two cadavers. But their shadows were bigger and I looked up and saw they'd come quite a bit lower: their heads were turning on their long gristly necks to keep me in sight as they circled.

Then I had to wait, squatting by the transceiver and covering my neck against the sun, thinking of nothing in particular, how hot it was, what the hell did the snails eat, the way she'd looked at her fingertips.

Tango.

Hear you.

I'll be keeping open for you from now on.

All right. I'm immediately outside the freighter and I'm

*going to leave the set here and take the mike inside on the
extension.*

Understood. Will you—

Then there was a quick fade, as if he'd suddenly put a
hand over the mike, and I thought the last two words had
probably been spoken to Diane as he asked her to leave
the radio room before I began reporting for the tape.

Onset of chill, the hairs lifting on my forearms. The
bodily changes due to the heat were being modified by the
psychic unease aroused when I'd turned them over and
looked at their faces.

Air crews are practical men with a high threshold of
fear and the durable brand of philosophy that is learned
by living with the elements and acknowledging their infinite power. I would expect them, as the mountainside
loomed through the fog or the explosion shook the airframe, to show natural and momentary fear before they
concentrated on whatever action remained open to them. I
would expect to find, on the faces of men who had died in
a plane crash, an expression of anguish, fear, or resignation. Not of terror.

The brain is concerned with practical considerations:
facts and figures, the interplay of kinetic and mechanical
forces involved in high-speed collision. The psyche is
more subtly concerned with abstracts ranging from ecstasy
to nightmare, including terror. The raised scalp, the trickle
along the spine are induced by things strange to us, or ab-
horrent: the silence of a slowly winding snake, a leaping
shadow, a howl in the deep of night.

I could think of nothing like this that could have struck
terror in these two men before they died. But our people
in London could. *Photograph their faces,* Loman had said.
I am merely passing on instructions from London.

The birds cackled above me, wheeling lower, perhaps
because I'd stopped moving. I wondered if I ought to go
over and do something to protect the two bodies: Holt
and his navigator wouldn't know what was happening but
I didn't want to have a thing like that on my mind as
well. In the end I did nothing because there wasn't anything to throw over them and even if I buried them the
birds knew now that they were there.

Loman.
Receiving.

Your voice faded out on that last signal.
Yes, I covered the microphone.
Telling her to go?
Yes.
Just checking.
Understood.

I disconnected the microphone lead and coupled it to the coiled extension, reconnecting.

Testing.
Receiving you.
I'm going in.

14. Frenzy

Silence.
    Heat.
    Darkness.
    A faint smell: the rubber casing of the torch. I slid the switch and light hit the skeleton framework of the fuselage. I went forward and stopped in the next second and stood off-balance, listening to the steady hiss from somewhere below. Forebrain desperate for explanation: a stream of images out of sequence. The sound becoming fainter.
    Sand. Sand dislodged by my feet from the drift the wind had brought in and pouring onto the metal trough of the midsection here between the pilot's deck and the freight compartment.
    Pulse slowing again. Rhodopsin was concentrating and my eyes were adapting to scotopic vision, the torchlight growing brighter. Other senses finely adjusting, hyperreceptive to stimuli: heat on the skin, marked absence of motion or even vibration as my weight shifted onto the floor of the pilot's deck. The entombing sand was deadening the motion normally set up by people entering a vehicle with sprung mass and pneumatic tyres.
    The door to the freight section was ajar and I moved the torch beam through the four-inch gap in a vertical sweep but it lit nothing except the ribbed wall of the fuselage. The urge was to go in there first, kick the door wide open and go in ready for anything, so I moved in the opposite direction because the urge was emotional: I was

afraid of going in there and wanted to get it over. It was safer to follow the instincts and reason.

London wanted to know things.

Loman.

Receiving you.

I'm now in the pilot's compartment. Throttles closed, under carriage control in the raised position, flaps at full. Fuel reserve at one quarter, all lamp switches in the off position. Instruments and controls compatible with a forced-landing situation by daylight. The crew got out of their 'chute harness, the 'chutes still on their seats. Radio is switched to 6 MHz, one set of headphones on the floor and an earpiece smashed: evidence of impact effects or possible haste to leave the plane.

The torch beam went on moving, sometimes reflecting from polished surfaces. Pair of worn flying gloves, photo of a Eurasian woman tucked into a panel over the left-hand seat, packet of chewing gum sticking out of the map pocket.

Can you see anything not normally found in the cabin of an aircraft?

This was obviously the first question on a list they'd given him. I spent a full minute on it with the torch.

No. One or two personal effects: pair of tennis shoes in an open locker, carved teakwood statuette in one of them, copy of Playboy. *Nothing else.*

Thank you.

Do you want pictures?

No.

It was the cargo they were more interested in.

The extension lead got caught on a seat strut and I freed it and moved back towards the freight section, my boots grinding on the loose sand across the floor. I didn't hurry because there were a lot of questions crowding in, one of them worrying me. If it was something in the cargo that had driven the two men out of here with the fear of Christ in them I couldn't see why the door was no more than ajar; the four-inch gap seemed too narrow to allow anything to attack through it, and obviously they wouldn't have stopped to pull the door shut after them.

It worried me also to think that the vultures had died with them, as if something had followed them out of the plane to kill anything that lived.

I looped the extension lead across one shoulder to stop

it fouling and opened the Pentax, setting it for flash and keeping it slung in front of me so that I could operate it with one hand. There was a chance that if anything happened when I went in there I could get a picture of it and if one day someone thought of processing the film they'd see what had finished me off.

Loman. I'm going into the freight section.

His voice was more distant now because the 2000CA was standing outside on the sand.

Understood.

I sent the torch beam through the gap and swung the door wider by one inch, stopping and listening, the nerves reacting again and the scalp tightening. Kept seeing their faces, and the gaping beaks of the birds. Another inch and stop and listen and take a grip and bloody well think with the brain instead of the plexus.

But it was difficult because the organism was aware of danger and preparing its defences, draining the blood from the surface to the internal organs, increasing the breathing rhythm to feed more oxygen to the muscles, dilating the pupils to admit more light and refining the nerves until they reached the state where they could be activated by stimuli below the normal threshold of sensitivity. The brain was being bypassed by the nervous system, the automatic defence mechanism that snatches the hand from a hot object, that snaps the eyes shut as a spark flies, without the aid of the brain.

Another inch and stop and listen. Nothing. The beam of light shifting in a calculated zigzag from high to low: the ribbed wall of the fuselage and alloy racks, an emergency hatchet clipped to a bracket alongside an extinguisher.

A depth of silence I couldn't remember having experienced ever before; the silence of the desert, of the dead.

Quiller.

The sound of his voice explosive.

Wait. Release the breath.

Hear you.

Is there any problem?

No problem.

I'd been off the air for more than a minute and he was having to sweat it out, couldn't see what I was doing, couldn't hear.

Swing it another inch and stop and listen.

Faint metallic clicking.

Not perfectly regular.

Quite close and below me.

It stopped when I held my breath and began again when I breathed. Satisfactory: the Pentax was slung from the neck and the case buckle was intermittently registering my heart beat when my diaphragm expanded and contracted in breathing.

Trickle of sweat into the corner of one eye, stinging a little. Shielded from the intense direct sunshine, the skin was releasing through the pores. The heat in here was of a different quality: it oppressed, stifling.

Another inch and the beam passed over a cylinder standing erect, clamped to the alloy rack, and I shut my eyes before I triggered the flash to minimize the effect on the dark-adaptation process but even so the torch beam looked almost yellow when I opened them again.

Loman. First picture: a cylinder, compressed-air type, four feet high, clamped vertically.

Only one?

So far. There may be others.

Forebrain thinking was becoming clearer: the psyche had been too dominant, concerning itself with occult responses, indulging in a sick belief in fiends, in spectral phantasy, dwelling on creaturehood rather than inanimation.

Nothing had moved, even when the flash had gone off. Nothing in here was alive. Logic found no case for a rigged trap of any kind: they wouldn't have left one themselves and nobody had been here since they'd died.

I swung the door at right-angles and took two shots.

General scene: freight compartment. Two frames.

Thank you.

They looked like people.

Some stood in a group, two or three of them leaning one against another; about a half-dozen had fallen, either to the floor or piled against the end of the rack at varying angles. They looked like people because at the top of each cylinder was a round protective shield fixed over the nozzle, and below it was the neck widening into shoulders. Scotopic vision had been affected by the last use of the flash and I couldn't see any details.

Two shots to allow for panorama montage.

Thank you.

*There are about twenty more cylinders, same size, and
the impact broke some of them away from their anchor-
age. It looks as if they were all stowed vertically between
buffers of foam plastic. The nozzles have got protective
caps. Three shots, close-up.*

Blinding light and I waited, shutting my eyes and
switching off the torch. First theories at random: the crew
had known what they were transporting on this trip and
they knew it was lethal and perhaps explosive in terms of
chemical expansion or in terms of gas compression sensitive to release. Possible risk of fire or gross reactive burning without flame, nitric acid, so forth. But I wouldn't
have thought this kind of hazard would have induced actual terror in reasonable men.

Slid the switch, the beam less yellow now.

There were four racks, two on each side, padded with
shock-resistant material and fitted with straps and clamps.
For some reason the cylinders couldn't be shipped horizontally or in crates and their stowage precautions had
been quite good to have left some of them still in place
after the high deceleration loads of the forced landing.
Five oblong crates filled the space between the racks, hard
against the rear bulkhead, and they had been protected
with a matte black liquid material with rapid hardening
qualities: Bostik or a thermal sealing product. Two domed
canisters were stowed one each side of the compartment
with restraint bands and protective jacketing. A red label
was common to every crate, cylinder and canister, with
the words *Flashpoint Zero:* the Lloyds designation for dangerous cargo.

I gave Loman a general picture and began on the indi-
vidual labels, starting with the containers that were easy to
reach without clambering across the disorder.

*Cylinder. Matte grey, three parallel red bands, metal
tabs reading PH/18179/M—Cat.IX. Next cylinder same
markings, tab reading PH/18180/M—Cat.IX. Next cylinder painted matte green with four yellow bands. Tab:
ZRG/635/2—Cat.XII.*

There were thirteen in one group, three in another, with
markings that tied with one of the domed canisters. The
crates contained identical material, all tabs the same.

His voice came faintly from outside.

Have you a problem?

What?

Have you a problem?

He meant was everything all right and I got annoyed because I'd only taken half a minute's respite: the heat was coming mainly from overhead and sweating was profuse. The need for concentrating on the labels was inducing nausea, the beam of the torch wavering, sensation of extreme fatigue.

No problem.

Matte blue, two white bands. Tab says: OTJ/487/A— Cat. V.

I'd been in this bloody oven for twenty minutes and I didn't want him to poke me to see if I was done.

And somewhere in the background the failure to understand the urgency, *he wished to inform me personally that your mission is the key to a critical situation of the highest international proportions,* a top echelon director sent in with his signature on a 6-K form and the death-pill in his pocket, a shut-ended crash-priority mission with the final phase now running, and nothing going onto the tape except these hieroglyphs. Cylinders of BCW gas or something newer than that, something more lethal, but surely it didn't matter any more how destructive a weapon was or what it was made of: within a given hour today or tomorrow the cities of New York and Moscow and Peking could effortlessly be laid waste and the present concern at the conference tables was how to dismantle, piece by piece, the structure of the kill and overkill. I didn't understand why I was here.

Matte red with black bands. Tab: YCJ/2829/E. There's no reference to any category on this one.

They wanted my report on the cargo of Tango Victor and they were getting it and it wasn't my concern to ask why. I was a ferret and this was the rabbit and my teeth were in its neck.

GF/A9/Cat.XII. A point here is that "Cat." might stand for "catalyst," not for "category."

Noted.

I began work on the cylinders that had broken out of their clamps and were lying askew on the cabin floor. The nearest of them had smashed its protective cap and the brass nozzle had been snapped off at the neck, and this I reported to Loman. The metal tab was edge-on and I had to kneel between two of the other cylinders to read it. The torch beam centred on it and I struck out blindly to force the thing away but it screamed and I hit a shoulder and crashed across the loose sand with the blaze of the sun bursting over me as the wind came howling and threw me whirling over the roaring dunes and I span dying, drifting and spinning, falling.

The world burning and the whirl of dunes rising as high as mountains round the dizzying horizons, dwarfing me and dominating, looming over me in darkness while the giant birds came screaming as they gathered for the carrion, red of eye and enraged and swooping on me, scream of the mad Arab in my skull repeating, repeating, *mountains in the sky, and great birds darkening the heavens,* their long necks stretching and reaching and the first strike of a beak and my hands too feeble, the terror trickling in the blood as the sun burst and I fell again and lay sand-drowned.

Sharp pain finger, hit again, hideous, the beak hooked, hooking and a talon tugging, horror and their red eyes raging and the foul wind of their wings beating at the air and the sand flying up, pain again and tugging and my living hand for carrion *they will not* and quicker and snatching at a wing with cunning, pulling and the gross black body closer, *I refuse* and my fingers stronger, pulling again and now the talons hooking in a frenzy and my red blood running but a killing to be made, the bald head turning on the gristly neck, my hands closing and twisting on the last thin scream from the beak and the others fainter now, their cackling farther away, my legs buckling but up again and I stood with it, a dead weight dangling from the broken neck and I swung it, turning, swinging the heavy scarecrow body in a circle till the dead wings caught the air and flapped open and I let it go, you redeyed bastards, show you, try it again, the stream of the far hills slowing, my hands and fall and breath knocked out and lying numbed, the sand bloodied and the nightcoming waves soundlessly breaking, drowning.

Tango.

Lightheadedness: the mind hollow as a shell but the few thoughts lucid and of an extreme simplicity, diamond-bright and surrealistic, a return to prematurity, A is for Apple, This Little Boy Has Killed a Bird.

Ague, the limbs jerking, I would like to be somewhere

warm, I am so cold here, S is for Snow but this is Sand. The big birds had attacked me and tried to eat me but I won.

The sand reddish, the spots becoming brown in the sun, one finger a curious shape and the white of bone shining, peck-peck yes I remember.

Remember all right, the memory functioning satisfactorily, somewhere the forebrain trying to seize on facts, desperate to know and to act but blocked, frustrating.

Tango.

They were circling, as they had been before. I thought I heard them making sounds like chickens, but the brain was so busy that it wouldn't let me listen properly to anything. It wanted to know the facts. Obviously psychochemicals but not related to mescaline or lysergic acid, not Sarin or the Soman-Tabun group although there was this jerking of the muscles but no paralysis yet. Vision unimpaired, on the contrary, the vultures had the exaggerated 3-D effect you see in stereoscopes, the outline of their moving wings very sharp against the sky.

Acetylcholinesterase, the memory superclear like the vision, the GF, GE and VX group destroying this substance and thus blocking the nerve signals to prevent resetting, my legs jerking worse than my arms, nothing definitive.

Blackout sensations, possible onset of coma, try to keep cerebration clear and coherent: the gas was heavier than air and the residue had stayed in the fuselage, pooling in the trough of the freight section, and that was why I'd been all right till I'd had to crouch over the fallen cylinders to read the tabs. The initial psycho-shock had made me think of a creature, something that had to be fought off, classic reaction: terror is ancient and animistic, fear of a predator, of being eaten.

Check time I'd been unconscious between ten and thirteen minutes blackout still threatening, secondary stage of the syndrome in some nerve-target agents is coma: muscular trembling, coma, death. Finger not good, bone exposed, *how can I tell extent of blood loss and its contribution to syndrome,* other injuries, the thing had pecked a lot, the dunes beginning to float and the dark aureole increasing at the rim of the vision field and I got up because they were drifting lower and I didn't want that again,

couldn't stand that again, the surrealistic clarity darkening
now and things becoming confused and the memory
going, what was tango, who was tango, *get up and hide,
can't stay out here.* The dunes beginning to roar and I was
running, falling, running again.

Tango. Tango.

Voice faint voice whose voice get up or they'll have
you, eyes out.

It was different this time because the terror was less.
The maelstrom was whirling round me and the birds grew
monstrous, cackling overhead and one of them making a
dive at me and going away and trying again, but the coma
was blunting the nightmare and there was room for an
area of almost rational thought: I was trying to run as far
as the group of rocks because if I fell again and couldn't
get up they'd come and squabble over me.

The rocks grew enormous and I thought I'd reached
them but they floated away and I had to run in a curve
because the desert was a vortex, circling round me, then
one of the birds was suddenly right against my face with
its hooked beak screeching and I felt the draught of its
wings and caught the acrid farmyard stench of the thing
as it came for me red-eyed with the talons spread from
the stiffened legs and the screeching didn't stop but when
my hands went into the storm of feathers it beat franti-
cally and there was blue-black plumage in my clenched
fingers as it rose out of my reach, my legs trying to buckle
but I stopped them because I had to run, go on running,
the sky was murderous.

Rocks loomed again and I tripped and crashed down
and slid across loose shale, really here, really home, a
dark cloud floating under me, the spread of fabric
rumpling into folds as I crawled deeper, deeper into the
niche where the lizards lived, where I would live, safe
from the cackling sky.

But they came nearer and I couldn't move any more,
their wings thundering close as they hooked and pecked
and I tried to move but they knew I couldn't, the ether
smell and the pain digging, I don't know, I haven't met
this kind of a thing in Europe, their green gowns and the
flutter of their hands, we'll just hope for luck, I guess, and
she said yes. They didn't screech any more, where are
they, where are what, leaning over me, wanting to hear
what I was saying.

"It's very fast-acting."

Some of them had gone away and the smell of ether was strong. I hadn't seen him before. I tried to say Diane.

"Diane."

Her head turned to look down at me and she said my God, what *is* that stuff?

"The brand name is Theratal and I gave him a 30 mg IM, a bit more than the normal dose. I've used it for pulling kids out of trips, though not with a dose that size." He was putting some instruments away. "This is nothing to do with ergot, you know—he'd be dead by this time."

My left hand felt like a boxing glove and I told them to take the stuff off but he just leaned over me again and lifted my eyelids in turn, nodding to her.

"Get this stuff off my hand."

"You feeling okay now?"

"I want to use my hand."

"You have the other one, don't you?"

He looked at her and laughed comfortably, pressing the two brass locks and picking up the bag. She seemed worried by this.

"Are you going now?"

"There isn't anything else I can do until tomorrow. He just has to rest and I'll leave instructions with the ward nurse: they have Diazon-3 here and it's the same thing with a Belgian brand name. He'll be okay."

She went to the door with him and I'd got half the bandage off by the time she came back and tried to stop me. She was wearing a zipped windcheater and her hair was in some kind of bandeau.

"Is it night?"

She said it was.

There seemed to be odd periods of blackout between periods of lucidity but they didn't worry me. I wanted to know things and she could tell me, and the lucid periods lasted longer than the blanks.

"Is base intact?"

"Yes."

"Chirac pull me out?"

"What?"

"Did Chirac pull me out?"

"Yes."

There were still three cylinders I hadn't reported on but London must have got enough or they wouldn't have or-

dered Loman to pull me out. He'd sent Chirac with a helicopter, the only way: that was why I'd heard their wings
thundering.

"Get this off, will you?"

She said it had to stay like that and I told her to shut
up and get it done, I don't like being one-handed even
when there's nothing particular to do. She fetched one of
the nurses who'd been here before. The nurse said the
bandage had to stay on and I managed to swing my legs
off the bed and sit up, nearly flaked out again and said to
Diane *listen I mean it* and she talked some persuasive
French, the *m'sieur* was feeling very frustrated because of
his accident and it would be better to do what he asked,
so forth, worked in the end because in any case I was in a
rotten mood and they could see I was going to tear the
bloody thing off if they didn't cooperate. But the whole
wall kept coming and going and I had to sit still for a
minute while it stopped.

Finger looked a mess. I told them how I wanted things,
just a No. 1 dressing on it and the others left free, especially the thumb, lose three fingers and you can still grip
things, lose the thumb and all you've got left is a hook
and a hammer.

"How is the mad Arab?"

"*Comment?*"

"*L'arabe fou, comment va-t-il?*"

She spoke English perfectly well: she was the girl
who'd fixed me up here yesterday and she'd talked to
Vickers, the big oil driller: but she was annoyed because I
wanted my hand done differently.

"*Je ne comprends pas, m'sieur. Écartez les doigts, s'il
vous plaît.*"

And she didn't want to talk about the mad Arab, either.
That was all right but there were one or two things beginning to needle me and I didn't like it: the American said
just now that it wasn't anything to do with ergot and I
could believe him. They were checking the bread supplies
as a formality while a more specialised medical team was
trying to find out the real cause of the trouble. There'd
been other Arabs, Vickers had told me, and what I wanted to know is how they'd got anywhere near that aeroplane without first knowing it was there, and how they'd
survived and reached Kaifra without broadcasting the

fact, because even in delirium they'd surely mention the plane, and that would have initiated an immediate air search.

But it hadn't. The Arab had been here in Kaifra at 1500 hours yesterday raving about the "mountains" and "great birds" out there but he couldn't have mentioned the freighter or the Algerian squadrons would have overflown the area much sooner.

Blank period and someone held me suddenly, tried hard to surface, no go. Memory throwing images for me but no sequence, the dazzle of the headlights blinding and fading and the trays on the waiters' hands and the storm of dark plumage against my face, keeping me upright, holding me steady, could hear my breathing, its rhythm slowing, a cold compress on my forehead, her eyes worried, Diane's, poor little bitch, been sitting prettily in the British Embassy ordering buns for the Queen's Birthday and then the bastards had shanghaied her and now she was having to wet-nurse something the vultures had left, not at all nice.

"All right."

They still kept a hold on me and I had to say it again *I'm all right* till they let me go, difficult patient, yes, I grant you, but don't like being held up, demoralising.

When the nurse had gone off I said:

"Go and tell them."

"Tell them what?"

She thought I hadn't been listening. The nurse had finally had enough of me and she was going to bring help and get me undressed and into a bed.

"If they try anything I'm going to smash the place up so make sure they understand because it'll save a lot of noise."

She went off a bit impatiently and I had five minutes to straighten out, steady deep breaths, muscles relaxed, one or two questions, why wasn't Loman here, he must be packing us up at base, the Arab could have been working in strict hush for the opposition yes but in delirium he'd have broken down, shouted aeroplane all over the place, something didn't quite add up in this area.

Opened my eyes and she was there again, her eyes worried, waiting for me to start collapsing but I wasn't going to any more, didn't intend to, the organism was trying to take over and I was going to let it.

"You tell them?"

"Yes." She stuck her small hands into the windcheater but she was obviously ready to pull them out fast to do something if I keeled over again and that annoyed me and I got off the bed and went a couple of paces and leaned on the wall and she had more sense than to help me, could see my face.

Very good being on the feet again. Therapeutic.

"Who was the doctor?"

"He's visiting the American camps."

"Where did Chirac land me?"

"At South 6."

"And brought the doctor along with me?"

"Yes."

"He'll be able to shoot that stuff into the Arabs now."

"The last one died in the night."

Turned away as she said it and turned back when I didn't answer. She looked quietly furious, not a bit worried now. I said:

"Getting on your nerves, is it, all this?"

Surprise, comprehension, frustration: she had wonderful eyes and you could read everything in them and that was why they'd been such bastards to use her, reaction-concealment capacity subzero and her hands too small to lift a gun.

"Do you always go on till you drop?"

"Oh Christ," I said, "don't you start." I leaned off the wall and tried walking about, not too bad, no pratt-fall. "Listen, they were in poor condition anyway, what d'you expect, a diet of dates all their life, or they inhaled more of it than I did. You'll have to find something better than me to worry about."

I walked some more, a few steps to the window and back, did it again and felt the hallucination thing starting up and their high cackling screech and the fourth one smashing into the instrument panel and stood and didn't do anything, hung limp, remarkable efficacy of total muscular relaxation, very old ferret, an instinct now, the wall steadier but I had to slow the breathing consciously, I didn't think she'd moved to help me, learned fast.

"We have do—" try again and get the slur out while you're at it, "Do we have a rendezvous Lo—with Loman?"

Possibly it wasn't good enough yet but I didn't want to repeat it, certain amount of satisfaction in having pulled out of the spasm without having to sit down and ask for an aspirin or anything.

I turned round, away from the wall, and looked at her. She wasn't looking at me, looking upwards, listening. I could hear it too.

"Not immediately."

I didn't understand. Traces still threatening the psyche, his upturned face and the expression on it and the way the leg had snapped when I'd hurled the thing away, I suppose I was a bit tired, that was all, it didn't help, not being in top form.

She was watching me. I saw what I looked like, because her eyes showed everything, and I turned away but the window was there with the outside dark making it a mirror, yes indeed, a sorry figure as they say, rather messed about with, one way and another. Saw her point now. Motherly little soul, wanted to tuck me up before the whole bloody auction had time to disintegrate.

So I walked about a bit to prove it wasn't going to.

"When's it for?"

"What?"

"The rdv."

She was still listening to the jet, head on one side. It sounded as though it was going into circuit above the airport.

"Later," she said, not looking down.

"What time?" And she jerked her head to look at me because I'd put a lot of force into it, fed up with not knowing things and not being able to talk properly or think properly, getting better but not nearly fast enough, upsetting.

She was watching me critically, trying to make some sort of decision. Her hands were still bunched inside the windcheater, and the weight of the Colt Official Police .38 was dragging it down at one side; you wouldn't have to frisk this pint-sized Mata Hari: you could see she was armed half a mile away.

She kept her voice low, moving closer.

"Loman has some orders for you. He insisted I didn't give them to you unless you seemed fit enough for some more work. Well, you're not fit but you won't give an inch so what can I do? He's at base keeping up a signals exchange with London in the hope that you'll be able to operate."

"That doesn't sound like Loman. He'd grind a blind dog into the ground."

"I don't think it's a question of consideration."

"More like it, come on."

"He wants you to do something he called 'sensitive' and if you can't bring it off he said the repercussions would be grave in the extreme. He also—"

Suddenly I was shaking her and she drew a breath and shut her eyes and waited and when I realised what I was doing I stopped and stood away and she didn't say anything for a bit, furious again I suppose because she was doing her best and I wasn't helping. Quietly as I could:

"Just put it in your own words."

Couldn't stand the man, that was all, a pox on his grave repercussions, if he meant the whole thing'd blow up if I ballsed it why couldn't he bloody well say so. Besides which I was badly shaken because they'd wanted me to go and report on Tango Victor and I'd done that so I'd thought the mission was tied up and now London had got second thoughts on it, they never let you alone, those bastards, drive you till you drop.

"Things have been happening," she said. "Soon after you went off the air we had an alert from London. We were asked to rebrief you for the end phase of the mission. We didn't know if you were still alive, but London said they were going ahead on the assumption that you could still operate."

The whine of the jet was thinning above us as it came into the approach path and I looked at the square electric clock above the instrument trolley. 2352.

"It's for tonight, is it?"

"Yes. I don't know it all. I can only tell you what I've been instructed. You're to know that a representative of the Foreign Office was flown out this evening to meet the Tunisian Minister of the Interior. It's been arranged that an aircraft of the R.A.F. Tactical Command will be permitted to land here at Kaifra tonight, at approximately midnight. Your orders are to meet it, receive a consignment and take it to base."

Final approach now and eight minutes early. I looked from the window but couldn't see anything of his lights in the sky. Then I moved away, not hurrying.

"All right," I said. "Anything else?"

The room wasn't big: nine short paces from this window to the one opposite. I counted the paces because I like knowing about things, especially about the environment I have to operate in. I hadn't walked this far since I'd been in the desert but the legs were holding up all right.

"Nothing else," I heard her saying, "till you reach base."

The glass of the window was black and I could see her reflection; she was standing there with her hands in the windcheater, watching me. The only light from below was from a street lamp, reflecting on edges and curved surfaces.

"The immediate thing," I said, "is to meet that plane, right?"

"Yes," she said.

I could hear it landing now, the jets screaming suddenly and then fading right out. I looked down from the window.

The other side of the building there'd been a Mercedes and a 404, both with their lights off. This side there was the small Fiat I'd seen at the Royal Sahara and a GT Citroën, no lights. They weren't just parked: you don't leave a car like that in the deepest shadow you can find; you put it under a street lamp if there is one, so people won't pinch things.

I said over my shoulder:

"D'you think you could've been followed here?"

It took her a couple of seconds.

"Followed?"

I came away from the window, again not hurrying, but it didn't matter whether they knew I'd seen them or not because it was too late to do anything about it: this place was a trap.

15. Trap

"I don't think so," she said.

She looked small and cold and hunched.

"Wouldn't you know?"

She didn't answer.

I hadn't meant to hurt: I wasn't even thinking about her. I wanted facts, as many as I could get and as soon as I could get them. She moved slowly and I said:

"No. Keep away from the windows."

She stopped at once, looking down.

I suppose she wanted so much to show me she was a professional, but everything she did was amateur.

"Did you get here before Chirac brought me, or after?"

"After."

I began walking about to get the circulation going. There hadn't been a psychic spasm since she'd told me about the Foreign Office sending out a man to see the president here: the end phase was being thrown at me like a fast-burn fuse and I had to do a lot of thinking and if the psyche wanted to act the bloody fool it wouldn't get any help from me.

They must be desperate in London. The R.A.F. back in the act and unofficial negotiations at presidential level: if they went on like this they'd shake the whole thing off its bearings.

"When Loman told Chirac to pull me out he must have known the mission was still running?"

She lifted her head and looked at me, ready to make another mistake and ready to see what I thought of it, bracing herself.

"I don't know what you mean."

"Oh, for Christ sake——"

Not thinking properly. Control. We were in a red sector and I wouldn't get us out of it by pushing this poor little bitch till she broke.

"Don't worry," I said, "they couldn't have followed you here. They don't know you. They haven't seen you since you set up the base and if they saw you in Kaifra before then it couldn't have meant anything: they don't know who you are."

The breach of security must have been through Chirac. He wasn't a professional either and Loman had got him airborne again at short notice and he'd had to bring me here from South 6 by road and the area was stiff with surveillance.

"All right," she said.

She turned away with her eyes getting wet and I suppose she could stand up to me when I was being a bastard but she didn't know what to do when I stopped.

"Listen," I said, "I want to know things. When Loman told Chirac to pull me out of the desert, he must have known the mission wasn't over, right? He was still in signals with London, wasn't he?"

"Yes."

"Then if the mission was still running and we were meant to keep it quiet, how could Loman send out a helicopter for me, right into the target area?"

This was something she knew about and her head came up quickly. "He said that after the massive air search by the Algerians no one in Kaifra would go on thinking that Tango Victor was in the region, so a single flight wouldn't attract much attention. But he told Chirac to gain full ceiling before he set his course, as a precaution."

"Fair enough."

Quickly she said: "Is that right?"

"It makes complete sense."

She nodded, feeling better, and I wished to God they'd found someone different to help us on this job, someone I could have ignored or disliked, a girl with glasses and a sniff or a yellow-toothed hell-hag with a barbed-wire wig, anyone but this downy-armed child with her courage and innocence who ought not to be here with me now, caught in a trap that could kill her unless I could spring it.

"Not too near," I said.

"No."

She turned back, keeping near the instrument trolley, the point farthest from both windows.

"Are we able to phone base?"

"No." Very emphatic about this. "Loman said it's possible the telephone exchange has been infiltrated. I imagine he means—"

"Got at."

I wanted to think and she sensed it and didn't talk for a bit. Proposition: it wasn't the cell that had set up the marksman for me or they'd be in here by now, at least four of them or any number up to sixteen or more, adequately armed and easily capable of taking us or leaving us for dead, the staff of the clinic powerless to stop them. It was the cell that had orders to survey us, find out where we were going, so that when the objective was reached they'd be there too. So far they hadn't done very well: Loman had put me into the target area and pulled me out again and they hadn't been good enough; all they'd done was lose a man in a ravine. Tonight they looked like doing better.

It was a proposition only: not an assumption. Assumptions are dangerous and sometimes lethal. They might be simply holding their fire till we went out there so there wouldn't be any fuss, nothing for the ward maids here to clean up afterwards. They *could be* that cell: the one with the marksman, the one with orders to stop me reaching Tango Victor wherever it was, in the whole of the Sahara. They hadn't done very well either: they hadn't stopped me reaching the target and reporting on it and getting out again; all they'd done was mess up a Mercedes and leave it full of shells. Tonight they were better placed.

It didn't matter which cell it was.

"You mean there's someone outside?"

I think she had to ask because she couldn't stand it any more, not knowing.

"Yes."

She nodded.

Her little nods were expressive: just now it had meant she felt better; this time it was acceptance. Nothing more than that because she didn't know the whole thing, she probably thought there was just one man, just one man watching.

"Where's Chirac?"

"He went back to the Petrocombine South 6 drilling camp. Loman said he must use that as his base."

Further operations: you don't need a base if you've finished operating.

A spasm came and I wasn't ready and they screeched and their black wings beat at me and I shouted at them without a sound, doing nothing with my hands, repulsing them with my mind, half aware of their unreality, only the psyche sensitised by the thought of Chirac standing by for further operations.

"Are you all right?"

"What?"

"Are you—"

"Yes."

Sweat running and respiration accelerated, normal symptoms of fear. If Chirac was standing by it could be to fly me out again, drop me back into the nightmare, not ready yet to stand it, even to stand the thought.

She was keeping close to me, watching me, wanting to help.

"You're all right now."

"Yes. You know it was nerve gas, don't you, you were there when I—"

"Yes."

"It's the one that puts the fear of Christ in you."

"I know."

I suppose they'd heard me yelling my way out of the freighter. A bit embarrassing but it wasn't my fault: there'd been photographs, a press release at the time when the stuff was invented, picture of a mouse in a cage with a cat and the cat was terrified of it, back arched and ears flat, spitting.

"Listen," I said and turned away from her, "what other facilities have been granted?"

When I turned back she was just standing still trying to think what I meant, trying to answer before I lost patience again. So I said: "The U.K.'s had permission to land a military aircraft here but I mean what else? Did Loman ask for any kind of assistance, police, army, secret service liaison?"

"I didn't hear of anything else. He didn't tell me about anything. I was there all the time while the signals were going through, till he sent me here to brief you."

"All right."

Paradox: the Tunisian government was prepared to receive a plane with R.A.F. rondels in Kaifra but I couldn't go down to the reception desk and phone the police and say there are four cars outside please have their drivers arrested on suspicion. But it wasn't quite like that: the Tango mission had been ultrasensitive from the start and a visit from the Foreign Office type with a request for immediate military overflying and landing rights could have tightened things to the limit.

We were strictly on our own.

The thing that worried me most was the timing. The plane was down and the crew was expecting me and I was here in a trap and I didn't know how long they'd wait or what they'd do with the consignment I was meant to receive.

"What is this thing, d'you know?"

"Which thing, please?"

"Whatever the R.A.F. are bringing in."

"I don't know. Loman called it 'the device.' "

"The what?"

" 'Device.' It's the word he used for it in signals."

"You didn't get any clues? Chemical antidote? Some sort of destruct system? Gas mask?"

She thought back and then said no. This was logical because if Loman had been allowed to tell me what the thing was he would have briefed the girl, instead of which he'd obviously made sure she didn't pick anything up during the signals exchange.

I kept on walking, the mind exercising the organism, wouldn't be possible in this condition to do very much if they came in for us, effort required, keep on walking and do it properly.

"Is there any kind of a deadline on this?"

"He didn't say so."

Logical too: the military aircraft had landed and I ought to be there to meet it because there'd be no point in letting it hang about the airfield. The deadline was already past.

I stopped by the window, the one at the front of the building, and looked down as I'd done before. It presented them with a model target, a silhouette with back-lighting, but that was all right because if they wanted to pick me off they'd have done it the first time and in any case they wouldn't have sent four vehicles with crews numbering up to sixteen if all they wanted to do was make a small hole in a skull.

It wasn't easy to see things through the reflections on the glass but the white oblong down there had a cross on the side and a penant mounted on the windscreen pillar, French style. It was parked about halfway between the gates and the front entrance of the clinic and from this angle I couldn't see if it was in sight of the Merc and the 404. They were in the shadow of the palms on the road outside and there was a hedge of desert tamarisk in their general line of vision: if they could see the ambulance at all it would be through the gateway.

"How many are there?"

I shortened focus and looked at her reflection in the glass. At this distance I couldn't see her eyes but her voice

had sounded steady enough, just a degree strident as if
she'd made herself say it. She was young and inexperi-
enced and would make the worst possible agent material
and if they ever pushed her into a mission where she had
to operate solo for five minutes that'd be as long as she'd
live, but she looked as though she had guts and I thought
the safest thing would be to tell her what the actual situation was so that she'd have a chance of saving herself if I
forgot to duck.

"There are at least four cars."

Her reflection gave a little nod. She didn't say anything.

I looked through the glass again. Conditions outside
were the same as last night when I'd walked out of the
Royal Sahara to the Mercedes: bright starlight, still leaves,
moonless and windless. Low natural visibility without
haze, acoustic irradiation conditions somewhere near a
hundred per cent with the hygrometer down towards zero
and the air totally static. I would have preferred low
cloud and a moist wind, the dark to hide in, the wind to
take sound away.

I turned and began walking again.

"What's the code intro?"

She was watching me with very bright, very alert young
eyes: she didn't understand what I meant and was trying
hard to think and get it right and not look stupid.

"What's the code introduction when I meet these
R.A.F. types? Password. What do I—"

"Oh yes—*Firefly*. They'll be carrying photographs of
you and you'll be asked to show them the scar on your
left arm. You must destroy the photographs immediately."

"My Christ, is that all?"

She just shut her eyes and stood there hunched up but I
wasn't even thinking about her because London had covered the code intro with actual pictures and a physical
feature so it wasn't just a gas mask they were handing
over: it was something so bloody classified that the Air
Ministry wouldn't deliver it before they'd forced the Bureau into providing treble-check identification. They
couldn't be standard aircrew on the plane: they were seconded from D.I.6 or Liaison Branch, or the Bureau
wouldn't have let those photographs out of the files.

I suppose she thought she'd got it wrong again because
of the way I'd said was that all. She only knew half of

what was going on and whenever I asked her anything she'd only got a fifty-fifty hope of coming up with the right answer and it was wearing her down.

"What car did you come in?"

She opened her eyes.

"The Chrysler."

"Loman's?"

"Yes."

"You came from base direct?"

"Yes."

"You know the way back?"

"Past the Mosque."

"That's right."

It was a three-minute trip.

If I could get her out of here she could be back in cover within three minutes but three minutes wouldn't give her anything like enough time to flush a tag and she hadn't been trained to overshoot base and take him onto neutral ground and do what I'd done to Mohamed. With four vehicles waiting out there I thought they'd probably just take her somewhere for interrogation and she wasn't trained to cope with that kind of thing either.

I'd have to leave her here and tell the staff to look after her while I drew off the opposition.

"What are your orders?"

"Orders?"

"What were you told to do, once you'd briefed me?"

"Get back to base."

She'd already briefed me: Foreign Office involvement, Tactical Command sortie, rdv, code intro, there wouldn't be anything else; it was a simple pickup job. So now Loman wanted her back at the Yasmina to man our communications and leave him free to make neutral ground contact with Chirac and perhaps others and I couldn't leave her here and ask the staff to look after her while I tried to break out.

I'd have to take her with me.

"Are you frightened?"

"Yes," she said, "very."

"That's good."

She wasn't exactly shivering: there was a tension in her body that was making her contract, hunching herself into the windcheater as if she were cold. It was the classic animal posture in the face of a predator, the body drawn in on itself to protect the vital organs and present a smaller form, the limbs at the same time contracted in readiness to strike or spring if defence were changed to attack.

"Why is it good?"

"You're producing everything you need: adrenalin, muscle tone, sensory alertness. No one else can do it for you and you can't get it out of a bottle."

She nodded.

I took another walk and passed the window and glanced out and went on. There wasn't any sign of life down there: the Mercedes and the Peugeot 404 made blocks of shadow among the trees and the ambulance showed up as a blur of white against the tamarisk hedge. In the building here I could make out voices but they were distant; twice since I'd regained consciousness I'd heard the lift working just outside this room.

"Has that thing got a full clip?"

"What thing?"

"That gun. Has it got a full magazine?"

"Yes."

"Is the safety catch on?"

She had to look, tugging the thing out of her pocket as if someone had said give me that bag of toffees I've told you before. Then she nodded.

"Yes. It's on."

She was pleased because she'd got her lessons right and I thought oh you bastards if you rope in a child again to help us in the kind of work we do I'll have your thumbs off first and then mind your eyes.

"Do you want it?"

She was holding it out to me.

"No. Put it away."

"All right." She got it back into her pocket and looked up at me again and the fear was still in her eyes, I suppose because I'd made her think we were getting ready for some kind of trouble. I'd only wanted to check on the safety catch because she might have to run and if she tripped and the thing fired it'd blow her leg off. I would have taken it away from her altogether and dropped it into a waste bin before we left here but it was just possible she could save herself with it if things got rough.

"Diane."

"Yes?"

"We're going."

"All right."

"There won't be much trouble."

"I see."

Light eyes and a firm mouth and her bright hair in a bandeau and out there in the night a bunch of thugs who'd do what their orders were to do, shoot her down or take her somewhere and put her through forced interrogation, anything they were told to do, anything they wanted to do. I'd say her chances were fifty-fifty, the same as my own.

But the alternatives I'd come up with were riskier still and I wanted to try the break-out before the opposition control decided to send them in for us. We'd be better off in the open, with room to move.

So I told her to find a couple of white coats, the linen things the doctors used, and she drew blank in the cupboards here and had to go out and across the landing and try her luck over there. I could still hear voices from somewhere below in the building but they weren't loud. It was almost midnight and activity in the clinic was at a low level.

She came back.

"Will these do?"

"Yes. Leave them here for a minute. We're going to walk across the room, past the window. Just slowly, talking."

"All right."

"No, this side of me." I took her arm. "I want them to see you clearly, But don't look out of the window."

We got moving and before we reached the window she'd begun trembling.

"Do I do all of the talking?"

"No. We're just in conversation. The main thing is not to look out of the window. This way a bit, a few inches this way."

If she passed too near the window she'd only present an almost black silhouette and if she were too far from it the reflected light from the walls would strike her face. I didn't want them to see her face but only the pale blue windcheater.

"Don't look out."

"How do you know I want to?"

"You want to see for yourself who they are. A bit

slower. But you wouldn't see them anyway, it's only a couple of cars parked under the trees."

"You said there were four."

"The other two are at the back of the building."

"I see. It's giving me goose flesh, knowing they're watching me now."

"Don't worry."

The trembling was still in her arm, under my hand.

"Why are we doing this?"

"They know you're with me here, because you must have passed this window a few times before I told you to stay clear of it. They could even have been outside when you drove up. I want to remind them, as late as possible before we leave here, that you're wearing blue."

We reached the wall and turned round and started going back, the window on my side now. She said:

"Why did you tell me to keep clear, before?"

"I thought there was a chance they'd shoot you."

"Why don't you think so now?"

"Because I'm still alive."

The other window wasn't important because from the Fiat and the Citroën they couldn't see the ambulance. She was still trembling and I said: "You'll feel all right once we get going; it's only the delayed action affecting your nerves. Can you drive a D.S. 90?"

"Yes. We've got one at the Embassy."

"Fair enough. There's a D.S. ambulance outside. I want you to go and start it up and bring it over to the front steps." We were clear of the window now and put on the white linen coats. "Keep that thing tucked well in: I don't want them to see any blue. All right, we'll take the lift."

There was nobody in the main hall. Posters about inoculation against cholera, preventative hygiene to fight sand-fly trachoma; a pair of sandals lying in a corner near the door; artificial flowers on the reception desk with a faded ribbon on them. Sand gritted under our feet; there is sand everywhere in Kaifra, even inside the buildings.

"Take off your bandeau and put it in your pocket."

"All right."

"See the ambulance?"

"Yes."

"I'll wait for you here on the steps."

She went down them and I stood watching her.

There wasn't anything else we could do but this; nothing that had as much hope of working out smoothly, provided they didn't get too close a look at us. I wanted to keep the action down because she had all her life in front of her and we had a mission to run and I wasn't in fit condition to risk a major mistake.

She walked nervously, her step springing a little, but she wasn't looking round her though I knew she must be wanting to. They couldn't see her yet: it would only be when she crossed the gap made by the gates that they might see her. I could think of no reason why they should shoot. It was just that she looked small and vulnerable out there where there wasn't any cover and I wished I'd gone with her but it was too late and anyway impractical because this was part of the whole setup: a change of image as convincing as we could make it.

She got into the ambulance and the sidelights came on and the engine started up and the pennant gave a couple of lazy flaps as she locked over and came towards the steps.

"I'll drive."

She slid across and I got behind the wheel as quick as I could because one of the voices I'd heard on the ground floor would belong to the ambulance driver and he'd know the sound of this vehicle and wonder what was going on. I would have preferred to let her drive: she'd already established the image behind the wheel and now we'd altered it but if they weren't satisfied with what we were giving them they'd tuck in behind and we'd have to lose them and she wasn't trained for that.

"Seat belt," I said.

She pulled it across and buckled it.

The fuel was at three quarters. I turned the facia-lamp rheostat to medium power, getting enough of a glow to show up my white coat but not to light my face. Then I put the heads full on and drove through the gates and turned left so that if they decided to follow us up they'd have to make a half turn first. I could see the blue flash of the roof emergency lamp in the mirror frames and thought about using the hee-haw but there was no traffic and it might be overdoing things.

There was a slight clang from behind us, probably the chrome-armoured tube of the oxygen unit against the cylinder because we were leaning in a close turn; and there was another sound, fainter and underlying the first and not easy to identify: possibly a piece of equipment shifting.

"You all right?"

"Yes, thank you."

"Don't worry."

"No."

I really thought they'd accepted the image and then some lights swung from behind us and I knew the sound I hadn't been able to identify had been the first of them starting up.

"Keep low in the seat."

"All right."

I kicked the throttle to bring the ratio down and the rear tyres lost traction on the sand but we weren't even picking up useful revs before the lights showed me the GT Citroën moving broadside across the road in front of us. There wasn't anything I could do because this was an avenue of close-standing palms and there was no point in trying a slide U-turn because there were lights in the mirrors now.

Their orders hadn't been to tag us. They'd been told to set up a pincer trap for anything that moved, and we were in it.

16. Hassan

No, this is Angela, with Robert.

They'll be coming over to see us while you're here, and I'm longing for you to meet them.

Yes, aren't they? And always hand in hand—they weren't posing like that for the photographer. Deeply in love, and we're so very happy for them.

On Tuesday, coming down from Cambridge. They're just dying to meet you—of course we've told them all about you.

No, that's our youngest. She—she was a lovely child.

Yes, I'm very sad to say. It happened in North Africa, one of those mysterious and dreadful things that sometimes happens to people when they're abroad.

We never really found out. It was sort of—hushed up,

and even our own Embassy advised us to let the enquiries drop. Yes, all very strange.

Murdered. But no one was ever accused. They say there were just some Arabs, and it was nighttime, and—well we don't let ourselves think too much.

Oh not a bit, no. That's why we keep her picture here, with the rest of our little family. She was such a lovely girl and it sort of helps, to talk about her to people. It makes her seem—well—still a little bit alive.

The Citroën GT was backing and turning.

The term in the personnel files is "an assault on the person designed to extract intelligence." If you've held out against it you get the 9 suffix to your code name but it's not exactly an award for meritorious duty or anything: it just means they can give you some of the high-risk jobs in the hope that you'll do the same again, refuse to expose the mission or the cell or the Bureau even though the light blinds and the flesh burns and the scream is private inside your skull, for pride's sake.

An assault on the person. Your own person. No one else's.

Backing and turning and coming in this direction, no longer blocking the road entirely, leaving me enough room to go through if I wanted to. But there wasn't any point: the Fiat was farther along the avenue with a muzzle poking out of a side window. The lights of the Citroën came on, full heads, and most of the scene was blacked out because of the glare.

"Shall I shoot at them?"

"No."

"Why not? They—"

"When you're outnumbered, the thing is to think, not shoot."

I turned my head sideways to avoid the glare. She was looking at me, her skin silvered by the brightness of the light, her eyes exaggeratedly blue because of the contracted pupils. She would have made a good photograph.

"What will they do?" she asked me.

"Nothing much. They want some information, that's all."

Because if they'd intended to kill, as the other cell had intended, they would simply have sent a marksman to wait for me to leave the clinic or they would have ordered an armed group into the building to do it summarily. And if they'd intended to put mobile surveillance on me they wouldn't have used four vehicles to set it up: they couldn't hope to do it without my knowing and in a small town like Kaifra it wasn't even necessary.

They wanted me for interrogation.

This idea would have worried me in the ordinary way, but not too much. I had twice explored this psychological terrain in earlier missions and I knew roughly what to do: the only possible way is to remove the mind from the body and to look at the situation objectively—the pain is expressed in the nerves and is perfectly natural but it doesn't have any significance; it's totally physical and there's no message; you merely want it to stop and you could say the word but you couldn't live with yourself afterwards so you might as well die now and if you're prepared to die then they've had it because once you're dead you're no more use and they know that.

The worry would have been about the unpleasantness, that was all, not about whether I'd break. And at the moment they wouldn't have a lot of success because there were bruises everywhere and the effects of the gas were still hanging around and they'd only have to push me a bit too far and I'd flake out and they wouldn't learn anything.

But there was a new factor involved tonight. I didn't know how long I'd be able to hold out if they went to work on Diane instead of me.

The Citroën pulled up and someone got out and walked up to us holding a submachine gun. For a moment his shadow grew immense, flitting across the bonnet of the ambulance; then the light blazed again and he came to the side and stood there waiting for something, the muzzle aimed at my head.

I turned to look at him. Except for the man who'd died in the ravine this was the first time I'd seen anyone from an opposition cell because they'd worked covertly for the most part: the bomb in Tunis, the marksman here in Kaifra. This man wasn't of any interest because he was just a factotum but I looked at him so that I'd know him if I saw him later.

There were footsteps on the loose sand and another man came up from one of the cars behind us and stood looking in at Diane.

"Get out of the car."

I noted that he was an Egyptian, with a Cairo dockside accent. I told her:

"You only speak English."

"What?" she called to him through the window.

He jerked his submachine gun.

"Get out this side," I told her, "with me."

"All right."

I opened the door and the one who'd come up from the Citroën got worried and jerked his gun at me.

"Get your hands up!"

"Oh bollocks."

He was Egyptian too. I suppose Loman must have known the U.A.R. was involved but hadn't been allowed to tell me, on the grounds that the less the ferret knows the longer he lives.

Diane followed me out and we stood waiting. Two other men came up, one from the Fiat and one from behind us, and both had guns trained on us. Only one of them wore a fez: the others looked inferior material, capable of subduing or killing but nothing more. By their speech they were all from dockside Cairo and they called the man in the fez by the name of Hassan.

"Bring the Fiat here," he told one of them. Then he turned to me. "Give me your gun."

"I haven't one."

I spoke in Arabic because at least one of the opposition cells had a dossier on me: Loman had warned me about that.

"Search him! Get his gun!"

Hassan was very nervous and I placed him fairly high up in his cell or even in the network: he had the intelligence to know his responsibilities and to know that if I got out of this trap he'd probably get a chopping.

One of the thugs frisked me and I didn't make it difficult for him.

"He has no gun, Hassan."

"He must have!"

I was frisked gain and they dragged open the doors of the ambulance and ransacked the compartments and then one of them said it was the woman—she had my gun. Hassan looked at me to see my reaction when they tugged the Colt .38 out of her pocket and I looked suitably upset.

"He gave the woman his gun," said a man, "but we found it!"

Hassan told him to shut up and turned away and spoke to the man who'd brought the Fiat alongside.

"Is Ahmed coming?"

"Yes."

The transmitting aerial went on waving, slower and slower.

I thought that Ahmed wouldn't be likely to come alone: he was obviously higher in the cell and would have at least one trigger man. So far there were only the four of them here, unless there were others who'd stayed in the Mercedes or the 404 and I doubted this because Hassan was nervous and would have brought every one of his men in to guard me. There was no hope of estimating how long it would take Ahmed to reach here from their radio base but it would need only ten minutes to cross the whole of Kaifra. He could be here within sixty seconds.

Hassan was watching me.

"Where is the rest of your cell?"

I said I was operating freelance and there wasn't an actual cell, and he just shook his head and didn't take me up on it. I think it was just a random question to try me out. He looked like a hard-working field executive, the eyes alert but unimaginative, a man who had reached the position of lieutenant in a small cell operating overseas. I thought he would put the requirements of the operation before everything else, and would work well with Ahmed when the grilling began. I would have given a great deal to know whether either of them would have the intelligence to use Diane as the means of persuasion; I believed they would, because it had two immense advantages over a single interrogation session: a man might easily hold out if the pain was his own but might as easily break if he had to listen to someone else going through it, especially a young girl; secondly the girl could be brought again and again to the point of mental unbalance while the man was left with a clear head and the ability to answer questions.

It would depend partly on how well Ahmed and Hassan understood the European attitude to things like this: an Arab would entirely ignore the suffering of a mere woman and it wouldn't be worth touching her.

"Where is the aeroplane?"

"I still can't find it."

The answers had to be acceptable: it was no good saying what cell, what aeroplane, so forth. He knew I was an agent operating in the local field and he knew I was assigned to the U.K. Tango Victor mission and if I could give him some answers that would fit in with what he already knew it might get him to think of a few more questions. The more I could persuade him to talk, the more he'd tell me.

"Do you think the aeroplane is somewhere near Kaifra?"

"Well," I said, "I don't know about near. We certainly thought it was, but it looks as if we were wrong."

He seemed about to ask me another one and I waited but he shut up and began stamping his feet impatiently, looking along the perspective of the palm trees to see if Ahmed were coming. I thought it was interesting to note that this was an Egyptian cell and not the one controlling the marksman; also that one of the other cells was Algerian and working at government level with immediate-category liaison, because Chirac had brought in five squadrons of desert-reconnaissance aircraft just by mooching around up there at dawn this morning.

"Feeling all right?"

"Yes," she said.

She was looking pale, the gold skin losing colour.

"Do not talk!"

Hassan had swung round nervously.

"You mean don't talk in English?"

"Yes. Talk in Arabic."

"But this woman doesn't understand Arabic."

"Then do not talk."

His olive-black unimaginative eyes stared at me to make sure I was getting the message; then he turned away and looked for Ahmed again.

He wasn't trying anything subtle: he was energetic and efficient but not educated and it was almost certain that his henchmen didn't speak anything but their own crane-hook argot but it'd be too risky to rely on that so I asked her in English:

"Did you leave the other gun in the ambulance?"

I didn't expect her to have time to answer: she hadn't heard about any other gun and anyway she'd be thrown because I'd just been told not to speak in English and here I was doing it.

He came round very fast, Hassan, and his teeth flashed in the light as the animal mouth delivered its speech, the expression more explicit than the words.

If you talk to the woman in English again we will kill you, I will not have my commands disobeyed, if you do it again you will die, so forth.

But I'd got the information I'd wanted because the other three had closed in on me almost by reflex action when they'd seen him swing round, and their submachine guns had come up to the aim. So they didn't understand English and Hassan didn't understand it either or he'd have told them to search the ambulance for the "other gun" instead of telling me off.

I just hoped Diane would work things out and make a careful note: I'd told her they wanted to interrogate me and she knew you can't interrogate a dead man so if we had to talk to each other urgently we could do it in English.

Hassan was still glowering at me and I could see he'd like to shoot me here and now just for disobeying his orders: he was terribly nervous about the whole situation and didn't really trust in his ability to keep me subdued.

"Oh come on, Hassan, I bet you talk a bit of English, if it's only Coca-Cola."

He spat, not too far from my shoe. We could hear a car somewhere, its exhaust note muffled by the phalanx of palms, and he jerked his head to listen, watching the end of the avenue. I was worried because there was so little time and because this situation couldn't be expected to improve. One man and one submachine gun would be enough to keep us immobilised, and this force—already overwhelming—would be augmented as soon as Ahmed arrived.

And I didn't like the thing about Diane.

I could only save her by getting her away and I didn't think I could do that. Once they'd got us in the confines of an interrogation chamber she wouldn't have a chance. Nothing very important of course would happen: a fledgling agent seconded from an embassy to an active cell would go into the reports as fatally injured during the course of a mission and the incident would be passed on to those responsible for spreading the blackout. Two young gentlemen with diffident voices and polished nails would call at the flat in Lowndes Square to break the news, bearing the personal sympathy of the Foreign Secretary and hoping it might be a consolation to know that this very courageous civil servant sacrificed her life for the sake of others, adding that since her duties had been of an exceptional kind it would be unfair to her memory if any demand were made for enquiries that could only prove abortive and at the same time undo much of the work she had so assiduously accomplished in the cause of active diplomacy.

We never really found out. It was sort of—hushed up, all very strange. They say there were just some Arabs, and it was nighttime, and—well we don't let ourselves think too much.

The avenue was still empty: the car was moving at right-angles to it, a good mile away, its note rising and falling as the sound was trapped and released among the buildings. Hassan turned back to us and fumbled quickly for a cigarette, breaking the first match before he could light it.

Nothing very important and it happens two or three times a year to experienced executives like O'Brien and Fyson and we never know how many smaller fry are neutralised. It was infinitely more important that when she began sobbing I should remind them that I hadn't yet been able to locate Tango Victor, that when she first screamed I should repeat that I was only a freelance without a local base, and that when she failed to respond to resuscitation I should tell them they'd been wasting their time simply because they hadn't believed me, and that they would only waste more of their time if they put me through the same treatment because if I didn't know where the freighter had crashed then I couldn't tell them.

Hassan went and leaned into the Citroën GT and put the headlights down to dipped so that he could watch the road without having to move away from us beyond the glare. The smoke from his Egyptian cigarette drifted on the air, tarry and perfumed. He was smoking it nervously, flicking away the ash before it had time to form more than a millimetre. I watched his cigarette.

Diane was yawning quietly, being afraid. It happens in the trenches and behind the *barrera* of the bull ring: the intake of oxygen for the muscles, the release of thyroid secretion for the nerves. I looked at her and nodded and said:

"O.K.?"

"Yes, thank you."

Hassan jerked his dark head to look at me but O.K. was international and that was why I'd used it and he didn't slam into me this time. I said in Arabic:

"The woman doesn't know anything. Why don't you let her go?"

He shook his head again, taking me seriously.

"We will find out what she knows."

I let it go at that and moved my feet round a bit, as he was doing, my hands behind me. The snouts of their guns moved, keeping me lined up. I wished I could help her get through the waiting, say a word or two; but she wasn't meant to understand Arabic and if I spoke English again he might tell one of them to go for the face or the dia-phragm to make sure I understood and that wouldn't do any good: I didn't think I could save her but it wouldn't make her any less frightened if she saw how helpless I was.

I stopped moving about and leaned with my back against the little Fiat, listening to the faint sounds of traf-fic on the far side of the town where the highway linked the airport with the drilling camps. I couldn't hear the sound of any particular vehicle nearing. Hassan was lis-tening too and I thought it probably wouldn't be long be-fore he used the radio to ask his base where Ahmed was.

That was the principle of the thing, anyway: Whatever they did to her, I wouldn't give them information. What-ever they did to me, I wouldn't talk. They could afford to work on her as far as the point where life ceased and the odd thing was that I was absolutely certain she'd hold out for as long as I did: it hadn't occurred to me that they'd get anything out of her. I could of course have been wrong but I didn't think I was.

She was watching me and glanced away but realised I'd seen her and looked at me again, one eye clear and ame-thyst, the other in deep shadow, the down on her face sil-vered in the light from the Citroën, her soft hair shining. One day she'd be a beautiful woman, would have been, yes, as you say, a beautiful woman, but there we are and I suppose there aren't many families without something to grieve for, it's Angela, really, who felt it the most, they were very close you know, terribly fond of each other, almost like twin sisters, but I mustn't go on like this the minute you arrive.

A query in the quiet regard: What's going to happen?

I didn't know.

Cursed them again till the sweat came and I looked away from her because I ought to have reassured her but couldn't manage it, cursed them for bringing in a child just because the machine they'd set up was running too fast, sweating in the cool night air, not wanting to make the effort I would have to make and very soon. Not only her life involved, butterflies are pretty too, you find them flattened in window jambs and the world goes whistling on, but my own life as well, not that I've ever thought of dying in bed, thank you. Two lives and a mission. Made you sweat.

Physical condition not up to standard: the bruising had left me wanting to keep still, every movement making it feel as though something was going to snap, a bone, a tendon. Mentally fed up of course, the horror still there at the fringe of consciousness, their talons hooking and the farmyard stink of them, quite apart from the worry about what was going to happen. Put it this way, the organism wasn't in awfully good shape for survival.

"Hassan."

I was still leaning against the side of the Fiat and I didn't straighten up when he came over to me. I was dead beat, he could see that. I said:

"The woman doesn't know anything."

"You have said this, but we will see."

"Let her go and I'll tell you everything I know."

He laughed, just a quick flash of his teeth in the brown skin, and turned his head to look at Diane, the cigarette flattened between his fingers as he raised it and drew the smoke out, the glow of its tip reflected like a spark in his eye and then dying.

They would use a cigarette like this one. Probably one of those in the pack he'd pulled out just now. What is the longitude, what is the latitude, or she will not see anything again, the glowing tip against the amethyst, tell us. They would use other things; they would be selective, efficient.

"You will tell us everything you know," he said, "in any case."

He'd laughed because I'd said something at last that he couldn't take seriously: if they let her go I'd tell them less, in the end, not more; and he knew that. Anyway the whole thing was academic because he was a professional and he knew that any man can be reduced to a gibbering loon if they take it far enough and it doesn't need more than an hour. The only drawback is that he might not be, at that stage, too articulate.

"You can't say I didn't try, Hassan."

He turned to me, his teeth flashing again.

"You tried," he said, nodding his dark head, "yes."

He dropped his cigarette end, putting his black pointed shoe on it, the loose sand gritting. Then he stood watching the roadway, listening.

The three men hadn't moved for minutes. Most of the time they watched me but turned their heads now and then to see what Hassan was doing, one of them staring at Diane until he saw me watching him, one of them looking sometimes along the road's perspective. Their submachine guns had fallen away from the aim since Hassan had told me off for speaking in English but this was normal for the situation: they were standing at ease, in the military sense, to avoid the onset of syncope that sends our guardsmen toppling with such embarrassment at the Trooping of the Colours. Their guns could swing up and fire within a tenth of a second and at this range the shells would go through me and through both sides of the Fiat and there wasn't anything I could do about it: Hassan was running an efficient little cell and this trap was man-tight.

Near the end of the avenue a dome turned white and then darkened again as headlights swept across the building, and Hassan's thin dark body stiffened, straightening. We could hear the car but it wasn't coming in this direction and he relaxed after a while, shifting his feet and getting the packet of cigarettes, pulling one out.

"Don't worry, Hassan, he'll get here."

He put the cigarette between his lips.

"Oh yes," he nodded, "he'll get here."

"Can I have one of those?"

He came over to me and I got some matches out, striking one for him. When he'd lit up he held the packet out

to me and I took a cigarette, putting the tip between my
lips and striking another match. It occurred to me, in one
of those stray thoughts that pass through our minds at unlikely moments, that it wasn't a very easy death I was giving him.

17. Marauder

They were Unicorn Brand but that was all I knew about
them. The important thing was that they were British
made and therefore likely to have fewer duds among them
than a Continental make, so that the odds against this
kind of operation succeeding were considerably lower
even though it was a strictly one-shot setup without a
hope of another go.

The oxygen carrier might have been anything, potas-
sium chlorate, manganese dioxide or possibly lead oxide,
with the usual sulphur for the flame-burst medium mixed
with dextrin, powdered glass and so on for the binding
and striking agents. The actual splint would have been
treated with sodium silicate or ammonium phosphate as
an impregnation against after-glow and although in this
climate it was tinder dry I decided to throw it directly into
the fuel tank orifice while ignition was still in progress
rather than wait for the flame to become established because the air rush could blow it out.

There was an area of danger during the actual setting-
up of the operation. I had gone to lean against the Fiat instead of the Citroën GT because there wasn't a hinged
panel over the petrol cap: a panel would have made a
noise springing open and I would have had to stand slightly
away from the bodywork to give it room, which would
have exposed my hands and the panel itself. With nothing
more than the half-turn cap to take off it had been a
pushover even with my hands behind me and no one had
seen what I was doing because finger movement alone was
necessary, the forearm and wrist remaining perfectly still.

The area of danger had involved the petrol cap itself
once I'd removed it: I couldn't put it into my pocket without their seeing it, so I'd had to leave it wedged between
my spine and the body panel in order to leave my hands
free to get the matches and strike them; and the whole op-

eration would have been abortive if for any reason I'd had to lean away from the car because the petrol cap would have dropped with quite a lot of noise.

There'd been a certain amount of strain on the nerves because the fact was that two lives and the end phase of a priority mission were now depending on a blob of chemicals literally as small as a match head and this resulted in quite normal but dangerous purpose tremor when the time came to bring out the matches: my fingers weren't steady as I struck the first one and I had to get over this by considering a simple enough fact: that if nothing at all had depended on doing this thing properly I could have done it at the very least a dozen times with perfect success. In other words I was on an odds-on favourite at twelve to one so there wasn't any real need to worry.

I think my fingers had been quite steady again in the instant before I struck the second match but there wasn't time to give it any attention. The operation was now in final sequence and almost automatic: the match had to be moved through a hundred and eighty degrees laterally and downwards approximately forty degrees from the horizontal and the eye would pick up the target at once because it was well defined as a dark hole in a light-coloured panel. The actual timing was critical but presented no physical problem: all I had to do was swing half round with my right hand moving downwards during the ignition phase, allowing almost two full seconds for the manoeuvre— more than twice as long as I needed for the muscular commands and responses.

The ignition was normal and I waited for the oxygen release from the carrier and the formation of sulphur dioxide with heat increase before I turned and threw the match into the fuel orifice. At this stage the chemical process was becoming rapid and the final oxygen release almost explosive and I got clear and let the petrol cap drop to the roadway.

Hassan didn't have any time to react. The mental process involving the sequence of surprise, suspicion, comprehension and physical avoidance commands was much too long and I doubt if he'd done more than assume the startle posture, head forward and shoulders hunched, before the fumes caught. He was standing, in effect, directly in front of a flame thrower.

The timing of the main explosion wasn't important.

Both Hassan and one of his men were in the immediate
flame area and were thus technically out of action as soon
as I threw the match. My target was the man standing
seven or eight feet away towards the Citroën GT and I
went for him in the same movement that got me clear of
the explosion.

He didn't have a chance and I knew that. His surprise
phase would last much longer than it would take me to
reach him: two seconds ago the night had been quiet and
he had been party to a situation affording him absolute
power and he was now faced visually with a conflagration
that covered seventy five per cent of his static field of
view and mentally with a reversal of concepts difficult to
accept without a sense of unreality. He was moving instinctively into a half crouch when I span the submachine
gun to break his hold on it and flung it clear and dropped
him and went for the other man.

There was bright flamelight now and a lot of noise.
Hassan was screaming and trying to roll over but he was a
torch and the petrol was still flooding across the roadway
and making a sea of fire and I had to keep clear as I went
for the fourth man. The one who'd been standing near
Hassan wasn't making any noise and I think the initial
burst of flame had asphyxiated him and sent him down
without any chance of getting away. I saw Diane still
standing near the front of the Fiat and starting to move
for the ambulance and then I was coming up on the
fourth man and having to dodge because he'd begun
pumping his gun as a reflex action and the stuff was going
into the roadway and sending up clods of tar before he
saw me and swung round and I felt the blast of three suc-
cessive shots as I went low and got his legs.

Sudden rattling almost as loud as the gun itself as the
aim went wild and the shells began hitting the Fiat behind
me, sharpness of cordite in the lungs and somewhere in
the middle of everything the unmistakable sounds of Hassan dying and then my hands closed and I dragged the
fourth man off balance with his feet kicking upwards,
split-second image of his face terrified in the flamelight
then I chopped once and took the gun and slung it skittering across the sandy road and finished him and started
back towards the ambulance.

Fell against something.

Oh Christ someone saying, fumes very strong, myself

saying it, get up but my hand slid, part of the Fiat, front end, couldn't get up.

The effort demanded hadn't been great but total resources had been called upon suddenly and factors like oxygen needs and blood supply to the muscles and brain had become involved, bad enough if I'd kept up the effort till the organism rediscovered its rhythm but worse because the relative fall-off in terms of effort was precipitous: all I was having to do now was move from the flame area to the ambulance and it didn't take much doing and reaction was getting time to set in.

Roaring and the red light blinding, hello we'll have to watch that won't we, hitting something again, bumpers, up but I couldn't then bloody well try again or you'll burn alive, a sleeve of the white coat catching you're in for it now if you don't take an interest but the fumes choking and the heat fierce look out that's the wrong way, this way or you'll fry and *get* that coat off *get it off*.

Lights through the dark, the billowing dark of the smoke and the lights flooding through it, greenish and very clear and not the orange-red colour of the fire, somebody moving a car and coming nearer, the ambulance why don't you *bloody well get up*. Yes better now, the air more breathable. The stars spinning headlong across the roof of the night and *look where you're going for Christ sake*, that's better, steady now there's no need to panic, everything's under control.

Door swung and I pitched in and slammed it.

She drove hard and just before we left the area I saw them lying there, three of them blackening, one of them still trying to crawl through the dying flames. This was satsifactory and it had been easier for them, even this, than what they would have done to her, and later to me.

She drove well but the sobbing wouldn't stop and she had to keep straightening up from the wheel, her tears bright in the backglow from the headlamps. She hadn't seen anything like that before and the spasms kept shaking her and when I could manage it I said all right, I'll drive now.

"Sorry I'm late."

"We've only just got here ourselves."

I thought it was civil of him. They were both in their flying suits, one short, one tall, no indications of rank or service branch, strictly incognito, but the Mk XI Marauder outside on the tarmac had the standard rondels on it: I'd seen it in the docking bay when I'd driven into the airport.

I suppose they felt they shouldn't go on looking at me like this without asking something about it because the short one said:

"Have you had an accident?"

"Not really."

"Ah."

It annoyed me because I hadn't had time to clean up since the petrol tank thing and I didn't have any time now so they could keep their bloody remarks to themselves.

"Are you Mr. Gage?"

"Yes."

"Would you like some coffee?"

"Yes."

We were in the bar alongside the Metropolitan Departure gate: they'd been waiting here because they couldn't miss me when I came through the main doors of the building, and their own coffee hadn't long arrived.

We sat down at the little table and I said don't wait for me so they started stirring and the short one said:

"Lovely weather, isn't it?"

There weren't many people round: the boy making the coffee behind the bar, a holy man wrapped in his *gandourah* and his dreams in the corner by the Kodak stand, a young French couple perched half asleep on a pile of baggage, a clerk in a fez coming through the doors and crossing the hall. There was no sound of any flying.

Thoughts not a hundred per cent coherent because the pressure had come off, total energy output in progress fifteen minutes ago and now I was waiting for a cup of coffee and the nerves were having to adjust. But present situation comfortable and that was a help and besides she'd have reached base by now: I'd dropped her as near as it had been possible without exposing the image of the ambulance all over the place, no this one's Diane, our youngest, we've just had a call from her today, as a matter of fact, from Tunisia, she sounded quite homesick but otherwise fit. Yes, isn't she pretty?

Satisfactory.

"What?" I asked him.

"I said the weather's nice."

"Yes. The trouble is it brings the insects out and you

get them all over the windscreen, one firefly after another."

So the tall one got the envelope out and gave it to me and I opened it and looked at the three photographs, mug-shot coverage with two profiles and a full face, and began tearing them up while they drank their coffee.

Everyone still looked all right but the clerk in the fez had gone into the phone box near the check-out counter and it occurred to me that they could have been his head-lights I'd seen in the mirror when I'd turned in to the car-park.

I drank my coffee. It was hot and bitter and I could taste the caffeine and I needed its heat and its alkaloid and I took it into my mouth slowly, as if it were ambrosia. They talked to each other about nothing in particular, a wonderful place to bring their wives, all those stars and palm trees, talked to each other as if I weren't there or wouldn't be interested, letting me drink in peace, perhaps, and gather my strength.

Presumably without significance: a lot of people would come here to the airport to use the phones, the post office wasn't open at this time of night.

"How big's this thing."

"I'm sorry?"

"This thing you've got for me. How big is it?"

I was getting fed up because one or two bits of glass were trying to work out and I smelt of singed hair and they were obviously wondering where the hell I'd been and I wasn't going to tell them, none of their bloody business.

Then they were talking in short embarrassed sentences and the penny dropped and I pulled my sleeve up higher, looking at my watch, after all they'd got their orders and they'd brought something pretty deadly for me in the Marauder.

"We could go and look at it," the short one said. "I expect you've been told it's flashpoint-zero freight."

"Well, I didn't think it was a piss pot."

They shut up for a bit and I finished my coffee, wondering how far he'd been, Ahmed, from the scene of the fire when I'd left there: he'd been on his way and the ambulance was a distinctive vehicle and I hadn't been feeling bright enough to worry too much about headlights in the mirror so long as they didn't come any closer.

I didn't know what he looked like, Ahmed.

Incipient torpor and I was aware of it objectively, didn't feel at all like making an effort but there was a lot to do and I jerked my head up and thought watch it you're not safe.

"Let's go and look at it then."

They said all right and we got up and they paid and the padded nylon legs of their flying suits made a faint *zoop, zoop, zoop* as we walked through the hall.

The clerk in the fez had left the telephone box and was crossing towards the main doors. I didn't know whether he looked like a clerk in a fez, Ahmed.

It was better in the fresh air and I lost the dangerous urge to fall asleep as the caffeine began working on the nerves. There was a police guard on the Marauder, a young Tunisian with a peaked cap and white gauntlets and a holstered pistol, very smart and rather self-conscious because he wasn't used to being on special duty. We walked into the smell of kerosene and hot alloys and PVC and the short one climbed aboard so I assumed he was the pilot and the tall one ushered me onto the metal step and followed me up.

The flight cabin was roomier than I'd expected, with a chart table and an astrodome and two freight lockers: the Marauder Mk XI was a modified version of the original Mk IX short-range bomber and Tactical Air Command used it for the kind of work that the standard models would have jibbed at.

"Shut that door, will you?"

"Right."

The pilot opened the lockers and brought out two black rectangular containers with top and end grips and brass combination locks, one of them looking lighter than the other by the way he handled them. Both had Bostik airtight sealing with ripwire opening provision but there weren't any labels and I assumed it was because anyone in charge of this cargo would know what it was without having to read about it.

I picked them up one at a time. The smaller one was very heavy, about four times the weight of a medium portable typewriter but not much bigger.

"What are they?"

"M'mm? Not sure, actually."

"Oh, for Christ sake, can't you—"

"No, we can't. Awfully sorry."

Typical armed services security attitude, so bloody coy about everything, of course they knew what this cargo was. In any case I didn't want more than three guesses because in London-to-base signals exchanges it was called a "device" so these were obviously two components of one unit and you'd have to fit them together before they'd work. The only thing I didn't really know was why Control was sending me a nuclear bomb with no prior instructions.

"I'll bring the car over."

"Fair enough."

They slid the door back for me and I climbed down and began walking across the tarmac and saw a pair of headlights just dimming out among the trees on the far side of the carpark where the ambulance was. Three more cars had got here since I'd arrived and I could see movement along the road from the town: a string of vehicles using only their sidelights. So he did in fact look like a clerk in a fez, Ahmed, and he'd called in the whole of his reserves and there wasn't a hope of getting that device as far as base, not a hope in hell.

18. Chronometer

Receiving you.

Shook him a bit: he was having to think.

Q-Quaker high Rharbi imp trans mat awheel.

Dation?

Croydon indigo.

I'd had to get him on the Embassy wavelength and use speech code because this thing hadn't got an auto-scrambler. Chirac had either left my KW 2000CA in the desert or brought it back for Loman to pick up and whichever it was he'd know I couldn't use it so he would have shut down that wavelength while he was in signals with London through the Embassy.

UMF?

I asked one of them and he said twelve minutes.

Synchronise please.

Double-oh two nine.

Plus twelve.

UMF double-oh four one.

He didn't say anything for a minute and I left him to it and looked down at the lights of a village as we began turning. The pilot had agreed we ought to set our course for Malta because that was where he'd told Kaifra he was going. Then we'd turn back and make a loop across the desert and go in from the south.

"Are we off their screens?"

"I don't know their range at Kaifra but fifty miles ought to be good enough because there's no other traffic."

He was in the navigator's seat, the tall one. They were both cheerful enough but we all knew it was going to be a real swine and some of the jokes had got a bit thin since we'd taken off.

I watched the glow of the village and the white dome of a mosque reflecting the starlight as we came round in the turn. I suppose we needn't have taken the trouble to head for Malta before we got off their screens but the Ahmed cell was badly up against it and they might decide to go into the control tower and ask questions at gunpoint.

Loman was still sulking. He'd been thinking everything was all right because when I dropped her I told her I was going to the airport to keep the rendezvous and pick up the device and now he knew everything was all wrong because I ought not to be somewhere over Rharbi at ten thousand feet and he was having to face an entirely new pattern of hazards at zero notice. Well that was what he was for.

"Feeling the cold?"

"We're not going to be stuck up here forever."

"Frankly I wish we were."

He laughed but we didn't join in. They'd jibbed at first but I said they'd got to try so they'd worked things out and the pilot had said all right we'll have a go but this dolly weighs sixty-three thousand pounds with the amount of fuel she'll have on board at our ETA and if we can't pull up she'll drag half the strip into the desert, so long as those oil-drilling chaps don't mind.

It occurred to me that base might have gone off the air.

Hear me?

Hear you.

Is Fred all right?

Perfectly.

Reprimand in his tone and he could bloody well keep it. Fred was the standard speech code name for any third member of an active cell and I wanted to know how she was because the last time I'd seen her there'd been tears running down her sooty little face and if any one of us survived this trip I'd see those scaly bastards wrote her off the books before they did anything else.

My eyes kept shutting and the navigator said something and I missed it and got my head up again.

"What?"

"Is there any chance of a flarepath on that strip?"

"No. They don't night-fly."

"I see." He said it rather stiffly.

"You've got landing lights haven't you?"

"Fortunately, yes."

He didn't like me any more than Loman did but I couldn't help that. I think he was trying to find an excuse to call up the Air Ministry through Malta and get official permission for the captain to hazard his ship but he couldn't do it in front of me because it'd be embarrassing: they'd been ordered to make this rdv with an overranking contact and that meant that whether they were pilot officers or air vice-marshals they still had to do what I told them, otherwise they'd have turned me down flat about the South 6 thing and I knew that.

Quaker.

Hear you.

Friday Croydon indigo.

Roger.

I gave them back the headset.

Friday was rdv so he'd meet me at South 6 and presumably I wouldn't have to lug these rotten things as far as base and that was something.

Then I suppose I just went to sleep because there wasn't anything else I had to do. She was rolling about in the flames and I was trying to pull her clear and he was saying we'll be down in three minutes so you'd better get into this thing.

"What thing?"

He was rigging some fabric stays across the freight-locker section and I gave him a hand because even if we

didn't hit anything we were going to turn on an awful lot
of deceleration on a strip that short and I didn't want to
go through the front window.

"Have you got room to turn round?"

"Just about."

"Okay, then turn round and squat down with your back
to it."

The pilot moved the flaps and we began running
through eiderdowns and they were both rather young considering their responsibilities so I said:

"I'm sorry about this."

"Oh that's okay. It's just that these dollies are so terribly expensive and we're always being told about the tax-
payers' money."

The noise was pretty hellish because of the surface and
the reversed thrust and I thought the nose leg must have
folded back on impact but the angle was still roughly horizontal. Then the brakes came on and I was pressed
backwards into the fabric sling like a pea in a catapult
and one of them was shouting to the other one, something
about *distance* but I couldn't hear the rest of it. A lot of
low-pitch vibration coming in as the airframe took the
strain, smell of hot rubber, be awkward if we hit a bad
patch and the lockers burst open, not that anything could
go off but we'd been to a lot of trouble getting it here, vibration starting to hammer and someone yelling *won't
make it* and I thought oh Christ can't we ever get anything right, the front leg taking the brunt of the shocks
and everything trying to shake loose in the flight compartment, of course they'd known it would be like this and
that's why they'd looked at me as if I was barmy when I
told them we'd got to do it.

Hit my shoulder when they dropped me through and a
hand caught at me and then there was a dreadful quietness and there was Loman sitting sideways on the front
seat with his arm hooked across the squab and his pale
eyes watching me and I said we got down all right did
we?

"Yes."

He didn't look very pleased.

I absorbed the environment: Chrysler. I was on the
back seat with a rug over me. Zenith: 00⁵
had been 0041. I don't like gaps in the ti

"What happened?"

"In what precise way?"

Talked like a schoolmistress. He was very rattled.

"To the aircraft."

"They wrote off the undercarriage."

"Is that all?"

"It's quite sufficient."

There was an engine starting up somewhere but I couldn't see anything. We were parked alongside the hangar and the echo was coming back, sounded like a chopper. I listened to it and Loman didn't talk: he'd stopped looking at me now and sat watching the road that ran from the main gates of the camp to the south end of the airstrip where the windsock drooped against the starfields.

"Is it for me?"

"What?"

"That chopper."

"Yes." He sounded edgy, even for Loman.

I suppose the waiting was getting on his nerves. The Ahmed cell had seen the Marauder go up and it wouldn't be long before they heard it had come down all over the South 6 strip instead of Malta and they'd get here as fast as they could. Loman knew they were on to it because if there'd been no one getting in my way at Kaifra Airport I would have left there by road.

The helicopter was being warmed up, a comfortable *throp-throp-throp* from its rotor, aurally hypnotic, my head going down, then she said London wanted to know the position, her voice about normal, not still upset or anything.

Loman said he'd send it direct.

Situ Croydon indigo point skygo redmins point Q-Quaker able light-time standby ending point object present go conditters point Tango out.

I thought he was being a bit optimistic but I suppose he was worried about getting a blast if he sounded too doubtful: they were already having to absorb the Marauder switch into their thinking and it didn't take much to send them hysterical. The whole of this area was on the plotting table at the Bureau and they'd just received a situation signal and in spite of Loman's optimism they knew we were in a distinct red sector because the Marauder had ot of noise coming down and every opposition l have been alerted: they'd got me out of the plane before anyone had come along to see what had made the crump but quite a gang of day-shift drillers had gone down the airstrip from the living quarters and the crew were still there explaining about engine trouble and forced landing conditions and all that cock and it wouldn't be long before every camel driver in Kaifra knew that a foreign military aircraft had gone into South 6 by night.

London would be sweating because what ought to have happened was that I should have taken the device by road from the airport to base for Loman to brief me on it and what had happened was that I'd arranged for us both to be sitting here with the thing on our lap and hoping to Christ nobody found us before we got airborne. At the first sign of an adverse party in this area Loman would quietly melt into the middle distance because the director in the field is never actually meant to operate *in* the field but only from local base on the double principle that he's not trained in unarmed combat and if a mission blows up there has to be someone to take home the pieces and have them analysed in the hope that one fine day someone's going to profit from the lesson.

Loman would take the device with him because it was expensive and injurious and that would leave me on my own to do what I could but I wasn't in a condition to do very much and although he'd told them that Q-Quaker was able they wouldn't think much of my chances. So London was having the sweats.

Tango.

Tango receiving.

Embassy wants a repeat on "redmins."

They can have it.

She went off the air.

"Is that my end of the blower you've got there?"

"No," he said.

I believed the little bastard. He'd told Chirac to leave my transceiver in the desert when he'd picked me up because I'd need it again and there wasn't any point in dropping it a second time in an area where there were rocks that could bust it up.

"Are you sending me back there, Loman?"

"We don't know yet."

"Oh yes you bloody well do."

* * *

Throp-throp-throp.
0117.

Chirac shut off and the rotor began slowing above our heads. I hadn't taken a lot of notice when I'd come aboard but I had a look round now and saw that the little necessities of life were here all right: two parachutes and the two black containers.

"What's in that thing?"

"Cous-cous, mon ami!"

"I'm not hungry."

"You will be," Loman said. He sat peering through the curved perspex like a goldfish in a bowl. From what I could see of it we were in a *gassi* between low dunes.

"Where are we?"

"In a *gassi.*"

"I know that."

Chirac set the fuel taps at off. "We are ten kilometres from Petrocombine South 5 and eleven kilometres from Kaifra."

I tried to think where that was, but any kind of mental effort induced a kind of grey-out and I gave it up because it didn't seem to be anywhere in particular.

"Why here, Loman?"

"It's neutral ground." He'd stopped peering through the perspex bubble and was watching me critically. "You have three hours in which to get some sleep, so I suggest you do that."

He looked so depressed that I felt sorry for him, as far as you can feel sorry for a man like Loman.

"All right." I wanted to ask him a few things because it was now 0118.55 on the Zenith and he was going to let me sleep till 0418.55 and that meant he'd got me lined up for a dawn drop unless Control threw us a new one during the night; but if he was in the mood to give me any answers I didn't want to have to work them out, singing in the ears, a sensation of floating, the *tick-tick-tick* of the chronometer near my head. "Loman."

"Yes?"

"Have we still got a mission running?"

All I heard as his voice went faint was something about London and I suppose he was saying depends on.

First stage, second stage and detonator.

He showed me three times: annular clamp, bypass conduit, main body-locking with three-start threads. It was easy enough but I didn't object to the repetitions because you had to do it properly or the thing wouldn't go off.

"It's essential that no sand enters these threads."

"Noted. How powerful is this model?"

"It has the equivalent of one hundred tons of trinitrotoluene. The Americans have used similar devices in the Sahara for blasting wells, but this one has been modified for a ground-burst operation, reducing fallout and giving a low Mach wave with a relatively small residual radiation range."

"In figures?"

"One thousand yards. In still air with low humidity you will be safe at one mile, and should set the timer accordingly."

So it was a mini but the soot-black finish and the castellated retaining nuts and the knowledge that it would bring down the Post Office Tower at one blow gave it a potent aspect. It was so very quiet, standing on its flat end with the three of us crouched round it.

"Pouf!" said Chirac, "hein?"

He turned away and opened the polyester picnic box and took out the thermos of cous-cous. There was no meat with it and we used two of the plastic bowls. Loman said he'd eaten not long before we'd make the rdv at South 6 and so had Chirac probably but you'll get a Frenchman joining you at any time and in any place and with whatever kind of menu but especially an hour before dawn in the Sahara if it's cous-cous.

I'd slept for most of the allotted period but Loman had been talking to London quite a bit and I'd partly heard some of the panic: a lot of the trouble was that the signals had had to go from here to Kaifra to Tunis to Crowborough to London and back and had involved three automatic scramblers and two codes and the normal telephone delay between Crowborough and Control, but most of the panic was over the need to liaise the Bureau's international monitoring facilities with the controller running the mission and to do it within the few hours left before dawn. The local situation here was known and the risks calculated, but additionally London was using what amounted to a scanner that would pick up any event in-

ternationally that might have a bearing on the end phase
of the Tango mission: if for example the president of the
United Arab Republic happened to be assassinated at any
given moment then London would get the news almost
immediately through the monitoring facilities and Control
might realise straight away that an Egyptian cell operating here in Kaifra could conceivably get orders to cease
all action.

I didn't think it would happen. Nor did London and
that was why London was having the sweats: I wasn't
long out of sleep but it didn't take a lot of brain-think to
see that Loman was now driven to mounting a last desperate throw, because the Marauder thing had made it clear
to every local opposition cell that I was still very much in
business and therefore the U.K. was still certain that
Tango Victor was somewhere in this area. Chirac had
made the short hop from South 6 to the *gassi* here without picking up a tag from any one of the airfields around
Kaifra but when we took off for the open desert we'd be
running a gauntlet of ground observers and acoustic units.

Loman had said I'd need something like forty minutes
after the drop to set up the device in safety and trigger it
and if Chirac could fly me into the target zone and leave
me with that amount of time to work in without drawing
in a whole pack of opposition agents I thought he'd be
bloody lucky.

"What's that glow?" asked Loman.

"The moon rising." Chirac spooned his *cous-cous*.

"Why is it diffused like that?"

"It is a sandstorm over there."

"Will it affect your mission?"

"Pas du tout. It is two hundred miles away and moving
to the west. I have been watching it and there will not be
any trouble."

Loman drew the spigots and freed the clamp and boxed
the device into its separate containers. I decided not to
look at my watch so frequently: it was becoming a habit
and it was a sign of nerves. If we took off at the ap-
pointed time we would do it in eleven minutes from now.

"So what does London say?"

Loman didn't look at me. He doesn't like briefing you
until there's precisely time enough left to give you the
whole story without leaving an interval before the go, and

he's perfectly right because it allows a psychological sag
and you'll start mulling over the thing and asking silly
questions but I couldn't help that. There were things I
wanted to know and he was going to tell me.

"London?"

"That place with the clock."

"The end phase has been approved."

"Oh come on Loman give me the bloody information."

Voice rather sharp and Chirac flicked a look at me and
I was very annoyed because my nerves were more touchy
than I'd thought and that's always dangerous and I'd have
to do something about it. It was the snivelling little organism, that was all, saying we don't want to go back there
with all those horrid birds and that nasty gas, always
worrying about its skin instead of the job in hand.

Loman went on sulking for half a minute and then
said:

"The objective has to be obliterated."

He meant I'd got to go and blow up the freighter.

"Why?"

There was no technical problem: he wasn't obliged to
say anything that couldn't be said in front of Chirac and I
could do what I liked about that.

"It's the only way of dispersing the gas." He checked
his watch and looked back at the diffused glow on the horizon. "The heat of a nuclear reaction is required."

I finished the *cous-cous* in the bowl and Chirac went to
dish me out some more but I shook my head.

"Is there any protein?"

Loman fished in the box and gave me a square packet
and I peeled the skin off and ate it slowly: by the taste it
was mainly processed soya. I said:

"You know some Arabs found that aeroplane, don't
you?"

"Of course they didn't." Still upset because I'd spoken
to him like that in front of Chirac.

"What did they die of then, those Arabs in the clinic?"

"Nerve gas."

He wanted me to ask him how they could have been
exposed to the gas without finding the freighter and I
wasn't going to: Loman had the knack of making you as
petty-minded as he was. I said:

"Some of the drillers think it was ergot. There's a medical unit testing the bread supplies. The nurses at the clinic say it was a magnetic storm."

He waited long enough to let Chirac see that I didn't know what the hell I was talking about.

"The properties of Zylon-K-Gamma are peculiar. By its nature it is humid and—as you discovered—heavier than air; and in addition it is given pronounced surface-adhesive characteristics by the manufacturing laboratory, enhancing its effectiveness as a weapon of war. When Tango Victor came down and a gas cylinder was damaged on impact, some of the gas remained in the aircraft, but some was evidently released by overspill and formed the characteristic bubble. This was invisible, freely afloat at ground level and of course subject to the influence of winds. It seemingly was blown across the caravan track between Ghadamis and Kaifra, since within twenty kilometres of Kaifra there were fourteen Arabs found dead, also their camels, also sundry birds of prey that had flown down to feed. The Arabs who died in the clinic had inhaled considerably less than their companions, and were able to reach Kaifra."

So that was why I was still here.

Their situation had been different from mine: they'd been caught in the open desert and couldn't escape but I'd been caught in a confined space, and could. They hadn't known where the gas was and they could have run deeper into it when they'd tried to run clear; inside the freighter I'd known where the stuff was and I'd known where to run to get away from it. There'd been other factors in play: moving slowly under the open sky, as they'd been doing all their lives, they'd been taken utterly by surprise and must have thought in terms of a visitation by fiends at the behest of a disapproving Allah, their fear transfixing them. My mind had already been conditioned to think in terms of a toxic gas, and inhalation had been blocked immediately by reflex as I'd started to get clear.

"Isn't there any kind of gas mask available?"

"You would have been given one, in that event. So would the crew of the aeroplane."

Their situation had been different from mine and from the Arabs': they'd been conditioned to the risk of a toxic gas leak but the crash landing had slowed their escape, either because they'd been partly stunned or the door had become jammed, possibly both.

"Who's been making this bloody stuff?"

Loman said nothing so I left it. There wasn't anything new he could tell me about that gas: when I went back inside Tango Victor I'd know what to expect.

"Where was it being delivered?"

"This is not the time to discuss—"

"I will go away, *mes amis.*" Chirac opened the starboard door and swung his feet through the gap.

"There is no need, Chirac. There's nothing to discuss in any case."

"*Quand même,* I shall stretch the legs."

He dropped through and I watched his dark compact figure moving away against the starlit flank of the dune.

"Algeria," I said, "or Egypt?"

Quickly: "You've identified a cell of the U.A.R. network?"

"Yes."

It'd be a signal for London.

"There are probably more than one."

"More than one Egyptian cell?"

"Yes."

I finished the protein and screwed up the paper and flicked it through the doorway. "This gas was made in England, was it?"

"Clandestinely, of course."

"By private initiative?"

"Certain members of an otherwise reputable laboratory have been interviewed by the Special Branch. Unfortunately the laboratory had been placed under government contract, and although the production of this gas was made in secret by criminal elements, you can imagine what would happen to the reputation of the U.K. itself if Tango Victor were found by—shall we say—an ill-wisher."

"And what's going to happen to the reputation of the United Arab Republic when we tell everyone they've been buying BCW material within six months of the Geneva banning?"

He turned slowly to look at me.

"What reputation? The difference is there. In any case it won't occur. The U.K. will tell nobody, since the gas was unfortunately made in England and any accusation would of course boomerang."

"There'll be a public trial for the people who made the stuff."

"Unavoidably. The image of the U.K. will receive a certain degree of damage. Regrettably, a criminal element has been manufacturing and selling a deadly chemical warfare material. Nothing more. We shall hope to avoid the disastrous outcome of much more serious revelations."

"You mean those poor bastards in the clinic have officially died of ergot in the bread supplies."

"You would oblige me by remembering that."

"And the outbreak in Mali? What was the death roll?"

"Three hundred."

"Jesus. An outsize bubble on the move. Was it lobbed there?"

"There's an Algerian missile site in the south Sahara and the gas was being tested for the United Arab Republic."

"In vivo."

"How otherwise would its precise effects be known? But in fact the Mali batch was too powerful: the intention was to induce an incapacitating state of anxiety for a period of a few days. The batch in Tango Victor is less lethal but still too strong. What Egypt would be seeking is of course the convenient dilution providing this effect, enabling her to take over control in Tel Aviv without casualties and therefore without too great an international motion of censure."

He looked at his watch.

In the background silence the tick of the instrument-panel chronometer was insistent, its illuminated dial sharply defined. There were four minutes to go.

"You'd better brief me."

"Yes."

He shifted his position on the observer's seat as he opened the map, and the Alouette moved slightly on its suspension. I rummaged in the rations box and found some dehydrated honey tablets and peeled one off the strip.

"Chirac will be using a flight pattern designed to confuse the acoustic observation posts as much as possible. You will go from here to the Petrocombine South 5 drilling camp and overfly the airstrip, setting course for this point here in the Roches Vertes complex and then flying for three kilometres along the scheduled air route from

Ghadamis to El Oued across the Algerian desert. You will then proceed at 203° direct to the target area."

I checked it twice and asked him where the listening posts were meant to be.

"From local intelligence we know there are four posts in this line from South 5 to No. 2 Philips radio tower. There may be others farther west."

I looked up from the map.

"What d'you think our chances are, Loman?"

He must have been expecting it but tried to look surprised.

"Of doing what?"

"Reaching the target area without bringing a whole pack of tags or interceptors into the air."

I'd made my point and he had the grace to give me a straight answer without pretending to consider the actual odds.

"Unpromising."

I suppose he was spiritually exhausted or physically over the edge of fatigue because he suddenly sagged, his hands resting loosely on the spread map and his pale eyes closing for a moment.

"That is the only possible flight pattern we can use."

"Taking us within seven kilometres of this end listening post." I'd begun sweating. "What d'you imagine their effective range is? About fifty?"

"Perhaps."

He was sitting perfectly still and I knew he was waiting for me to blow up in his face but I wasn't going to do it because it wouldn't help us and Christ we needed help and a new question was coming into my mind and I tried to get rid of it before it could do any harm, before it could bring down the last few bricks of the mission that still appeared to be standing. But it wouldn't go.

Question. When does a director in the field start losing his sense of proportion? When does the strain of watching the slow demolition of his plans begin to tell on him and take him beyond the point where reason can only be ignored with fatal results? *When does he break?*

Perhaps it is when he finishes up sitting in a helicopter on the edge of the Sahara in the early hours of a sleepless night and awaiting the dawn of a hopeless day, his hands lying unnerved on a map where the only uncharted feature is the ruin he knows is there but refuses to recognise: those last few tumbled bricks of the thing he was trying too hard to build.

I wouldn't expect a man like Loman to abandon a mission if success or even survival looked unattainable. I would expect him to keep on working at it, no longer for what he could make of it but for its own sake, once it had gone beyond the stage where any useful purpose remained. I would expect him to become obsessive, to make a shrine of it: and I would expect him to regard his executive in the field as a natural sacrifice.

"Loman," I said, "when did you get London's directive on this end phase?"

He was now genuinely surprised, couldn't follow me.

"Just before 0300 hours."

I didn't think he'd actually lie about a thing like that. I didn't think he'd lost his reason: I just thought reason was now being subjugated to the point where he might have me killed off for nothing.

"Have they been given total intelligence on the disposition of those listening posts?"

Then he saw what I meant.

"I'm sorry, Quiller. The objective has to be destroyed. London insists."

"For what reason?"

Because you can ask questions if you think your life is being moved into a specific hazard: they don't bind your hands behind you and drive you blindfold against the cannon.

"There are two reasons," Loman said. He sounded perfectly calm and I thought this is how they sound when their fantasies have had to take control of them to save them from the reality they can't any longer face. "It requires several days of exposure to the ultraviolet rays in sunlight to alter the atomic structure of Zylon-K-Gamma and render it harmless. If anyone attempted to move the cargo in that aeroplane, not knowing what it was, enough gas could be spilled to wipe out the population of Kaifra, particularly since the *ghibli* is a south wind. The United Kingdom would be responsible. Secondly a nuclear explosion would not only change the atomic structure of the gas instantaneously, but would obliterate the aeroplane: and this is essential. It will be known that a new BCW weapon was being manufactured in the U.K. long after the banning of such weapons by the Geneva Convention, and even though it was done clandestinely it can only be embarrassing and the government will have to explain how it was allowed to occur. This is bad enough. It would be disastrous at this moment when Israel and the Arab world confront each other if it were also known that a consignment of chemical warfare gas had been flown from the U.K. to North Africa. Allow me to borrow the old cliché of a spark in a powder barrel."

I watched his reflection in the glass of the black-dialled chronometer. He was looking at me, waiting. His face was as calm as his speech had been: reaction concealment was second nature to him and that was why I was worried when he'd suddenly sagged a few minutes ago.

He would remain perfectly calm, I assumed, after his mind had slipped its focus. He would give careful and cogent reasons for driving his executive headlong against the cannon.

Decision necessary: stay with the mission or get out. Trust this efficient and merciless little bastard all the way or take a step back and see him for what he might be: an intelligence director turned psychopath.

Chirac, a dark figure against the pale flank of the dune, waiting. The chronometer ticking in the quietness, the face of Loman reflected on the dial, waiting.

Do what he says and do it even if you know it's likely to kill you, even if you know he'll never grieve. Or save yourself, tell him no, no go.

The scream of a ferret in the dark.

Or refusal.

19. Epitaph

The slam of the wind and the known world gone, the sky on the ground and the sand overhead, spinning.

Sink rate rising.

Tumbling now and a lot of noise and the collar of his flying suit flapping because the zip had pulled open when I'd jumped, Chirac had lent it to me, helping me on with it in the predawn cold. A good man, Chirac, a man I'd like to see again and probably never would. *Adieu, mon ami.*

It was a low level drop at low speed and the conditions were different from the first time: he'd only given me two hundred feet to do it in and that wasn't much, even over sand, but he said there was rising ground towards the northeast, the remains of an eroded escarpment, and it could conceivably bounce our acoustic irradiation and fox the scanners, you never know your luck. You've got to try everything when you haven't got a hope in hell. Everything.

Blood pooling in the head, the eyes swollen, the air noise very loud and the terminal velocity coming up close to a hundred knots so pull the thing, lying awkwardly face up but there's not much room left so *pull it.*

Canopy deployed.

Pendulous oscillation setting in and I tried to control it with the shroud lines but couldn't, hadn't the strength, because the opening shock had jerked me upright like a puppet and the harness webbing had bitten into old bruises and all I could do was hang in the air getting my breath, nausea threatening because of the oscillation, fight it.

Swing, swing, swing.

Cheer up, the worst is over, so forth.

Very queasy and I got hold of a line, two lines, pulled on them, an improvement, going almost straight down like a shuttlecock. Don't think about the ground: it's not going to be comfortable so we'll just settle for that and shut up about it.

I caught sight of the supply chute three times during the drop, lower than I was because I'd shoved it overboard before I'd jumped, and not bad timing: it was nearer the rock outcrop, almost on top of it.

It would have been nice, yes, if Chirac could have landed me in his Alouette and waited for the estimated forty minutes while I fiddled with the thing and then taken me away before the bang went off, a civilised approach to the end phase of a mission, a taxi for the exeiutive in the field. But the listening posts were going to pick us up on their scanners unless the rising ground to the northeast diffused our sound wake enough to fox them, and there was a chance they'd take us for a prospecting crew or one of the Algerian desert-reconnaissance machines.

But if Chirac put her down they'd get an immediate fix

on our position and I wouldn't have time to set up the bang before we got smothered in ticks. No go.

Sand coming up fast don't think about it.

The first light of the day was spilling across the horizon, touching the tips of the rocks with rose and colouring the crests of the dunes and leaving the last of the night pooled in the hollows. Chirac had done his homework and the timing had been precise. With the opposition cells alerted by the Marauder's switch to South 6 we couldn't hope to repeat a night approach by sailplane: this time we had to go right into the target area with a zero margin of error so that I could set up the device as soon as I landed, trigger it and leave an escape-delay on the detonator sufficient to get me clear.

Nor could we night-fly the mission all the way because dead-reckoning was out of the question: it would demand a margin of error and we couldn't afford one. Chirac had to see the rock outcrop, home in on it and overfly it and do it without altering speed so that the doppler factor would remain constant on the scanners. Nor could we fly by daylight all the way without being seen, even if we flew at dune level from the south.

So Chirac had flown through the last of the dark with an ETA of dawn plus one over the target area and he'd got it spot on.

I could still hear him, heading southwest for Ghadamis on a decoy run before he turned back to Kaifra.

Estimate five seconds to go, relax or you'll break a joint.

I tried to turn bodily but it set up the first swing of an oscillation and I didn't want to land at an angle so I stopped. In any case there was no problem: the supply chute had been close to the rocks when I'd last sighted it.

The decision had been made rather formally. He is like that, Loman. Even when the chances of a successful end phase are almost nil and he's staring straight into the brick dust as the mission collapses he remains rather formal.

The situation, Quiller, is simply this. Even if we have only a one per cent chance of completing our mission, London would appreciate our making the attempt.

Then he'd got out of the observer's seat and dropped onto the sand and walked away in the direction opposite from Chirac's, to stand there with his back to me. His gesture was symbolic, accurate, and characteristic: he couldn't go far from the helicopter because if I accepted the end phase we'd have to take off in three minutes, so he went as far as he could and indicated by turning his back that he was to all intents and purposes out of sight. The final decision was to be my own and no pressure was to be put on me by my director in the field, even by his presence.

Ground close watch it.

The situation, Quiller, is simply this. Even if you have only a one per cent chance of surviving the end phase, London would appreciate your making the attempt.

One always has to paraphrase just a little, with Loman.

Then I'd called to Chirac to start up and I was here because I was an old ferret sharp of tooth and I knew my warrens and I'd run them before and I'd run them again because the chance I believe in is the one-per-center and that is the way of things, as I see them. Pure logic, of course: the high risks of my trade drew me to it and that is why I ply it, and the greater the risk the more I am drawn and when the risk is expressed as a one per cent chance of survival then I'm hooked and damned and hellbound and don't get in my way.

Their small heads, I suppose, were raised there among the shadowed crevices of rock as I drifted down, a great circular petal reflected in their gold-rimmed eyes.

Side of a dune and I was badly placed and pitched flat and the sand burst red singing fire dream.

The supply chute was draped across a spur of rock like a sheet hung out to dry. The shroud lines were badly twisted and I had to cut some of them before I could free the two containers, and with each jerk of the knife everything went red again and I had to rest, leaning on the hot surface of the rocks. When I could manage it I dragged the canopy down and folded it and stuffed it into a fissure: all they needed was a landmark but we were all right at the moment because there were some vultures coasting not far away and they'd have sheered off if there were any aircraft about.

When I'd looked at the containers I went across to the niche in the rocks where I'd left my camp. Chirac had found the transceiver when he'd come for me last evening, and stowed it here out of the sun's direct heat.

Tango.

Loman wasn't going to like it.

He would have been trying to call me up, I knew that, but I hadn't set to receive before I'd dragged the canopy out of sight. Chirac would have picked him up in the *gassi* an hour ago and dropped him somewhere near base and since then he'd been trying to call me and by this time he'd be certain we'd failed and he was right and he wasn't going to like it when I told him.

Tango receiving.

I could hear them scuttling, perhaps in fright at his voice, sharp and metallic and amplified.

I said I was in the target area.

What was the delay?

Bad landing.

Are you injured?

No.

Then I saw the vultures drifting away and knew that there wasn't any doubt left: we'd hit a dead end. We'd thought this mission had an all-or-nothing end phase, either I'd blow Tango Victor off the face of the earth or the oppositon would get here and kill me before I could do it. The idea of a compromise hadn't occurred to us: that I'd get here for nothing, and too late.

I would appreciate your situation report.

Talked like a bloody schoolteacher. I'd soon stop that.

We've had it, Loman. The timer's been smashed.

Five seconds.

Please repeat.

I suppose he had a point. When you're sending the last signal of a mission you might as well make it clear what you're saying, if only for the record.

The supply chute came down on the rock outcrop and the impact has smashed the timing mechanism.

A longer pause. I waited, listening to the sky.

My lips tasted salty, had blood on them. It had been dripping onto the shale and I'd only just noticed it and I wiped my hand across, well what would you expect, I'd hit the side of the dune with my face and opened the stitches.

Loman asked:

What is that noise?

Helicopters.

Silence from the black speaker grille.

In his mind he was trying to reorganise the end phase, signalling London for directives, re-creating the ruins I'd just told him about. And he couldn't do it.

How long have they been there?

About a minute and a half.

How far away?

Five kilometres, maybe six.

I watched them. There were three of them.

What is your situation appraisal?

I wiped my hand across my mouth again.

They got us on the scanners but not too accurately. They're starting a square search due east of me, three of them.

Are they moving towards your position?

No. Directly away, at right angles.

I didn't see it could matter. I didn't see it could matter to him or the mission or London because if they found me I was a dead duck and if they didn't find me there wasn't anything I could do here. I wished he'd stop asking questions, too tired for it, not on form.

Are they military aircraft or civilian?

Oh for Christ sake Loman we've had it, I've told you the timer's been smashed, didn't you hear me?

Are they military, or civilian?

I shut my eyes, let them water, sand had got into them when I'd hit the dune.

I can't see from this distance. They're close to the sun.

Ten seconds.

I am going off the air for thirty minutes but please keep open to receive.

Silence.

Thirty minutes: he'd signal London now for a directive, ask them what to do, but there was nothing to do. He'd tell Diane to use the phone and contact Chirac and request him to stand by with the helicopter but it'd only be a gesture because Chirac wouldn't be able to pick me up without exposing the target area and if he came in after they'd found me there wouldn't be anything to pick up anyway, nothing alive.

I opened my eyes and squinted towards the horizon. The three choppers were moving back along their initial course, farther south by one prescribed strip of their

sweep. They could see these rocks but they couldn't
see me because I was in shadow and sighting through a
gap in the shale. I'd buried my chute under the sand before I'd come here, and last evening Chirac had taken
down the fabric shelter I'd set up near the plane, so there
was nothing for them to see.

The birds had come down five hundred yards away and
I watched them. They'd obviously been there when I'd
landed and the chute had startled them and now they
were back, feeding on the pilot and navigator. The helicopter crews couldn't have noticed them or they'd come
to investigate because they'd know that the presence of
vultures marked the presence of recent life.

Urge to sleep now overwhelming. I took a final look at
the timer to make sure it hadn't been the subject of hallucination but it hadn't changed: two of the brass lugs were
snapped off near the flange and half the main body of the
mechanism had been so badly impacted that I could see
one of the intermediary gear trains lying askew and
thrown out of mesh. Strictly no go.

I crawled deeper between the rocks because of the dark
nightmare shapes over there: they reminded me of terror
and I didn't want them to see me, to come for me in my
sleep.

My eyes closed and the great weight of my head came
to rest against the rock face, a last thought, we got close,
tell London we got close.

Said I could hear him.
Caught me in a low sleep curve, groggy.
Zenith 0631.
I have been in signals with London.
They were still there, I could just catch their distant
purring, *throp-throp-throp.*
Can you hear me?
Hear you.
What is the position of the helicopters now?
Damn his eyes, won't ever leave you alone.
I reached for the water bottle and got the cap off and
drank, tasting the blood on my mouth. The sun's heat was
beginning to strike into the niche and I couldn't get my
legs in the shade. Took my time, thirsty, and he said
could I hear him and I didn't answer till I'd finished my

drink because that was more important. Then I told him:

They're shifting to a second square.

How clearly can you see them?

About distance shot.

Could they see you, if you went into the open?

No.

Of course I should have known.

Will you please verify that the timing mechanism is out of action, irreparably?

Verified.

Is there any damage to the main components?

No.

Please verify.

I should have known by his insistence on these things.

There's no external damage. The timer took the shock.

What is your physical condition?

I need sleep.

He considered this.

Are you capable of carrying the device as far as the freighter?

Should have known, shouldn't I, what he was going to do to me.

Perfectly capable.

Silence for half a minute. I thought he was calculating something. Maybe he was.

Quiller.

Hear you.

London would like you to proceed with the end phase.

How the hell can I do that if the timer won't—

I didn't finish.

Got it now.

The sun was burning on my legs and I drew them up, forcing myself higher against the rock face, the effort increasing the circulation and bringing me fully awake. I would have to think about this. He was saying:

Control has asked me to point out that your action would be seen as generous, and therefore much appreciated.

Death sentence.

Civil of them.

He didn't say anything; I suppose he was giving me time to think. They were all being very considerate.

Give me ten minutes, Loman, will you?

Of course. There's no immediate hurry.

I clipped the mike back and stared through the cleft in the rocks. They were still at it, their ragged plumage fluttering as they jerked about, hooking at the meat. That, at least, I would be spared.

Of course the potential expendability of an executive is part of the contract and we know what we're signing. The Bureau is the sacred bull and its first credo is that the mission is more important than the man, otherwise you wouldn't be issued with a capsule if you wanted one, on your way through clearance. And after all, providing you accept the fact at any given time during an operation that you've become expendable the actual means of despatch don't matter: all we ask is that it shall be quick and the only thing quicker than a cyanide pill is putting your thumb on a nuclear detonator.

I couldn't assess my chances when they shifted their search over this area and found me: the thing was that I'd want to initiate some kind of hostile action and they'd finish me anyway. That situation was entirely academic in any case because if London wanted me to complete the mission I'd have time to do it before I was seen.

And I didn't have any choice. I had contracted to hazard my life if the needs of a mission demanded and that was that. I was only taking time out to think about it because if there was an alternative I wanted to use it, but I knew there wasn't one: Loman would throw me to the dogs if it suited his purposes and his present purposes were to go back to London with his instructions carried out and Tango Victor obliterated. Technically there wasn't an alternative because we didn't have time to send for a new delay mechansim and without one the only way to detonate was to press the button myself.

Sense of unreality creeping on me because the whole thing was so calculated: I'd come close to dying in Tunis among the flying glass and in Kaifra when the marksman had me in his sights but there'd been no time to think about it, and now there was.

Bloody little organism up on its back legs and whining, don't want to die, *shuddup*.

My ten minutes wasn't up but I'd had all the time I needed and it was no good sitting here with this strange hollow feeling, the almost physical sensation of the life-blood beginning to drain away. Possibly normal: a question of mind over matter and when the mind knows that death is imminent the body starts dying automatically, it happens in Africa, put a curse on a man and he'll die without a mark on him.

Irrelevant.

Mission running, end phase initiated, instructions perfectly clear, so go on, pick up that mike.

Loman.

Receiving you.

Just tell me again, will you, what exactly I'm going to achieve?

No change of tone when he spoke. He'd known I'd have to do it. He'd known, earlier this morning when he'd walked across the sand and stood with his back to me, that I wouldn't refuse. And so had I.

They're bastards in London, mean with the money and slow on promotion and that sort of thing, but certain gestures are made in the name of decency: despite the contracts we sign they like us to feel that we're not irrevocably committed, that when the crunch comes we'll still have a part in the decision-making. But it's only a gesture, the same as being asked if you'd like a blindfold before the bolts click back.

It is less a question of what you'll achieve than of what you will vouchsafe your country to avoid. If the objective is not destroyed, the influence of the United Kingdom at the international conference tables will be gravely enfeebled, and her work for peace tragically undermined.

I waited but that was all he said. The second half of the equation was tacit: compared with these disastrous eventualities, what value had the life of one man?

All right, Loman.

Pause.

You are prepared to complete your mission?

Did you think I'd back out?

No.

Never make a mistake, do you?

Wished I hadn't said it but an hour from now he'd be alive and I wouldn't and I hated him for that, for that alone and for nothing else.

The most important mistake I could have made, Quiller, would have been to choose an executive in the field

*with a sense of responsibility less admirable than your
own. Please accept my compliments.*

A certain style: the man had a certain style, give him
that.

Good of you.

She'd be there, I supposed, listening and not liking it,
her own fault, she shouldn't have looked for work in this
trade, her downy arms and her sooty face and her quick
little way of nodding, all I knew, really.

Loman, is that girl there?

Yes. Do you want to—

*No. Just do something for me. Get her out of it when
this mission's over, get her out of this bloody trade, it's
not for her. Do that for me.*

Then it occurred to me that this was the final signal, so
I ended it the way the little bastard would want me to,
right out of the copybook.

Tango out.

20. Detonation

They flew up screaming as I neared them, one of them
with meat hanging from its beak. I remembered them
from the nightmare, and had to stand still for a while, the
sweat running on me, until something inside the spirit of a
dying man was roused to his last needs, and I managed to
go on towards the freighter, the weight of the two containers slowing my feet through the sand.

The birds didn't go far away: I'd interrupted their feeding and by the time I reached the doorway they'd settled
again. I thought it odd how the chemical processes of life
were still going on: a minute ago I'd drunk the last of the
water, and these birds were busy absorbing nourishment,
but very soon we would no longer exist. The scene was
surrealistic: a man and some birds perpetuating the motions of life in a desert landscape, without purpose.

*The influence of the United Kingdom at the interna-
tional conference tables,* so forth. Purpose, yes.

I took great care going into the freighter because some
of the cylinders had been lying at an angle and could fall
if I caused vibration. This is characteristic of the end
phase of a mission: you take pains to see that at the elev-

enth hour you don't wreck everything you've been working for.

I didn't think I could go into the actual freight section
and set up the device without the risk of inhaling gas: the
movement of my feet could stir up the bubble pooling
there. The flight deck wasn't contaminated because it was
at a higher level, so I carried the containers inside and slid
the door closed after me, switching on the torch.

Stifling heat, tendency to claustrophobia, not because
the cabin was small but because I knew I would never
leave it in the form of a living creature. Rapid increase of
sweating, pulse accelerated, mouth dry: the organism
mortally afraid and the forebrain alone driving it on, forcing its hands, arranging the movement of its fingers, performing the necessary motions that would assemble the
black-painted components as required.

Annular clamp, the brass threads smelling of silicone
lubricant and an additive, the toggle action precise and almost silent as I brought the levers home and set the pins.

By-pass conduit, the channels lined up by a sprung
ball-and-socket: I listened for the click and the lingering
musical tone of the spring.

Main body-locking, the three-start thread fairly coarse,
but even so there was provision for alignment by sighting,
to avoid the risk of crossing them. Push-fit pin location,
precise to less than a thousandth: the entire mechanism
was built to maximum-security specifications, giving me
confidence in it.

It had to perform with absolute satisfaction and somewhere in the last confused interplay of thoughts I felt ada-
mant about this: since I was prepared to detonate it I
didn't want it to fail me because of slipshod work at some
stage during its manufacture.

Oven heat.

Aware of my breathing, rather loud in the confines and
faster than normal. Sweat in the eyes, stinging. Some area
of the brain noting the immediate environment, instinct
plus training: appraisal of physical factors in hazardous
situation. Instruments and controls, parachutes, pair of
tennis shoes in the open locker, carved teakwood statuette,
copy of *Playboy*, so forth. Nothing significant.

As I worked I could hear them cackling outside. The
sand was still piled against the perspex windows and I
couldn't see them but they were much in my mind, adding

to the incipient terror that was trying to overwhelm conscious thought.

Cackle cackle.

The awful thing was that I couldn't hear them without seeing them in my imagination, tugging and pulling as they fed. If they'd been doing anything else, if they'd simply been flying around like ordinary birds, they would have kept me company in these last minutes. As it was, the world I was leaving had the aspect of nightmare.

But I was ready now.

The activator was a cylindrical spigot, not very different from a press-button but two inches across, its surface grooved to mate with the grooves I'd seen on the timing mechanism. The extent of travel was less than half an inch, the extent by which the activator stood proud of the casing. Thumb pressure would suffice: the mechanism of the timer had been sensitive rather than heavy. I put my thumb on the grooved surface.

The organism was at this point in a state of excitation: the blind instinct to preserve itself was in fierce conflict with the will. I think it would have been easier for me if I'd been in fit condition: there wouldn't have been this need to drive a bruised and terrified subconscious into contributing to the final act of extinction. In the confused cerebral state there was only one area with any kind of ability to reason, and here the technician in me was observing the situation in his own terms and noting things like the complementary factors of requirements and facilities available, the requirements being to press the activator and detonate the device, the facilities being my thumb and its motor nerves.

At some time this idea became linked with philosophical considerations containing a marked awareness of self: the activator has to be pressed, therefore all we need is pressure; I can exert pressure with my thumb, but I'd rather it were something else because if I press this thing with my thumb it's going to kill me.

Cerebration is very fast and I doubt whether more than half a minute had passed before the whole idea took shape. I could still hear them cackling, and another sound, a kind of secret laughter, gloating and vengeful, rising from the vortex of my own subliminal.

Vaguely aware that I was laughing at the birds out

there, the horrible sounds inside me echoing theirs, but not a lot of time to think about it, the need was to move back from the edge of clinical hysteria and perform acts.

The first was to remove my thumb from the detonator.

Of the various objects on the flight deck I thought the carved teakwood statuette was most suitable. For a little while I held it, feeling its shape with my fingertips. It was a couple of feet long, the carving quite good except where the tool had slipped and one of the feet had been narrowed; or it could have been damaged at some time and the break smoothed off. It was Nahudian, obviously a god, wide nosed and with tribal markings on the forehead, a burning brand held at the side: perhaps it was N'Gami, god of lighting.

Other material was available and I wedged the nuclear device on its flat end between the seats and moved the throttle levers parallel with each other, driving the feet of the statuette between them to inhibit lateral movement. At the other end I used the parachute packs as lateral guides, so that N'Gami's body lay horizontal, his head resting on the grooved activator. And while I made these simple arrangements the unnerving muted laughter went on inside my skull, echoing the noise of the birds outside, perhaps defying them.

Because it would be difficult to do what I would have to do now. I had done it before, to save my life; and I would do it again, to save my life; but this time it would be more difficult because I would have to make myself do it, in cold blood. Nevertheless, I would do it.

The daylight struck in as I slid the door open, and for a minute I stood listening, my eyes closed against the glare. But the noise of the birds overlaid the more distant sound and I had to go outside before I could note the difference in volume: the helicopters had moved westward and were flying the same north-south pattern. I could see them more easily now because they were nearer, but their configuration was much larger than mine and I discounted the immediate risk of my being seen on the ground.

On this side of the freighter, the lee side, the sand had barely drifted across the top of the cabin, and I climbed there, feeling the solidity of the mainplate root somewhere under me. As I dug with my right hand, bringing the sand away, I saw that Tango Victor had been overtaken by a storm and had turned to head into it, some time before landing blind: the flight-deck windows were abrased to the point of opaqueness. But they were translucent, and that was all I needed.

Then I came down and looked at the birds against the glare coming up from the sand, nausea starting in me and bringing doubts whether I could do it. The heat pressed on my back and I stood swaying, watching them.

All right, they were merely feeding and we all do that, all living creatures have to feed; but it was their ruby red eyes and their bald heads and their white necks that sickened me, and the fact that their meat had once been man.

Sleep was trying to blot everything out: fatigue plus the soporific aftereffects of the gas, and this was dangerous because there was a chance of staying alive if I made an effort, pity to let it all, slope of sand and my hand to break the *get up* spin of the blinding sky *get up you bloody fool*, near one.

That was a near one all right.

Stupid bastard, get moving, do what you've got to do, think where you are: no more water left and the tissues already drying out, helicopters moving closer, a matter of half an hour before they're over here, you going to stand here till you drop, stay here till you fry, Christ sake put some effort into this thing or you've had it and you know that.

Still hadn't moved but now I did, going down the slope towards them, jerk jerk, cackle cackle, towards them.

When I was within a dozen yards of them the nearest one flew up, shrieking its alarm cry. The others chorused it instinctively, some moving away but all turning to face me, one lifting its ragged wings and waddling towards me, threatening.

I dropped onto my knees and rolled over and lay face down with the sand's heat burning under me and the sun's heat on my back. Already their cry had changed from the alarm to a desultory cackling and the one that had flown up came drifting across to rejoin the others. I lay watching them, catching their foetid stench on the air. There'd be no danger if I fell asleep. If I slept, they'd wake me.

Cackle.
Very close and in front of me.
Sense of *déjà vu:* I'd lain here on the sand before, in

this or another lifetime, and the bird had come for me, cackling. It voiced again and I opened my eyes and from between my fingers I saw the thing standing close to me on its wide-straddling legs, the head forward and the hooked beak open, the wings raised, menacing, the guttural racketing in my ears.

Difficult not to move, not to yell at it, not in some way to show defiance. But I mustn't even show life.

Others were coming, encouraged. They came waddling, their heavy bodies moving from side to side under their bald white necks and heads, their red eyes brilliant. It was the biggest of them that had come over to me first, and now it came closer, taking a single hop with the black wings spreading and folding again as it landed and stood over me. I felt the draught it had made, and began taking slow shallow breaths because of its smell. It voiced again, uncertain of me, knowing that minutes ago I'd been alive and moving. As the sound rattled from its throat I saw the sharp red tongue stiffened in the gaping beak and the small eyes glaring.

Lie still.

The others came waddling and I heard the hiss of the sand as their feet displaced it; but the big one, standing over me, gave a low cackle and lifted its head; and they stopped. This was the leader, and according to the protocol of the flock it would be the first to take meat.

Lie still.

Peck.

Shocking in its force, part pincer and part hammer blow, numbing my wrist. I didn't move. I could do it now because the thing was close enough but it was still uncertain, hopping back after taking the first trial peck in case I reacted. Now it came closer again, more boldly, the hooked beak half open for the strike, this time to feed.

Then I took it.

The beak struck but I went for the legs and got a grip on their scaly hardness and held on and tried to stand up but its weight stopped me and I rolled over and buried my face against an arm as the shrieking broke out and the wings beat in a frenzy to churn the sand and send it clouding and scattering, the strong legs tugging as I held them and one pulling free and its talons hooking at my face and hooking again, the gross body swinging from its single tether while I found a purchase on the sand and

stood up, lurching and snatching for the free leg because
the talons were murderous and if the other leg snapped
and the thing got free and flew away I was done.

Then I got it and held on and let it struggle, the wings
thrashing and the beak striking and striking again and
again at my wrists and arms as I walked with the thing to
the aeroplane while the rest of the flock wheeled screaming overhead.

I had left the sliding door to the flight deck fully open
and now I hurled the bird inside and shut it in and came
away and dropped to the sand and began walking, began
lurching into some kind of a run towards the rock outcrop, hearing the mad shrieking behind me as the thing
battered at the windows for escape.

Cerebration minimal now but I knew that I'd done
what I'd meant to do: the rest would depend on chance.
If the flight deck had been totally dark the bird would
have fluttered aimlessly, disorientated, and that would
have been dangerous. I'd cleared the windows so that it
could see the daylight, and for a while it would beat use-
lessly there until its frenzy tired it, leading it to look instinctively for a perch.

N'Gami, are you a god for me or for them?

The screaming was fainter now because of the distance.

I took the transceiver from the niche among the rocks
and cradled it against me and tried to run with it but
couldn't manage, had to make do with a shambling lurch
through the sand, stopping sometimes to listen. I could
hear the distant cries of the flock as they circled the
freighter, disturbed by what had happened to their leader.
The one distinctive cry, with its note of panic, was no
longer audible. Perhaps the bird was tiring now.

A throbbing was in my head as I made what pace I
could, in my head or in the sky, and I stopped again, turning to look back.

The helicopters had broken off their search and were
moving in to the target area at dune height: they'd seen
the vultures and knew from desert experience that there
must be carrion below, or some kind of living prey. When
they landed I would go back there and talk to them, a vol-
untary captive parched for water, and show them the
freighter, telling them what I'd found inside it, and arranging at the most convenient moment that the little god
should summon his lightnings.

I thought I was already beyond the residual radiation range but I turned and went on again because if they landed I would hear them. I would give myself until then.

The weight of the transceiver was dragging me forwards and I fell twice, the second time pitching down off balance and lying prone, a flashing in my head as I got onto all fours and dropped again, sudden rage rising, can't stand being feeble, *Christ sake get up*, trying again and hanging on the sand like a dog, *get up and get on,* trying again, no go, trying again as the dunes in front of me turned dazzling white and I squeezed my eyes shut, dropping again and groping for the transceiver, hitting the switch.

Slowly the white light was dying.

Beneath me the desert shuddered.

Mission completed.

They would hear it in Kaifra. Loman was waiting for it and until it came he'd be staying open to receive. There wasn't any hurry because the sound would take nearly a minute to reach there, but I called him up straightaway because I didn't know how long I could last out here on the burning sand, under the burning sky.

Tango.

He didn't answer immediately. Wasn't expecting a signal.

Tango receiving you.

About time.

I did the bang.

Of course he started asking a lot of questions but I cut him short, told him where I was, north of the rocks, told him to pull me out.